THE
SUBS
CLUB

D1736936

THE **SUBS** CLUB
BOOK I

J.A. ROCK

RIPTIDE
PUBLISHING

DEC 1 1 2015

Riptide Publishing
PO Box 6652
Hillsborough, NJ 08844
www.riptidepublishing.com

The Subs Club
Copyright © 2015 by J.A. Rock

Cover art: Kanaxa, kanaxa.com
Editor: Delphine Dryden, delphinedryden.com
Layout: L.C. Chase, lcchase.com/design.htm

ISBN: 978-1-62649-344-5

First edition
December, 2015

Also available in ebook:
ISBN: 978-1-62649-343-8

THE
SUBS
CLUB

THE **SUBS** CLUB
BOOK I

J.A. ROCK

RIPTIDE
PUBLISHING

For Becky, Shannon, Heather, and Brian.

TABLE
OF
CONTENTS

CHAPTER
ONE

S krillex was blaring when Miles, Kamen, Gould, and I walked into Riddle—one of two BDSM clubs in the city, and the only one we bothered hanging out at anymore. Riddle's owners had a real hard-on for dubstep. Even tonight, at the Kink by Candlelight party, which had the potential to be a wonderfully atmospheric event if someone would just swap the violent sub-bass for some monastic chanting or Vivaldi. Or Enya. Bitches love Enya.

The place was already packed. The couches were full, so we had to stand. Most people weren't even using the changing area; they just peeled off their street clothes there in the lounge and put on their harnesses and corsets and . . . capes? Yep, someone was definitely wearing a cape. Candles had been set up in the three playrooms as well as the lounge, and we were just waiting for the DMs to light them and turn off the overheads so we could get to the fun. Or at least what I hoped would be fun, though I was already starting to doubt it.

At the very least we might get to see a cape catch fire.

I glanced at the entrance to Tranquility, then made myself look away. Checked out the dry bar instead.

There was a guy standing at the end of the bar, rocking a glass-bottled root beer. In his forties, probably. Big-boned, a little paunchy even. Fucking pornstache, which normally would have been a deal breaker, but his was combined with some additional rugged facial hair that mitigated the situation. And he was mountain man-ish enough that the 'stache seemed not only right, but also necessary. His face was wide, his jaw square, and he wore his light-brown hair in an uneven crew cut. I was digging the long-sleeved polo, jeans, and loafers in a *yeah, daddy* kind of way. He caught me staring, and his pornstache twitched slightly. Then he turned away with a vigorous sniff, rubbing under his nose with one finger. He seemed vaguely familiar, but I couldn't figure out why. He looked up again. Made eye contact.

What da fuck, Pornstache?

"It's been seriously forever since we were all here together," Kamen said over the music. I turned away from Burt Reynolds Stars in *Boogie Nights* and faced my friends.

"Uh, yeah." I scratched my neck, which was inexplicably warm. I'd never met a mustache that made me feel this way. "I know."

It wasn't the first time we'd come to Riddle since Hal, but it was the first time we'd attended an event, and the first time we'd wordlessly committed to trying to enjoy ourselves. I felt responsible for how the night went, like an enthusiastic dad overseeing a lame family vacation. I'd hustled everyone into the car this evening and sung along too loudly to the radio and pointed out a new special on the Golden Corral billboard as we'd driven by. But now that we were here, my gaze kept finding Tranquility's doorway, and I could tell Gould was having the same problem. So I focused on the other attendees.

"Oh my God." I tried not to point too obviously. "There's Rachel. They'd better keep an eye on the candles."

Kamen's gaze followed mine. "Wait, what?"

Miles glanced at him. "She's the rope top who turns people into human menorahs. You've seen her. She does the rigging all across their arms and makes rope candleholders . . .?"

"Oh, yeah." Kamen nodded, but I didn't think he had any idea what Miles was talking about.

"I let her do me last Hanukkah. It was fun." My gaze flicked back to Pornstache, who drained his root beer and threw the glass bottle in the recycle bin for plastics. This bad boy made his own rules. Rawwwr.

Yeah, I put my glass in with the plastics. Yeah, I have a mustache even though it's no longer 1978. Yeah, I wanna put my dick in your—

Gould clapped my shoulder, and I jumped. He looked at me strangely. "Anyone want drinks?"

We all put in our orders. Gould headed to the bar. I figured he wouldn't want to talk much tonight. Not that he was ever a social butterfly, but he'd made the most effort of all of us to steer clear of Riddle over the past year. This was gonna be rough on him.

Pornstache was wandering toward Chaos.

Each of Riddle's three playrooms had a name. Chaos was the largest and loudest, and had equipment for intense scenes—medical table, crosses, cages, ladders, stocks, and a dentist's chair. I usually made straight for Refinement, which was quieter and smaller—spanking bench, bondage horse, rope frames. Tranquility was the smallest room and contained only an elegant, multipurpose bench and various steel rings on the walls and floor. There was no music, and the doorway had curtains and a velvet rope to keep the space private for whoever was doing a scene there. For some reason it struck me as strange that Tranquility still existed. It seemed like everyone should refuse to play there, out of respect or fear or whatever. Like it should have at least been repainted, the furniture rearranged . . . something.

Some girl was talking to Kamen. Of the four of us, Kamen got the most attention when we were out. People generally assumed he was a dom because of his size. I gave it about twenty minutes of chatter before Kamen—friendly as a golden retriever and often completely oblivious to what people wanted from him—figured out this girl was trying to get him to tie her up.

Miles, Kamen, Gould, and I were like a nineties' boy band. Kamen was the heartthrob—six foot four of hulking, WASPlicious, buzzed-headed jock. I was the boy next door—silken of hair and blue of eye and straight of teeth. Gould was the shy one—short, a little stocky, huge mop of curls. *Adorable.* And Miles was sort of a weird combination of the bad boy and the middle-aged, straitlaced accountant who got pulled up onstage to dance during a concert and was mortified but secretly thrilled. He was smart as hell, and he was the only pain slut in our group. If someone asked him to try pulling a barge through the Erie Canal with a chain attached to his PA piercing, he'd probably do it. But you'd never know that about him, because he dressed like a minister's daughter and behaved like the easily scandalized maiden aunt in a British drawing room play.

Cardigans in muted colors aside, he was gorgeous. He looked like a young Mos Def. I'd told him that once, and he didn't know who Mos Def was. He did, however, know the difference between a fish fork and a fruit fork. So WTF?

I nudged him now. "Bowser. Ten o'clock."

He followed my gaze. Bowser's scene name was DorianGreat, though everyone called him Bowser. He was mostly into medical play. Like hard-core, let-me-speculum-your-ass-until-I-could-drop-a-grapefruit-in-there play. Miles was the only one of us who'd scened with him. His laugh was exactly like Bowser's in *Mario 64* when you tried to open a locked door in the castle and didn't have enough stars. It was, in a weird way, kind of a turn-on.

Bowser caught Miles's eye. Smiled at him. A surprisingly intimate smile given that the two of them had only played once.

At the door, a girl in a feathered tutu and a man in a red sequined devil costume were filling out the first-timer paperwork—a ten-page contract full of confidentiality agreements, disclaimers, and house rules. It made me long for the leather bar I used to frequent on 6th, where you could walk in, drink actual alcohol, then get your ass reamed and suck some daddy's cock without having to sign a goddamn waiver.

Heterosexuals. Seriously.

I immediately felt guilty. Because Hal. Because rules were a good thing—*if people fucking followed them.*

Looking at you, Bill Henson.

Gould came back from the bar, two cups in each hand. "Sprite. Sweet tea—" He handed Miles and me our drinks. "And Kamen, they were all out of Mr. Pibb. So I got you water."

"Aw, no! I hate water." The expression on Kamen's face was tragic.

Gould grinned and handed him a cup of Coke. "Kamen, you're so easy."

"I don't know about easy." I took a sip of tea. "He turned down a play date with Maestro last week."

Kamen was stabbing ice cubes with his tiny straw. "He's not my type."

I snorted. "Is any human being not your type? You love everyone."

"I hate Bill."

None of us spoke. Skrillex continued thumping.

Kamen was engrossed in stabbing ice and didn't seem to notice the rest of us exchanging glances. During all the shit that had gone down over the last year, I didn't think I had ever actually heard Kamen say Bill's name.

I drummed my thighs. "So are we gonna stand around taking attendance, or are we gonna go get some action?" I searched for Pornstache. I was anxious about being here and caught up in thoughts about Hal, and so the less sophisticated parts of my brain had latched on to the least appropriate, most obviously heterosexual person in this club and had decided it was this man's destiny to bend me over and scrub my asshole with that mustache.

Gould's gaze was on the door. GK, one of Riddle's owners, had just walked in. Ohhh boy. I snapped my fingers in front of Gould. Nothing. I patted his curly hair, and he whipped around, looking embarrassed.

"You're drooling," I whispered.

Kamen crushed his cup in his fist. "We gotta wait for the lights to go off before we play."

Kink by Candlelight was a twice-yearly event where Riddle turned off all the lights in the club and everyone played . . . well, by candlelight. It was awkward as fuck, and people inevitably fell off spanking benches or got sensitive bits caught in body bag zippers. But it was a tradition I never wanted to see die.

"I'm definitely not going to be graced with a suitable partner," Miles grumbled.

I plucked at his cardigan. "Well, maybe if you didn't come to a fetish party dressed like Mr. Rogers. Are you here to get your ass beat or catch a trolley to the Neighborhood of Make-Believe?"

Miles straightened his sweater. "I can work a damn cardigan. But I'm in the mood for knives and the only one here right now who can do a decent knife scene is Bowser."

"So play with him."

"I am most certainly *not* in the mood to feel like I'm running toward a transmogrifying painting of Princess Peach. Besides, if we play with his scalpel, then he'll want to get out the rest of his toys and do a full exam. Before I know it I'm leaving with a lollipop and a prescription for prednisone."

I started singing the castle theme from *Mario 64*. "*Doop. Doop. Doop. Da-doo-DOOP. Doop. Doop—*"

Miles whacked my arm. "Stop."

"C'mon."

Miles joined in, and we started moving our heads back and forth in unison like meerkats. "*Doop. Doop. Doop. Da-doo-DOOP. Da-doo-doo-doodoodahdoodoodoo-da-DOOP-DOOP. Dah-nah-nah!*"

"Well, well, well," came a sardonic female voice. "If it isn't the fab four."

Miles and I stopped abruptly and turned, along with Kamen and Gould.

Behind us stood a woman—about thirty, tall and fit with bright red hair and a long, thin nose.

"Cinnamon." I made no attempt to hide my distaste.

"David."

Cinnamon was apparently a big deal in the pony world. She'd won a bunch of awards at shows and stuff. But as a human, she sucked. I hadn't seen her since Bill's trial, and I'd been hoping never to set eyes on her again. "Where's all your horse shit?" She was wearing a black leotard, but no pony gear.

"I haven't changed yet." She rocked on her stiletto boots—because yes, nothing made me think "pony" like a set of heels that could impale a man of substantial breadth—her hands on her hips. "Surprised to see you here. I didn't think you were members anymore."

"Still members." Miles regarded her coolly. "We've just cut back on the amount of time we spend here."

I was sure Cinnamon was going to say something sarcastic. Instead, her expression softened and she hesitated before she spoke. "I heard the memorial service was really good. I would have gone, but—"

"You threw a shoe?" I said sarcastically.

"Dude," Kamen whispered beside me.

"I'm sorry, but if she's gonna talk about the service being 'really good,' like it's an episode of *True Detective*—"

"I cared about him too!" Her voice broke. And were those . . . *tears* in her eyes?

"Then how come every fucking thing you said in court helped Bill Henson's case?" I demanded.

Gould stepped in. "It was a nice service. Dave's just being his usual charming self."

There was a time when any mention of Bill's name—or Cinnamon's—would have made Gould damn near hysterical with anger. But now here he was acting like I was the one who needed to be monitored.

Cinnamon wiped under one eye with her finger. "I know," she said in a small voice.

And the fucking SAG award goes to . . .

"Sorry." I shrugged. "I didn't mean to *stirrup* trouble. It was nice of you to come over and say *hay*."

She rolled her eyes and sort of laughed. "Oh my God. Really?"

"Why so annoyed? You *mustang* out with the wrong people."

She shook her head and started off. "Bye."

"What, are you *bridling* at my criticism?"

Gould clapped a hand over my mouth.

"Good-bye, asshole," she called over her shoulder.

Gould slowly took his hand away. "You're so pleasant, David."

I swirled my tea around in the plastic cup. "How can you of all people defend her? Besides, I can't stand furries."

"She's not a furry. Ponies are different." Miles, the walking, talking BDSM encyclopedia. I didn't care about the distinction; any kind of animal play made me uncomfortable.

"She might as well be a furry."

Kamen tossed his empty cup into the wastebasket several feet away. "Why do you hate furries so much, man?"

"They just weird me out."

"I always think one of these days you're gonna break down and tell us some crazy story like in *Team America: World Police*, where the dude's talking about how he doesn't trust actors because of that time the cast of *Cats* gang-raped him."

"I promise I was not gang-raped by furries." I looked around for Gould, but he'd wandered over to talk to GK and Kel, Riddle's owners.

God, why did I feel like I had to keep him in sight? We were all big boys.

"Look at that," I said to the other two. "Look how happy GK and Kel are to see Gould. He's like their favorite nephew. Any minute now they're gonna pull a twenty and a Werther's out of their pockets and ruffle his hair."

"Pardon," came a voice next to me. "I couldn't help overhearing." The accent was British but sounded fake.

I turned. A man with a weasel face and a waterproof jacket was grinning at me, showing off long, yellowish front teeth. "I've never understood the furry subculture myself."

Really? Cuz you look like you'd fit right in, Sir Ferret of Windbreakersham. I stared him up and down. "Who are you?"

He held out a hand. "Dennis." He laughed. "Regina said I ought to introduce myself. Said you and I might have similar interests. Discipline?"

I glanced over at the bar. Regina stood behind it. Sweet girl; biggest hair I'd seen outside of a Winger video. She knew everyone's name and what they liked, and was always trying to *Hello, Dolly!* the shit out of the club. She waved at me. I forced a smile and waved back.

"Dave." I shook Dennis's hand grudgingly. I glanced at Miles, who sipped his drink and raised his eyebrows at me.

"So what do you say?" Dennis the all-weather weasel asked. The accent was definitely fake.

I gazed around the club. *Come save me, Pornstache.*

I thought I glimpsed his crew cut through the doorway to Refinement.

But, I mean, don't, because I'm not attracted to you and I'm not here to have fun. I'm here to reflect on how stupid-lonely I am, and how I prefer meaningless sex to relationships, and meaningless spankings to meaningless sex.

I took a deep breath and flashed my weasel familiar a smile I didn't feel. "Yeah. I can be a real pain in the ass. I like a guy who's willing to do something about it." I'd said shit like this a hundred times before, but for some reason the words put a bad taste in my mouth tonight.

Dennis nodded. "Ahh. Okay, okay. I like to give a good spanking. To a boy who deserves it."

This was going to be a disaster. Dennis seemed like the kind of guy who spent an hour and a half waiting for a pizza delivery because the restaurant had forgotten his order. The kind of guy whose wife had divorced him by changing all the locks in the house while he was at work and just counting on him not to protest. He couldn't credibly have told a dog to sit.

But I was horny. And destined to die alone, so gather ye rosebuds and whatevs. At least Dennis didn't give off a danger vibe.

I exchanged nods with Miles—he'd look out for me. Then I turned to Dennis and jerked my head toward Refinement. "In there?"

He followed me through the doorway. A year ago, I'd never have played with someone like him. I'd have picked a guy who would know to grab my arm and march me over to the spanking bench, swatting me along if I resisted. Who would tell me that if I whined, he'd rip off my underwear and gag me with it. But tonight, I was almost grateful for Dennis's bland passivity.

A small crowd had gathered around the spanking bench to watch a woman dressed as a cowgirl cane an older woman who was not dressed at all. The older woman was taking it quietly; she barely moved as the cane *thwipped* against her bare ass over and over. I shuddered, thrilled and horrified. Canes were the one implement I couldn't do. I leaned over to Dennis. "Let's wait for the bench." No way did I feel like going over this guy's knee.

As I scanned the room, I spotted the 'stache I'd never known I needed. He was watching the caning with impassive blue eyes. The more I stared at him, the more blood rushed to my dick, and the more I thought he looked like a genetic hybrid of Teddy Roosevelt and that guy who cut his arm off when it got trapped by that boulder. Suddenly I had this vision of him holding a paddle and going all stern seventies dad on me. The entire fantasy actually took place in the seventies. There was orange shag carpet, and my hair had been blow-dried and conditioned, and I was wearing rust-colored bell-bottoms that stretched tight across my ass when he bent me over. It was groovy as all fuck.

Come on, Pornstache. I know you want to spank me.

And then marry me and become my forever companion—except don't, because relationships are doomed and marriage is an outdated and restrictive institution and hope is futile.

"Hey." Dennis nudged me. "They're done."

The cowgirl had released the bottom and pulled her up into a hug. They went together to the shelf with disinfectant and paper towels and started wiping down the spanking bench. The crowd dispersed, and it didn't appear that any of them had been waiting to use the bench, so Dennis and I laid claim to it. I was a little disappointed to see Pornstache on his way out. I wouldn't have minded putting on a show for him.

Your facial hair is stupid, but I still want your penis inside me.

He didn't turn back.

And then one day they'll make our babies in a test tube and we can feed each other ice cream on the beach while our children play in the sand and then we can grow old together and fart in bed during reruns of Community.

But, like, I get it. You're straight, and it's cool.

Ugh, relationships. Who needed them? In my early twenties, I'd made a career out of getting fucked by strangers in bars of dubious repute. So why, over the past few years, did coming to Riddle increasingly make me wish I lived in a house with wainscoting and someone who would love me forever?

Pornstache vanished into the crowd without so much as burying his face in my ass and giving me mustache burns on my taint. Life was cruel.

To my right was a little alcove that housed a padded table. A tall, thin man was tying down an eager-looking bottom. Like my mustached hero, the thin man was familiar, and I started to wonder about my memory. I hadn't been away from Riddle *that* long, and yet I'd lost the ability to put names to faces. Or, in this case, bodies. I couldn't see the thin man's face. He was *so* skinny though. It was kind of gross.

"Pants off, and get on up on that bench, boy." Dennis's accent was slipping.

I grimaced as I unsnapped my fly. I took off my pants and underwear and knelt on the bench, leaning forward over it. It was facing the alcove where the thin man was doing his scene. Well, at least I'd have some entertainment while I was spanked. Dennis lifted my shirttail halfway up my back. I tried to concentrate on wanting this.

A DM was going around lighting the candles, so they were probably getting ready to turn off the lights. "Safeword?" Dennis asked.

"Red-yellow. Don't touch my dick. No canes. Paddles are fine if you've got 'em."

"All I've got's my hand." Dennis patted my ass. "Okay, boy, get ready for your spanking."

"The moment we've all been waiting for!" someone yelled in the lounge area.

I lifted my head. Through the doorway to my left, I saw the lights in Chaos go out and heard a cheer. I readied myself for Refinement to be plunged into near-darkness.

At that moment, the thin man in the alcove turned so he was facing me. I stopped breathing, sure that my eyes were playing tricks.

No way.

No fucking way.

All the rage and fear and bitterness that had simmered so close to the surface over the last year threatened to boil over. In a flash, I saw Hal being rolled toward Riddle's door on the gurney. Felt GK's arm around me, keeping me in place.

Bill Henson stared back at me, looking as shocked as I felt.

Then the lights went out.

CHAPTER
TWO

I met with Kel Bowles—aka Darknyss—and Greg Kummets—alias GK—at the Finer Things Café Saturday morning, in a corner where hopefully we wouldn't be overheard. I was still pissed about Friday night, and I really wasn't in the mood for Teatime with Tops. But I needed to talk to them.

Kel and GK had opened Riddle three years ago. I always thought of Greg as GK, but I could never bring myself to think of Kel as Darknyss. They were both only in their midthirties, but very experienced. They'd taught workshops all over the country, and they did their best to make Riddle an educational forum as well as a play space. They were simultaneously wicked and parental, total badasses and yet such a normal couple. Kel would have been my number one choice if I'd ever decided to get my het on—gorgeous curves, blinding smile, mess of black hair piled in the most interesting configurations on her head. GK had the goddamned softest-looking brown skin. Dark eyes, long lashes. And he looked dashing in leather.

They'd never liked me much, but they *loved* Gould. If my friends and I really were a boy band, Gould would be the one GK and Kel had posters of on their wall. And they'd know his whole backstory too—that he wasn't simply the shy one, but also the one who'd survived some rare childhood disease. Gould just had a face like he'd struggled to overcome some unthinkable obstacle in his past. Even though I was pretty sure the only thing he'd ever actually struggled through prior to a year and a half ago was *God of War III* in Chaos mode.

Kel and GK bought me a tea and asked how my job was going. I forced myself to be polite and asked about their jobs and about the latex conference I'd seen on Fetmatch that they were attending next month. But I couldn't relax, and finally I blurted the reason I'd asked them here. "Bill was at the party last night."

Kel scratched her mug with one long, purple nail. "We know."

"Why?" I needed some help with this one. "Why the hell would he be there?"

GK exchanged a glance with Kel before turning back to me. "Because we reinstated his membership."

"Are you *kidding* me?" I would have accepted literally any other explanation for Bill's presence in Riddle last night, from *Spider-Man'ed up the side of the building* to *apparated*. "After what he did?"

Kel could barely look at me. "Dave. It's been almost a year since the trial. He wants a chance to be part of the community again."

"You can't be serious. He *killed* Hal."

GK winced. "I know this is hard. It must have been a shock to see him."

To put it *mildly*. "Gould's not allowed to be within a hundred yards of him! Gould could have been arrested just for being at the club last night."

Kel made what I thought was supposed to be a sympathetic face. "We really didn't know you four would be there. You haven't been around in so long."

"Aren't you afraid he'll hurt someone again?" I demanded.

"Bill has made a huge effort over the past few months." Kel was intensely interested in her mug. "We're keeping an extra-close eye on him to make sure he plays safely and responsibly."

"Hal's death was tragic," GK said. "But it *was* an accident."

"I know. I can't count how many times I've *accidentally* strangled someone during a sex game." I looked around and offered an air high-five to several people in the café who were staring at me. "Amiright?"

"David." Kel's voice was quiet but firm, and she was finally looking at me. "I don't know if you can imagine what it's been like, trying to restore Riddle's reputation. We lost ten percent of our membership last year, not to mention countless potential members who won't choose our club because they've heard what happened there. And what we went through when the court was trying to determine *our* liability—"

"How many more members do you think you'll lose by keeping that fucker around?" I was so furious I was shaking. "And since *when* is this a numbers game?"

"*Listen.* We want to try to repair the rift in the community. Reach out to anyone who needs help understanding and processing what happened. And that includes Bill Henson."

"No." I stood, jostling the table, and watched GK make a dramatic grab for his coffee mug. "It does *not* include reaching out to a murderer. What you need to do is send a clear message that Riddle won't tolerate unsafe players by never letting Bill through your door again."

"Bill had been in the scene for *years* without hurting anyone."

"That you know of."

"Mistakes do happen in this lifestyle."

"Quit calling it a mistake! A mistake is when you send your mom a text meant for the guy you're fucking. *Killing* someone is a *crime.*"

The hipster at the next table glanced over at us.

"The point is—" GK lowered his voice "—Bill's been through a rough time too. Many of Riddle's members have extended support, and Kel and I have worked with him personally to help him come to terms with the incident. We think allowing Bill back into Riddle might help *everyone* heal."

"*The incident.*" "*What happened.*" Nobody would come out and call it what it was. Even I had trouble with the word "murder." I'd go to say it, and there'd be this second where I wondered if it was too intense, too ugly, too unfair to Bill. And then I hated myself for caring.

"Well, get ready to lose four more members." I snatched up my cup. "Because I won't play anywhere he's allowed, and neither will my friends."

All the stern seventies pornstache daddies in the world couldn't drag me back into Riddle now.

I trashed my tea in a nearby bin, aware that people were, once again, staring.

I walked out the door.

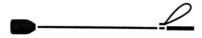

The story goes like this:

Once upon a time, we were a group of five. Kamen and I knew each other from high school, and were surprised to meet each other again in a leather bar two years after graduation. Miles we found at a munch a few months later, and he knew Gould.

And Gould knew Hal.

Gould and Hal were casually dating at the time. It was a rocky relationship, at least what I witnessed of it. It was hard to imagine anyone having a rocky relationship with Gould, who was disconcertingly innocuous. But Hal and Gould together were explosive. That was mostly Hal's fault. Hal was Gould's opposite—tempestuous, reckless, hella fun; you'd slide down the metal rails outside the art museum with him, but you wouldn't trust him to, like, remember to feed your cat while you were out of town. Yet Gould kept Hal in check, and Hal brought out Gould's adventurous side, as well as getting under his skin like no one else could. The first time I'd ever heard Gould shout was during a fight with Hal.

Anyway, the five of us started hanging out. We were mostly the same age, and while our BDSM tastes varied, we had a common interest in the theoretical aspects of the lifestyle as well as the practical. We liked workshops and discussions and, in Miles's case, reading every piece of BDSM literature ever published. Gould and I got along particularly well and had even messed around a little before he and Hal became official. We all joined Riddle the same year and grew, for lack of a better cliché, inseparable.

They were my only close friends at the time. I had plenty of casual friends—I loved socializing, and I could shoot the shit with just about anyone. But close friends, not so much. My parents moved to Canada after I went to college. Just up and left, like they'd been waiting on the edge of their matching leather recliners for me to move out. So Miles, Kamen, Gould, and Hal weren't just my friends; they were my family. Gould and Hal broke up after a year, and while things were slightly tense between them after that, we'd been lucky in that it hadn't affected the group dynamic much.

About a year and a half ago, Hal had wanted to play with a new dom who'd been hanging out at Riddle. Bill Henson was tall, scarecrow-ish, reasonably good-looking, and his Fet profile boasted an impressive résumé. Claimed he'd led workshops at leather conferences. That he was experienced with edge play and TPE. But in reality, he was arrogant, and he didn't seem to think there was anything more to domming than giving orders and getting pissed off if they weren't obeyed. Hal thought he was hilarious.

"I wanna do a scene with him," he'd told me that night.

"Don't be an idiot."

"I'm serious."

"He's the worst!" I steered Hal toward the bar, where Bowser was drinking a Coke. *"You want something outside the box? Play with the medicine man."*

Hal hated being told what to do, and later that night, I saw him in Tranquility with Bill. I figured he was doing it mostly to piss me off. So I left him to it and went to the bar for a soda and then outside for a smoke.

Diet Dr. Pepper. I can't remember what time it was or how long passed between when I saw Hal alive with Bill Henson and when I saw Hal on the gurney. But I do remember enjoying the refreshing taste of regular Dr. Pepper with none of the attendant calories.

I'd been in front of the building when the ambulance pulled up. Two paramedics got out, pressed the buzzer, and were admitted immediately. Morbidly curious, I followed them through the door and up the stairs to Riddle. I kept asking them what was wrong, but they ignored me. When they opened the door to the club, the lights were all on. They strode across the lounge, and I tried to follow, but GK stopped me. *"Dave,"* he said. *"Dave, stay here."*

When I didn't listen, he put his arms around me and held me in this bizarrely gentle embrace that tightened when I started to struggle. *"Stay here,"* he said. *"Just stay here."*

CHAPTER

THREE

Gould and I lived on the first floor of a neat little brick duplex near downtown. We had a stone porch, arched doorways, three bedrooms, and a bunch of plants and colored lights, courtesy of Gould. The living room looked out onto quiet Wayne Street—where Miles swore crack dealers lurked in the shadows—and the kitchen was roomy enough to accommodate the massive lacquered dining table my dad made me before he and my mom moved.

Gould was reading on the living room couch when I got home from the café. I'd been monitoring him closely since last night, but so far he seemed okay.

"Hey," he said without looking up.

I left the front door unlocked and went to the couch. Leaned over the back to drape my arms around his neck. "I met with GK and Kel." I spoke into his hair. "To talk about Bill." No point in keeping it from him.

He stiffened. Slipped a parking ticket into his book to mark his place, and twisted to look up at me. "And?"

I stared at the book. "Did you get a ticket?"

"No, you did. Last August."

"Oh. Right."

"You ever gonna pay it?"

I kissed his cheek and let him go. "Probably not."

Gould set the book—*I Hate My Hips: 50 Ways We Sabotage Ourselves with Negative Thinking*—on the arm of the sofa. I headed to the three-legged table under the window to sort through the mail.

"So GK and Kel said what?" Gould asked.

"They're gonna let him keep playing there." I tore a credit card offer in half.

"No." He didn't say it angrily. Just a simple, quiet *no*.

"I know. I'm sorry. I gave them hell, though. I figure we can—"

"*No*, they can't." Gould so seldom raised his voice that when he did, it was terrifying. For a second I was back in those days after Hal's death, when I'd seen a side of Gould I hadn't known existed.

Kamen walked in from the kitchen, carrying a huge plate of toast. "Wait, Bill's still allowed there?"

"Kamen, Jesus." I took a deep breath. "I had no idea you were here."

Kamen plopped on the couch next to Gould and sent the book crashing to the floor. "I wanted toast."

"Can you not make toast at your place?"

"You guys have the really good bread."

"You are aware this bread is available to the general public? At literally any grocery store?"

Kamen took a bite of toast. Crumbs fell all over his lap. "Why'd they let Bill back in?"

I tried to think of a diplomatic way to phrase this. "Because he wasn't convicted of murder, and they think he deserves a second chance."

Gould was staring at the carpet.

"So I figured we could drop our memberships to Riddle," I added quickly. "We don't need to hang out there anymore."

Kamen licked butter off his finger. "Ricky wanted us to take him this weekend."

Ricky Chuy. People called me a twink, but Ricky made me look like Tom Selleck freebasing Rogaine. Vietnamese, 5'5, hairless, and so thin he could have worn a wedding ring as a belt, Ricky was new to the scene. And so, so eager to learn. We'd taken him to Riddle on occasion to help educate him, but it was like bringing the goddamn Little Mermaid to a bondage club. Every implement, every piece of furniture or costume—he wanted to know what it was called and how it worked. It was exhausting. He'd charm some dom out of a genital whip and add it to his collection of whosits and whatsits galore. He'd pick up a Wartenberg wheel and use it to comb his hair. The most magical thing I could envision would be if a sea witch stole his voice. Permanently.

"Maybe we could take him to Cobalt instead," Gould suggested. I could hear how carefully controlled his tone was.

I went back to opening mail. "What if Kamen's mom's there?"

"Aw, shit," Kamen said around a mouthful. We'd all stopped going to Cobalt long ago. It actually had a bigger gay contingent than Riddle, but Kamen's mom frequented Cobalt, and we'd decided it just wasn't worth the risk of running into Mrs. Pell and her string of fuzzy-chested play partners each time we went. Plus, Cobalt was like the White Castle of fetish clubs.

I opened an envelope from the electric company. Stared. "Gould. Our electric bill is almost ninety dollars."

Gould propped his leg up on the coffee table. "Quit leaving all your shit plugged in."

Kamen slapped crumbs off his lap. "My mom's not usually there on Sundays. She has church."

I checked the name on the bill to make sure it really was ours. "Well, we can't spend our lives avoiding her."

"I do," Kamen mumbled.

"You don't. You're such a mama's boy."

"We should just be mature about it," Gould said. "She has needs, just like we do."

Kamen picked up another piece of bread. Butter ran down his fingers. "Ugh, don't talk about her needs."

I plunked myself between Kamen and Gould, bill in hand. "It is kind of awkward seeing her at the club. She feels too much like *our* mom."

Kamen paused with toast a few inches from his mouth. "That's awesome. Do you seriously think of my mom as your mom?"

"No," Gould said, at the same time I said, "Well, she did buy us that slow cooker."

I tossed the paper over the back of the couch, then leaned against the cushions, staring at the ceiling. "What are we gonna do about this Bill thing?"

Gould glanced at me. "Well, you just threw it on the floor, so I don't—"

"No, the Bill Henson thing." I sat up.

"I don't know, man." Kamen licked his finger and used it to pick crumbs off the plate and eat them. "Maybe we should keep going to Riddle. To show that we're, like, not gonna let Bill ruin it for us."

"Buddy." I caught Kamen's eye and nodded toward Gould.

"Oh, shit!" Kamen said. "I forgot. Sorry."

"It's okay." Gould didn't look at either of us. "You guys are allowed to talk about it. I don't care."

Bill had taken out a restraining order against Gould a year ago due to an incident we generally took great care not to mention.

I shifted. "If we wanna club, I say we go to Cobalt."

"You two can still go to Riddle." Gould sounded irritated. "Seriously, it's fine."

Kamen crunched his way through another piece of toast. "It just sucks that GK and Kel let that douche bag back in."

I sat up suddenly. "Douche bag!"

Kamen and Gould both looked at me.

I stood and hurried to the kitchen to get my laptop. "*That's* who was at the club." I brought the computer over and set it on the coffee table.

"What?" Kamen asked.

"There was this mountain man guy there on Friday." I fired up the laptop. "I, like, wanted to have his children and shave his face but also feel his mustache sanding my balls and have him teach me how to smoke venison. It was a bounty of contradictions."

Kamen's brow knit. "You want to have children?"

"No, not at all; I want to die alone and unloved. Anyway, I thought he looked familiar. It was the Disciplinarian."

"Ohhh." Kamen leaned forward as I brought up Fetmatch. "That guy's legend."

I logged onto Fet and found the Disciplinarian's profile. Yep, the picture was Pornstache—rugged, virile, and glowering at the camera with his pale-blue eyes.

"He's meant to be a total hard-ass, right?" Gould let his leg slide off the table. "You have to, like, bring him the head of a dragon to even be considered for a session."

I cleared my throat and read the profile statement out loud while Kamen looked over my shoulder.

"'Obediance,'" I read, "—spelled wrong—'*is what I expect. I see boys by appointment only, and I train them in the art of obedience. I use corporal punishment to do this. Under my tutelage, many boys are transformed. If I select you to do a scene with me, I will expect your absolute submission. I am experienced with a variety of whips, canes, paddles, etc. You will be subject to my rules and my decisions.*

"'*I am dominant in all areas of my life, and I do not tolerate disobedience, rudeness, or negative attitude. You are unlikely to find anyone as skilled as I at administering the discipline you need. But know that my training will not be easy.*

"'*You must be under 30, in good shape, and able to hold position through a long punishment. You must also be able to think creatively about the ways you will satisfy me.*

"'*If you are interested in a session with the Disciplinarian, please fill out the attached questionnaire. Serious inquiries only.*'"

Below the profile summary was a six-item questionnaire for potential applicants, as well as requirements for answer length— between three and five sentences—and formatting. *Dear Sir* was the required salutation, and *boy* the sign off.

Oh my God. To think I'd wanted this fucker to spank the seat of my fantasy bell-bottoms.

I brought up the questionnaire.

1. Why do you need to be punished?
2. Were you physically disciplined as a child? How?
3. Are you prepared to surrender complete control to me during a disciplinary session, and to allow me to determine the length and severity of a punishment? To submit to punishments that include: spanking, corner time, mouth soaping, enemas, body scrubbing, writing lines, housework, denial of bathroom privileges, figging, scolding, chastity, forced exercise, and rectal temperature-taking?
4. Do you understand that "punishment" is intended to be unpleasant—no chickening out and safewording?
5. What do you hope to get out of a session?
6. What are your feelings on the outdoors?

"Dave, that totally sounds like your thing," Kamen said. "All the punishment stuff."

"Uh, *yeah.*" I scrolled through the questions again. "Except for the safeword-equals-chickening-out bullshit."

"Oh, right."

"What a *dick.* I can't believe I wanted to feel his mustache in all my secret places." The man's profile reminded me of the stories I'd heard from other subs about Bill Henson. How Bill had liked to "push limits" and demand "real submission." But underlying my anger was the uncomfortable knowledge that this man, with his demands and his arrogance and his use of the word "tutelage," actually was the sort of guy I would have jumped on a couple of years ago without a second thought. Bill Henson himself I'd found incredibly unappealing, but I'd played with guys like him. Guys like the Disciplinarian. Guys who thought they were the shit. I'd *liked* that.

"Mmm, the outdoors," Gould said. "Maybe he wants to make you sleep outside."

I reassembled my righteous outrage. "Under thirty and in good shape? *He's* not either of those things."

"He's kinda hot, though." Kamen nodded at the profile picture.

I eyed Kamen's plate. "Buddy, that bread's like five dollars a loaf. You're really not gonna eat the crusts?"

"I am! I'm just eating them last." He picked one up and stuck it in his mouth to demonstrate. Looked at the screen again. "I thought you were into guys who take charge."

Kamen was right. That kind of role-play—*I'm gonna beat your ass and I don't care how hard you beg me to stop*—had always been my thing. I'd seized on any opportunity to rile doms up, to cause trouble. I wanted to be punished. Wanted an ass-whipping that would leave me sore for days. Wanted my hole jackhammered by some bear while he told me what a spoiled brat I was.

But the past few years had changed me. One of the first workshops I'd attended at Riddle had been on the topic of mutual respect in a scene. It sounded dumb, but it was the first time I'd really thought about getting to know someone before I played with them. Prior to joining Riddle, I'd mostly cruised the leather bar downtown. I'd go up to any daddy in there and pout and whine and stick my ass in his face and demand he buy me a drink until he took the hint and pulled me into a dark corner to show me who was boss.

Formal BDSM—negotiations, red-yellow-green, *do I actually like this person?*—had been fairly new to me. To Hal too, I was pretty sure. I sometimes thought if Hal had come from a more informed background, he might still be alive. Maybe his determination to play with Bill that night was a vestige of the days when it wasn't so easy to get online or go to a club and find safe, responsible gay doms willing to have an actual conversation before a scene. Hal had seen a good-looking guy. The good-looking guy had wanted to do more than Hal could handle. Hal had gone along with it because it had meant he'd get laid.

"I'm gonna apply," I announced.

Gould turned to me. "Are you kidding?"

"No. Because here's what we need to do. We need to play with some of these dick doms, and we need to call them out on being so . . . what's the word?"

"Dickish?" Kamen offered.

"No. I mean, yes, but there's another word . . . Miles would know. Entitled, maybe?"

Gould kicked at a fly on the coffee table. "Yeah, entitled's good."

"Like, think how many times we've all received messages on Fetmatch from doms who act like we're already their sub. No 'Hi, how are you?' Just, '. . . once you're on your knees, choking on my cock . . .'"

"Guys usually ask me how I am," Kamen said.

"Of course they do. Your profile sounds like little orphan Annie grew up and married the sun and they had a child made entirely of the unblemished souls of infant animals."

"What?"

Gould propped a foot on the table again. "Your profile's so nice, guys probably can't help but be nice back to you."

I half listened to Gould and Kamen talk about their profiles while I went to work on the Disciplinarian's questionnaire. I was humble, simpering, and anything but honest in my answers. I used *Dear Sir* and signed off with *boy*, as instructed. I'd met enough asshole daddies to know the kind of shit they liked to hear, and I was confident I'd be accepted. When I was done, I hit Submit and closed my laptop. "There." I felt quite smug.

Gould looked up. "You seriously did it?"

"Hell yeah, I did it. God, can you imagine what a pain in his ass I'll be? He doesn't tolerate rudeness, attitude, and disobedience? He won't know what hit him."

Gould opened his mouth, then closed it again. I knew what he wanted to say. *Be careful.* We thought it now, all the time. But we never said it.

I gave him a brief smile. *I will.*

Let the games begin.

CHAPTER
FOUR

I received a reply two days later:

> boy,
> *Thank you for your interest. At this time I have no appointments available.*
> —*The Disciplinarian*

That pissed me off. *Appointments?* Like this fuck-cake was in such high demand he couldn't take a couple of hours out of his day to spank me? I mean, how was this guy still in business? He wasn't that hot, his attitude was insufferable, and just the thought of his mustache made me want to . . .

Rub off on the fucking throw cushion.

God. Damn. It.

I redid the questionnaire, answering not with what I thought he wanted to hear, but with what I wanted to say.

> *Dear "Sir,"*
> *I don't know who exactly you think you are that you can vet potential subs based on a questionnaire, but let me tell you a little about myself—and I do expect you to read this, because I took the time to read your ridiculous profile.*
> *I don't submit easily. I don't expect doms to make me feel like shit about that. But I do need someone who's gonna enjoy keeping me in line. So if you put me over your knee and spank me, I'll fight you, but I'll be glad for it later. I don't consider my childhood your business, so if you're expecting me to write you a little jerk-off fantasy about the time Aunt Jane took a coat hanger to me, I'm afraid I have to disappoint.*

Here's the thing: No way am I gonna do a CNC scene with you first time out of the gate. I don't know you. What if your idea of punishment is to smear me with raw beef and toss me to starving Rottweilers? I need a way out of it if you turn out to be really twisted, which, based on your profile, you might be. I don't mean that as a flirty compliment, I mean it as a "Who the fuck says 'Under my tutelage, many boys are transformed'?"

I'm down for all the punishments you describe. The outdoors is an awesome thing to look at from inside. Here's where I am right now: I'm not thrilled with the way you present yourself, but you sound like someone who's dedicated to the art of discipline. I am dedicated to the art of earning it. So you can either invite me into your secret clubhouse and we'll see if we're a decent match, or you can tell me again that you're the master of the universe with so many eager subs falling at your feet you don't have time for me. Your choice.

—David

The response came much sooner this time.

Dear david,

I do not own or know any Rottweilers. I am twisted but will respect limits. If you are interested, meet at the Finer Things Café Thursday at 7 p.m. Wear comfortable clothes. We can decide from there whether to proceed to the secret clubhouse. In the event that we do, wear white briefs.

—The Disciplinarian

Oh, Pornstache, I know you did not just lowercase my name.

Wear comfortable clothes? As opposed to what? Chain mail? A hair shirt? As for white briefs, screw you, dude. My underwear, my business.

And if I was getting hard from being told what underwear to wear, that was only because I'd had a long day of hearing from customers at Teamendous why I sucked, trying to figure out how many stamps to put on a birthday card to Canada, and fantasizing about the days when casual sex was easy and fun, the handjobs flowed freely, and no erection of mine had gone untouched by a stranger's hand.

This was a total stress boner.

I read the message over and over. So far, there was nothing truly odious about him. I'd expected some affronted-ness in response to my goading, and possibly a *fuck off*. Something to fuel my anger. I would just have to settle for being enraged about the underwear. And the fact that the fucker *lowercased my name*.

I arrived at the Finer Things Café Thursday night wearing a snug black T-shirt and a pair of black and teal cutout PPU briefs under jeans so tight they had effectively flattened my balls. I'd combed my hair, then artfully mussed it. Adorned my wrist with a leather cuff, and shaved and moisturized my ass.

I glanced around and spotted him at a table for two. Not even a corner table—one in the center of the room. He wore cargo pants and, once again, a long-sleeved polo.

And God, how that mustache gently beckoned me.

Everyone else in the café was either a hipster or a university student busy on a laptop—or both—and he looked like he'd wandered out of an episode of *Survivorman*. I walked up to him.

"Are you the . . . Disciplinarian?" Dude could've provided me with a name.

His gaze settled briefly on my crotch. Game on. He leaned back and grunted softly. I was struck again by his surprising handsomeness given that he looked like the kind of dad you'd find manning the grill at a Fourth of July picnic in khaki shorts and knee-high white socks with sandals. "I am. Nice to meet you, David."

His voice was gruff, deep. Okay, fine: sexy.

It bothered me that he hadn't shaken my hand. I wanted, despite myself, to touch him. To see if I got the same jolt of heat and pleasure I did when I looked into his dumbass blue eyes.

He is a man who thinks safewords are for wimps and that you need to be tutelaged. If you get hard for him, you get hard for danger.

I sat across from him and slouched. His coffee smelled good and looked *extremely* black. Like tar. And he'd gotten it in a real mug, which meant we weren't leaving for a while. I wondered if I ought to wait to start the brat stuff until we were back at his place. But his online behavior had irritated me enough that I was ready to start the performance right now.

I slouched even more defiantly. A few seconds later, though, I was itching to sit up. It had to do with the way he looked at me—not predatory, not disapproving, but mildly disappointed, like he'd expected something better than this. Or maybe I was reading too much into it. His lips were mostly hidden under his mustache, so it was hard for me to nail down his exact expression.

"Can I get you anything?" he asked, at the same time I said, "You gonna take me home and beat my ass or what?"

His thick eyebrows slanted inward. "Coffee first?"

I shook my head. "Makes me jittery."

"Jittery," he repeated. His gaze dropped to my left leg, which was bouncing under the table.

"This is normal. I've been known to hover six inches off the ground when fully caffeinated."

He took a swallow of his coffee. It almost looked as though he was trying not to laugh.

"So do you have a name? Or am I just supposed to call you the Disciplinarian?" I flashed him a sweet if insincere smile.

He set his mug down precisely in its condensation ring on the table. "My name is David."

"Shut up." I grinned for real this time and straightened. "Are you serious?"

"Yes."

"Then you'll need a nickname so we don't get mixed up. Can I call you Big D? Or just D?"

"My name will not be an issue, since you will address me as 'Sir' from now on." He spoke slowly, deliberately, but not in that affected commanding tone I heard from a lot of doms. Maybe I was wrong. Maybe he didn't man the Fourth of July grill. Maybe he was in a coonskin cap, one foot up on a shovel, staring into the middle distance on some Americana postcard.

I placed my chin in my hands and widened my eyes. "Mmm. And what if I don't?"

"Then we will discuss it." Something about the way he said *discuss* made my stomach tighten. I was way more interested in this guy than I'd expected. He wasn't the sort of waxed and toned gym bunny I'd pursued during my late teens. Or the wrong-side-of-middle-aged biker bear type I'd developed a brief fetish for in my early twenties. He had his own thing going, and he was, physically speaking, the most stereotypically *manly* man I'd ever considered playing with.

Don't forget. You're here to teach him a lesson.

I went up to get a tea. Made sure to lean against the counter and stick my ass out. But when I glanced over my shoulder, he wasn't even looking. I returned to the table and watched him take a long, slow sip of coffee. Usually by this point I had a potential dom all excited and ready to go. But he seemed like he could sit here indefinitely, holding me with that stoic gaze.

"Warm out tonight, huh?" I asked.

Another slow sip of coffee, during which he didn't break eye contact. "I dislike small talk."

"Well, I love it." My jeans were making my balls itch. I couldn't wait for the part where we were at his place and he saw that I hadn't obeyed his stupid underwear rules.

Which suddenly didn't seem like the best idea I'd ever had. I kept looking at his hands, which were huge. Broad and thick, with long fingers. Even through the ugly shirt I could tell his arms were powerful. He probably spanked *hard*.

I took a sip of tea and accidentally spilled some down my front. Tried to play it cool. "So if you don't like small talk, Big D, maybe we should head to the secret clubhouse."

"It's not looking promising."

What? "What?"

"Do you really want to be here?" he asked quietly.

I furrowed my brow. "Obviously. Or I wouldn't be here."

"David." He spoke in that same gruff, matter-of-fact voice. "I am not here to fight you. I have few requirements, but—"

"*Few* requirements? Just fit and under thirty and not a wuss and totally compliant and obsessed with you and your mastery of the art of discipline?" I lowered my voice. "I guess you're accustomed to composing lists of stipulations and assuming that because you call yourself a dom, they'll be obeyed?"

He leaned forward. "If you don't think you can obey me, you might want to head on home, little boy."

Nuh-uh. You did not call me "little boy" in public. I leaned forward too. "No way. I wore my tighty-est, whitey-est pair of briefs for you. I wanna see what you can do, big man."

My breath caught at the almost manic hunger in his gaze. He didn't want to send me home. He wanted me over his knee—and seeing how much he wanted it made my cock press hard against taut denim. He stared at me, his eyes less blue now than a sharp, dark silver, like a stone slicked by rain. I could imagine his huge hand between my legs, his dick sliding against my hip, his tongue tracing a cord in my neck . . .

"Show me." He said it softly, but I knew I hadn't misunderstood.

"Show you?"

"The underwear."

"Uh . . . here?"

He nodded. "Pull the waistband of your underwear out of those ridiculous jeans and show me."

My face was hot, I was squirming, and fine, my briefs were damp. Didn't mean this joker had won. "They're not ridiculous."

"They're ridiculous. Pull your underwear out."

I glanced around the café. Then I pried my jeans away from my hip, snagged the band of my briefs, and tugged it out.

He looked down for all of a second, then met my gaze again. "David." His voice held an edge so fine it could have cut me without my knowing it. "Do you have difficulty telling black from white?"

I tried for a cocky smile, but my heart was pounding. "Not at all."

"What color is your underwear?"

"Black." A slight catch in my voice. We might have been the only two people in the café in that moment. "And teal."

He closed his eyes and nodded—an almost spiritual-looking gesture. Opened his eyes again. "Why?"

"Because it's the underwear I wanted to wear. You *earn* my obedience, Big D. You don't demand it. And you don't lowercase me unless we've discussed it."

I felt "I'm Every Woman" for about three seconds. Then he asked, "Are you hard?"

"Huh?"

"Do you have an erection?"

"Pssshhhh. Don't flatter yourself." I swallowed, shrugging with a nonchalance I didn't feel. "I'm sitting here thinking, this guy's full of himself, but what the hell, maybe I'll do him a favor and let him have a go at me, since he's drooling like one of those old cartoon wolves."

He leaned closer still, his mustache inches from my lips. "I'm thinking this boy's cocky as hell, but maybe, just maybe he can be taught to respect his elders."

"Not a chance."

"I can try."

"Go for it."

"You've been spanked before?" he asked.

"Hundreds of times."

"Ever had an enema?"

"Barium, molasses, saline, and soap. Do your worst."

"Figging?"

"Never."

"Never have or never will?"

"Never have. But I would."

"Soap in your mouth? Fish oil?"

"I'm allergic to seafood. Make it castor."

"Limits?"

"Canes."

"Shame." He raised his brows. "They'd do wonders for you."

"You think?"

For the first time, I saw a hint of amusement in his expression. "Oh, David. I *know*."

I could feel his breath against my lips. If I leaned just a little closer, I'd be kissing him.

I was hard for danger.

He leaned back, breaking the tension so suddenly that I actually sighed with relief.

"You didn't follow protocol when you messaged me," he said. "You showed up here in clothes I doubt were comfortable when you put them on, but are probably excruciating now that your little cock is hard. And—"

"My cock is huge. Porn stars and horses got nothin.'"

"—and you haven't shown me a modicum of respect since we met."

"I tried to ask about the weather, but you—"

"*This is your last chance to go home, son.*" It was the loudest I'd heard him speak.

I froze.

Cock, meet jeans. Jeans, please contain cock.

He lowered his voice again. "Otherwise we're going to my place. And what happens there isn't going to be as much fun as you think."

I managed a shadow of a grin. "Take me home, sweetheart. I always wanted to get it from the Brawny paper towel guy."

He finished his coffee and stood. He was shorter than I'd figured—I actually had a couple of inches on him. But those arms. Those *hands*. He went up to the dish tubs and placed his mug in the bin meant for plates.

I tensed as he returned to the table, waiting to see what he'd do.

He took my elbow and pulled me up. He was gentle yet firm. I could understand how to everyone else in the café it must have looked like a helpful gesture rather than manhandling.

I planted my feet, pleased to think that if he tried to drag me, it would definitely look like manhandling.

Except he didn't drag. He reached around, quickly and discreetly, and pinched my ass. I yelped and leaped forward, my thighs slamming the table. How he'd done that with such discretion, and how he'd managed to actually get my ass through my denim force field were mysteries to me, but it stung like fuck and surprised the hell out of me.

Several heads turned.

He raised an eyebrow. "David. You're in public."

I glared at him and rubbed the throbbing spot with my free hand. "So are you."

His grip on my arm tightened, but he passed his thumb lightly over my elbow. My stomach fluttered. The skin prickled where he'd touched it, and heat spread from my neck down. "No more trouble," he said quietly.

Aw, sweetheart. I'm just getting started.

I hid a smirk as he steered me around the table and out the door.

CHAPTER

FIVE

"Where're you parked?" I asked as we exited. I was trying to maintain a sense of outrage over him *pinching* me, but it was difficult when what I really wanted was for him to back me against the window of the café and stick his knee between my legs so I could rub off on him in front of the whole damn evening crowd.

"I walked." He let go of my arm and started striding at twice the pace any normal human would opt for. "I'm just a block over."

I caught up and fell into step alongside him.

"Walk in front of me."

"Why?" I asked, suspicious.

"Because I want you to."

This was a far from satisfactory answer. But he slowed, and I moved in front of him.

My ass clenched with each step because now that I was in front of him I was very aware of how tight my jeans were and what he planned to *do* to me. I loved tormenting guys at clubs or play parties by waving my ass at them, but when I was about to get spanked, suddenly I kind of wanted to be wearing a bustle and a crinoline.

"What am I in trouble for?" I asked, hoping to get a sense of what he was planning.

"We'll go over all that when you're at the desk."

"The desk?" I looked over my shoulder at him.

"Next house on your left."

It was a one-story brick deal with ugly brown shutters and battered clematis on the lamppost that looked like it should be named Gladys and have a smoker's cough.

"Wait here." D strode past me.

I was in the middle of the yard, and I assumed he meant I should at least follow him to the porch, but he turned around when I started after him. "*Stay. There.*" He didn't raise his voice, but he sharpened it, and I felt it in my groin.

I stopped walking and barked. When he whirled toward me again, I grinned.

He shook his head, but once again it looked like his lips were twitching under the mustache.

He went to the porch, unlocked the front door, and disappeared inside. I glanced around, feeling alone and a little chilly in the dark. I leaned against the lamppost, purposely mushing the clematis.

After a moment the porch light went on and he appeared in the door, chugging water from a bottle.

"You can come in." He recapped the bottle.

I sauntered.

He held the door open, and I walked past him into the house. The place smelled like leather and cedar and pine needles and the sweat of labor. Possibly he had some kind of Paul Bunyan-themed Glade PlugIn. I stood in the hall, not sure where to go from here.

"Drink?" he asked.

I shook my head. Glanced down at the front of my pants to remind him I was still hard. He stepped uncomfortably close to me and held eye contact just long enough that I shifted.

"Once I start the scene," he said, "I don't want to break it. For a scene with a new partner, I stick to spanking with my hand or a paddle. I also do mouth soaping, writing assignments, and corner time. I need to know if any of those are hard limits for you."

"Nope."

"I may also take you by the arm or ear, and if I soap your mouth, I may pinch your nose to get your mouth open."

"Fine."

"If I'm pleased with you, and we agree to further sessions, I'll expect you to accept punishments that could include enemas, figging, spanking—with crops, straps, paddles, or whips—and forced exercise."

"What's forced exercise?"

"You get on my treadmill and you run. Or you do laps around my yard. Or push-ups."

I leaned against the wall, hooking my thumbs in my belt loops. "What if I'm not pleased with *you*?"

"Then I imagine we won't agree to further sessions."

I nodded. "Here are *my* stipulations. You discipline me, but you don't degrade me. I can take a hard punishment. But if I think you're being gratuitous, I'll safeword."

"What do you mean?"

"Safeword. It's a word that—"

He rolled his eyes. "What do you mean 'gratuitous'?"

"I mean don't be an asshole about it. I'm not gonna choke on your cock as punishment, or let you pee in my mouth or anything. And don't make fun of me. Like, don't make fun of how I can't take enough pain or anything like that."

I saw his shoulders twitch, once, like he'd just swallowed a laugh. "I won't pee in your mouth. But I do incorporate humiliation into my punishments. And while I will respect your limits, once the punishment begins, I decide when it ends. The safeword is for emergencies only."

Every muscle in my body tensed. "The safeword is for any time I feel like using it."

"It's a punishment. It shouldn't be pleasant, and it should take you out of your comfort zone."

I pushed off the wall and stepped toward him. "I agree with not pleasant, but I'm not gonna let you tell me when I can and can't use my safeword." *Go on, you fucker. Just try and argue with me.*

He nodded. "What's your word?"

"'Red' works for me."

"Any health problems? Allergies, mental or physical disorders, past injuries?"

"I don't know. You want to examine me, doctor?"

"Answer the question."

"Allergic to cats, flax, and authority. And shellfish."

"Anything else you want to discuss before we begin?"

"Who cuts your hair? You should run them through with their own thinning shears. You have a wonderful face, and so much wasted potential for—" He stepped forward and grabbed my ear. "Ow!"

I gritted my teeth as he pulled me down the hall and toward the back of the house. I tried to dig my heels in, but when someone's got ahold of your ear, the only one you really hurt by digging in is yourself. I muttered and grabbed his wrist, but he twisted my earlobe, and I dropped my arms, my mouth open in a silent cry.

He led me into a room at the end of the hall. The floor was hardwood, the walls off-white, and there was a tiny, old-fashioned, red wooden school desk at one end with a sheet of paper and a pen on it. At the other end was a much larger, headmaster-style wooden desk and a high-backed, armless chair. The far wall had a long rack with three rows of pegs, and on it hung canes of various sizes, a riding crop, a black paddle the size of a small nation, a tawse, approximately eight billion other paddles, three floggers, and a gleaming razor strop.

Just hanging on the wall. What the hell did he tell guests who wandered back here looking for the bathroom and found this den of horrors? Near the desk there was a tall, varnished cabinet, which probably held other nightmares. He let go of my ear, and I gave it a good rub. Noticed what looked like a framed piece of leather on the wall above the desk. "What's that?"

"That is the first hide I ever tanned. Literally."

"You . . . make your own leather?"

He removed his jacket, folded it, and placed it over the high-backed chair. "Yes. There is nothing more tragic, David, than the death of the American man."

"I'll bet if you really tried, you could think of something more tragic."

"I doubt it."

I pretended to continue examining the leather while checking him out peripherally. "Why do you think the American man's dead? You mean because men don't know how to make leather anymore?"

He came to stand beside me. "Among other things. In this culture of participation awards, this society where everyone is special and legitimate skill is the mark of a bygone era, we have ceased to quantify accomplishment. I look around and see a generation of useless, overprivileged men who have all been taught to express their opinions rather than get things done."

"Aren't you expressing an opinion right now instead of getting things done?"

"Good point." He reached again for my ear.

"No! No, wait." I laughed, scooting away just before he could grab me. "I'm not through admiring your collection." I walked along the wall. "I like being a modern man. I like being able to talk about my feelings and watch Pixar movies with my dude friends." I started touching the paddles. "Did you make these?"

"Most of them. And two of the floggers."

I was fascinated by how slowly he spoke. Like he was in no hurry, ever, for anything. "They're gorgeous."

"Eleven paddles, five hairbrushes, ten canes. Six floggers. Three riding crops, a quirt, a single-tail stock whip. A nightstick. And then miscellaneous implements—wooden spoons, rulers, spatulas."

"You could have one fucked-up twelve days of Christmas. Did you say a nightstick?"

"Mm-hmm." He pulled a police baton off the wall and handed it to me.

"Jesus." I hefted it. "You could kill someone with this."

"I can't take it to clubs. It's illegal to have one in public. Not that I really go to clubs."

"So I just got lucky the other night?"

He didn't answer.

"I saw you," I pressed. "At Riddle."

Still no answer. Then, very quietly: "I saw you too."

I studied the baton again. "Have you ever killed anyone with this?"

"No."

"Maimed?" I thumped the stick against my palm.

"Bruised. Superficially. As per the boy's request." He took the nightstick from me. "It's more of a psychological tool than a physical one. You can scare someone without even touching them. Same with a rubber hose."

"You're scaring me now." I checked the walls for bloodstains. Claw marks. Places where the plaster had been weakened by salt tears. I saw nothing.

D snapped his fingers and pointed at the school desk. "Sit."

I debated resisting, but decided not to overplay my hand. I crammed myself into the tiny desk, forty-five percent sure my jeans were going to split. My knees jutted, and the wood under my ass was hard and unforgiving. I rubbed my ear again.

D clasped his hands behind his back and circled me. "From here on, you will address me as 'Sir.' You will obey my instructions promptly. I don't recommend testing me on that."

I always complained to my friends about doms who seemed to have memorized a cliché-ridden script; who deepened their voices and barked orders and thought that was sexy. I also complained about doms who had no script, whose instructions were disorganized and inarticulate. I needed a balance. D almost had it. He sounded rehearsed but also sure of himself.

"Yes, Sir," I said politely. Let him think I was cowed. Let him think he had me.

He wouldn't stop *staring* at me. My cock rubbed against damp nylon and tight denim. All I could see if I gazed ahead was the wall of implements. So I tried studying the desk. The blank piece of paper and pen.

"Look at me."

I did, and suddenly felt about the size of a figure in a snow globe.

"Do you have any questions?"

"You still haven't answered my last one. About who cuts your hair."

"Stand up." His voice was soft.

The desk creaked as I extricated myself. I stood in front of him. Had he gotten taller?

"Hands behind your head."

I raised my arms and clasped my hands behind my head, which pulled my shirt up a few inches and exposed the trail of hair running down under the waistband of my jeans. I'd done it all before, the bending over, the counting the strokes, the assuming of various positions of submission and contrition. But right now it all seemed new. My skin tingled like it was electric, my breathing was shallow, and my heart pumped too fast.

He reached into his pocket and pulled out his wallet. He removed a business card and slid it into my pocket, which took some time, since my jeans really didn't even leave room for a piece of paper. I stopped breathing for a second as his knuckles grazed my bare hip.

"My stylist's card," he said. "Now take your hands off your head and *sit down*."

I sat, my knees knocking the desk. "They're uneven."

"What?"

"Your sideburns."

"They're not." For the first time, he sounded uncertain.

I'd been studying them in the café. They totally were. "The left one's shorter."

He shifted. I could tell he wanted to look in a mirror. *Gotcha.*

"I could do a better job." I smiled. "I love cutting hair. I'm thinking about going to school for it. I do my roommate's hair sometimes, and he's got crazy curls. You'd look good with a—"

His hand came down hard on the desk. I jumped.

He pointed at the paper. "I want you to write me a description of every foot you've put wrong since we met. Make sure I can read your writing. You have five minutes."

He turned and walked across the room. I rolled my eyes. Write about How I Was Bad—how original. I'd never been so torn between being an asshole and behaving myself. I wanted to impress him with my *obedience*. I also wanted to make him grit his teeth until they cracked. "No fuckin' problem."

I expected him to snap at me, or come back and throw me over his knee, but instead he went to the bureau cabinet and opened it. I watched him take out a small porcelain bowl and a decanter of water. He set them on the desk. Then he took out a wrapped bar of Ivory soap and closed the cupboard.

Fuck. Should have seen that coming.

I pretended to be writing when he looked at me. Glanced up a second later to watch him pour the water in the bowl, unwrap the soap, dip it in the water, and start rubbing the bar until it was foamy.

I closed my eyes. I hated soap. Only one dom had ever used it on me, and I actually had caved and stopped being a brat just to make it end. D put the lathered bar into the bowl, then went to the Wall of Implements. He took down a large wooden paddle. With holes.

No fucking way.

He placed the paddle on the headmaster desk beside the soap and sat. I tried to focus.

Write about every foot I'd put wrong. I peered down at my feet.

I started to write: *My left foot is a size eight point five. It has a high arch, and my big toe is longer than my second toe. There is a light smattering of hair on the top of my foot.* I paused and stuck my left leg out, studying my shoe. *Right now I am wearing Nike Frees for m—*

"Bring me your paper."

I glanced at my paper. "I'm not done yet."

"One . . . two . . ."

I brought him the paper.

"Put your hands on your head."

You do the hokey pokey and you turn yourself around . . . I put my hands on my head and stood there while he read it.

"Shirt off." He didn't look up.

I took my shirt off. He still didn't look at me.

"Drop your pants,"

"I don't—" I started.

"*Drop* your *pants.*"

I pushed my jeans down to my thighs. Pretty sure they left skid marks on my hips.

"To your ankles."

I shoved them all the way down. Straightened. Remembered to put my hands back on my head. I felt considerably less confident now than I had earlier in the evening when I'd gleefully chosen to ignore his underwear request. The PPU briefs were my favorite—a sort of jockstrap-inspired male garter belt. A teal pouch covered my dick and balls, while black elastic bands went around the tops of my thighs and my waist. There were strategic cutouts exposing rectangles of skin just under my hipbones and along the sides of my ass. Normally I felt hot as fuck in them, but right now I felt uncertain and a little embarrassed.

"Why did you wear these tonight?" he asked calmly. He was staring at the front pouch, which was straining to hold my dick.

"I like them."

They were my favorite underwear to be spanked in. They cupped my ass just right and left me exposed in creative places. They made me feel like I was in gym class and on a runway at the same time.

No other guy I knew had underwear like these. But I wasn't going to tell D all that.

"Hmm." He reached out slowly and let his fingertips brush the bare skin to the left of my groin. I shivered and tried to stay still. He hooked his finger in the band around the top of my left thigh and snapped it gently. I allowed a small whimper to escape, and he glanced up. "Because of this?" He drew light circles along the naked sides of my ass.

"Yes, Sir." I let the words out on a breath. My knees softened as he touched the edges of the fabric. I closed my eyes and dipped my head. He traced the vertical straps that ran from the waistband down to the thigh bands then followed the thigh bands around to the back. I shifted, off-balance.

His head was level with my belly, and I could almost feel his breath on my cock through the fabric. I could smell his aftershave, and every inhalation that carried the scent was more exciting than the last. I wanted to touch his hair. Wanted to press my body to his and kiss him.

Wordlessly, he placed one hand on the small of my back and one on my stomach, and turned me so I wasn't directly facing him. He bent me forward. My legs quivered as he increased the pressure on my lower back until my ass stuck out. He rubbed a slow circle on the seat of my briefs. Leaned forward and whispered in my ear, "Are they what I asked you to wear?"

I shook my head, swallowing. "No, Sir."

He pinched the lower curve of my right cheek. Ran his nail lightly along my skin. I pushed my ass out further, hoping he'd keep going.

"Take that underwear down," he whispered.

I did. I hovered there, naked except for the pants and briefs around my ankles, breathing harshly. My cock was standing up and at an angle, a single bead of clear fluid shining on the tip.

I tried to look up without breaking position. Watched his face for any sign of admiration. The porn stars and horses had been an exaggeration, but my cock was decent sized, and my ass was epic. Ain't braggin' if it's true. I worked out to keep it just firm enough that you could see some muscle dimples but not so unyielding that it didn't bounce when smacked. I angled myself so he'd have a better view.

Now that I'd snapped out of whatever trance I'd been in for the last few minutes while he touched me, I was peeved at myself. What happened to coming here to confront him?

"Am I in good enough shape for you?" I asked, trying for snide, but falling short.

"I'm sure you know you're in very good shape."

"I just find it funny that you require your subs to be in shape when you're kind of all about the bass, right?"

That was probably going too far. A bad habit of mine—I liked teasing people, but I didn't always know how to quit before feelings got hurt. He seemed unfazed, though.

"Come here."

I was nervous. Not normal, pre-spanking jittery, but genuinely nervous. Because I knew I should be angry that he'd tried to tell me when I could use my safeword, but instead I fucking wanted him to like me.

"You clearly aren't taking this very seriously." He watched as I edged closer to him. "So you have two options. You can leave right now. Or you can apologize to me and take your punishment."

I shivered.

He waited.

"I'm sorry," I said quietly.

"For what?"

"Describing my foot." I gave him a charming smile, which withered quickly under his stare. It was hard to be charming with your pants around your ankles. "But here's the thing. I don't think you can set rules or ask for absolute submission until you've *earned* those rights. I really believe that."

He reached out and set a hand on my hip. I flinched. He waited until I was looking at him again. "I choose boys based on their ability to follow instructions. Or in your case, because I saw a hint of potential in your self-conscious posturing."

Heat crept up my neck. "Self-conscious?"

"You're afraid to give up control." He stroked my hip very gently with his thumb. "To submit."

That got to me. Triggered something I didn't entirely understand, and my throat tightened. I started talking before I could think.

"Ah, yes. I forgot: you're a dom, so you automatically know who I am and how I feel. Or did you gather all this from the 'introductory questions' I had to complete in order to land one magical night with you?"

"Why did you answer those questions if you didn't like them?"

I forced my voice steady. "So that I'd have a chance to tell you to your face that you're a dick. And that most subs like to be treated like human beings, not job applicants."

"When have I not treated you like a human being?"

Why did he keep asking me questions? Why didn't he *fight*? "You're— You act . . . *entitled*."

"Explain."

"You act like you deserve to be listened to. Why? I don't know you." A sharp, sudden memory of the door to Riddle closing behind the paramedics. The other players in the club clustering around, asking questions, crying, shouting. It hit me harder than it ever had that when I played, I placed my trust in strangers. Strangers who could hurt me any number of ways. I gripped the edge of the headmaster desk, trying to ground myself. The room seemed to tilt. "And you said in your profile that safewording is chickening out."

Miles played without safewords. Dude wouldn't say "stop" unless he was serious. And I'd rarely negotiated safewords back in the leather bar days—not unless the other guy brought it up. But now, just . . . fuck it. I wanted a word. And he had no right to make me feel like I shouldn't need it.

D's hand slid from my hip. "That's not exactly what I meant."

"Well, it's what it fucking sounds like."

He snapped his fingers again, and I wanted to fucking bite him. "You may tell me how you feel. But be respectful."

All my anger poured out of me at once. "Oh, how kind. I *may* tell you how I feel. May I also piss, shit, blink, breathe, and sleep?" I braced myself, but he didn't touch me.

"One last warning. Lose the attitude."

"I'm not playing anymore."

"Neither am I."

We glared at each other.

His mustache twitched. "I get a lot of requests for sessions, and—"

"I'll bet that really feeds your ego."

"I get a lot of requests," he went on, as if I hadn't spoken. "And I'm looking for boys whose interests match my own. If you're not ready for this level of discipline, maybe you should head home."

"Not ready? I've taken way more than a paddling. And I've written enough 'I'm a Bad Boy' essays to publish a greatest-hits collection. And you can't send me home because I was already leaving." *Ooh. Good one, Dave.*

I yanked my underwear and pants up, except they got stuck on my dick, which ached so badly I swore under my breath. My head throbbed, and my skin felt too hot, and I wanted to be home.

D watched me go without a word.

CHAPTER
SIX

I stewed for three days, but I wasn't sure why exactly I was angry. D hadn't actually disregarded my boundaries or tried to pressure me into anything I didn't want. And despite the claims he'd made on his profile, I'd played with doms way rougher and more demanding than he was.

When I was eighteen, I'd hooked up with a guy who'd had a very private backyard—wooden fence, hedges, no neighbors directly behind him. He had put a glory hole in the fence, in a little hedged alcove, and twice I'd gone to his backyard, where he was waiting for me with his giant cock sticking through the hole in the fence. I'd suck him off and leave. I never saw his face, but he'd mutter through the fence, stuff like, *"Take it boy,"* and, *"Suck me, you little cum whore."* On my third visit, I wasn't in the right mood or something. I felt weird about the things he was calling me, and I wasn't turned on. I just wanted to go home. So I stopped sucking him and stood. Started to apologize. And he'd said, *"If you walk away now, I'll kill you."*

He'd sounded dead serious. Part of me knew it was ridiculous—he was behind a fence, presumably naked or partly so. If I ran, I could be back at my car before he was even out of the yard. But my imagination had gotten the better of me. I'd imagined he had a gun pressed against the boards, ready to blow my brains out. Or that he'd had plenty of practice pulling his pants up and vaulting the fence in two seconds flat to attack little cum whores who didn't finish blowing him.

So I got back on my knees and sucked him until he came. Afterward, he'd let me go without a word.

He was still on Fetmatch. He'd Liked one of my pictures last month.

That was kind of fucked up, wasn't it? Not as fucked up as an actual murderer like Bill Henson getting to remain a member of Riddle. But still pretty fucked up. Like, maybe that was just Glory Hole's thing—the threats, the name-calling. Maybe lots of guys got off on it. But it wasn't something he'd warned me he was going to do, and it had scared the shit out of me.

But I still jerked off sometimes to the memory.

So what was I supposed to do about the fact that some of the things that seemed the most dangerous or cruel or terrifying about the lifestyle were often the most exciting?

Two years ago, Fetmatch had put a policy in place to prevent members from using the site to make rape or abuse allegations against other members. A few months after that, a group on Fet had petitioned the site to change its policy and allow victims of abuse to publicly call out their abusers—at least by screen name. They'd used Bill and Hal as an example of a tragedy that might have been stopped if there were a forum where members could identify dangerous players in their communities.

The debate surrounding it had been ugly. For every person who signed the petition and asked Fetmatch to stop silencing victims, someone else argued that finger-pointing was a "slippery slope" and was "just going to lead to drama." Fet had issued a public statement explaining that, as a social media site, it could not be responsible for hosting confrontations between alleged victims and their alleged attackers. *We offer resources for those in need*, the site said, *but the best way to stop a criminal from striking again is to report the crime to the police.*

A sub named Maya had been one of the most vocal petitioners. She'd written countless posts about why victims were often unable to go to the police, and why it was important for submissives to be able to warn one another about predators in the community. She'd argued with commenters who said things like *If it was real rape, the victim would go to the police* and *If you don't feel comfortable taking legal action against your attacker, you have no business calling them out here.* But in the end, she'd had to give up the fight. Fet wasn't going to change. Doms like Bill and Glory Hole were going to get away with whatever they wanted to do or say. And subs like me were going to enable them by putting up with it.

I had to stop. Had to quit playing with arrogant pricks.

So on my third day of being angry at D and being horny and wanting to punch him but also apologize to him and just generally not understanding what the *fuck* was going on in my head ... I had an idea.

A crazy idea.

But one that just might work.

"Thank you all for being here today." I looked across the table at Miles, Kamen, and Gould. I'd made them all sit on the same side, so they looked like a panel of judges at a pie contest. "I have something important to show you."

Miles adjusted his glasses. "If it's porn, please don't bother. I can't stand another reminder of how not-laid I'm getting." Miles's cardigan today was dark blue and oversized.

"Nice sweater." I nodded at it. "Neighbor Aber been by lately, or ...?"

"I am in no mood for your sartorial appraisals, David."

"So *is* it porn?" Kamen sounded excited.

"Better." I turned my laptop screen to face them. "Behold."

"'The Subs Club,'" Gould read off the top of the page. I leaned over the screen to read with them. The blog was done in a tasteful beige and hunter theme. Right now it only had one follower—me—but that was about to change.

"What is this?" Miles looked up at me.

"It's our new blog. We're going to use it to get people talking about doms."

Gould frowned. "Doms?"

"Yeah. Like about what makes doms either good or shitty. We can talk about our own experiences, invite other subs to share theirs, and, like, start a dialogue about what doms need to do in order to not be assholes." I checked the screen again. "And we don't really have to call it the Subs Club. That was just a lame placeholder title I put in."

Kamen crossed his arms on the table. "It makes me want a sandwich."

None of them seemed to be jumping on board.

Gould squinted. "Did you do this in WordPress?"

"Yeah." I tilted the screen so he could see it better. "Ricky helped."

"It looks nice."

"Thanks."

Miles tapped the table with his finger. "You know, this is a very interesting idea."

"I know." I nudged him. "And you'd be really good at it. You love writing and thinking and stuff."

"And I actually like 'the Subs Club' as a name."

Kamen nodded. "We're like the Baby-Sitters Club. Except instead of babysitting, we're face-sitting."

"Kamen, gross," I said. "Now I'll never be able to read the Baby-Sitters Club books the same way again."

Gould glanced at me. "Do you still read the Baby-Sitters Club books?"

I cleared my throat. "Moving on. All of us need to come up with usernames, to protect our privacy. We can invite subs we know to become members of the blog, and they'll be able to comment and submit posts. It'll be a private blog. That way, submissives have a safe place to talk about, like, if a dom abused them or whatever. Basically, everything Fetmatch *won't* let us discuss, we'll discuss here."

Miles did not look pleased. "Are we equipped to mediate that sort of discussion?"

"Why not?"

He shook his head. "I don't know. Remember the last time we tried to have a group blog?"

"You mean the Log Blog?" The four of us had once started an ill-fated blog where we posted pictures of noteworthy shits we'd taken. We'd developed quite the rabid fan base on Reddit before we took it down.

"Yeaaaaahhh!" Kamen slapped the table. "The Log Blog!"

I made a face. "We were super immature back then."

"It was two years ago," Gould pointed out.

"Exactly. Now we're all grown up and ready to have a serious adult blog."

Kamen leaned back, stretched, and scratched his chest. "My shits were the best, right?"

Miles rolled his eyes. "Kamen, yours defied the laws of nature, and everybody in this room thought you should see a doctor."

Kamen turned to Miles and offered his hand for a high five, but Miles didn't return it, and Kamen slowly put his hand down. "Gould never even participated," he muttered, rocking his chair back on its hind legs.

"Because I don't feel like sharing my bowel movements with the internet," Gould said.

"It was anonymous!"

Gould was easily embarrassed, especially by bodily functions. I'd known the guy for years and had yet to hear him fart.

"So what do you think?" I moved my laptop from side to side, letting everyone take a good look at the screen. "The Subs Club. Who's in?"

"I am." Kamen righted his chair with a *thunk*. "I suck at writing, though."

"I'll spell-check you, buddy."

Miles nodded. "I'm in." Miles never missed a chance to show off his BDSM knowledge or voice his opinion on anything kink related. This would be right up his alley.

Only Gould remained silent.

"Gould?" I asked.

He looked up at me. "What if we reviewed doms?"

"Reviewed?"

"Yeah. What if we listed doms we'd played with and let people rate them on, like, safety and skill?"

"Ooh. Gould!" I could totally get into that.

"Noooo," Miles said. "Terrible idea."

"Why?" I asked.

"It's a legal minefield."

"We wouldn't use anyone's real names. Just their Fet names."

"Still, it's a public persona. And you think these guys won't know who wrote the reviews? If we're, like, describing specific scenes?"

"We can have a sign-up form to join the blog," Gould suggested. "Make sure we only let submissives in. Doms never have to know it exists."

"Yes, because that's how the internet works. What happens when a member forwards the blog to one of the doms we're writing about?"

I jumped in. "It's not illegal to talk about people in the community on community-oriented forums. Remember that review on Fet a couple months ago trashing that rope group's demo?"

Miles's cardigan buttons clicked against the table's edge. "But a group like that, they're putting themselves in the public eye in a way that individuals aren't."

Miles and I had always been the most likely in the group to clash. He was more practical and rule abiding than I was, and sometimes the amount of time he spent on his high horse drove me crazy.

"I really think we'll be fine," I said, "as long as we don't use names. And obviously, we do not publish *any* details about where the doms live, work, or whatever. Though in the case of doms who are genuinely unsafe, I see absolutely no reason not to link to their Fet profile, provide details of exactly what they did, and share any pics they've made available under their profile names, so subs'll recognize them if they ever meet in a club."

"The problem," Miles insisted, "is that the doms who don't give a shit about hurting subs in a scene are the ones who'd be crazy enough to retaliate if they're outed."

"So we should let them continue to scare their victims into keeping quiet?"

Miles sighed.

"Hey." Kamen raised his hand.

"Yes, Kamen?" I said.

"If someone posts that, like, a dom is abusive, how do we know if they're telling the truth?"

"That's the same debate Fet was having last year, buddy. A bunch of dicks were saying that calling out abusers would turn into a witch hunt."

"But why are they dicks for thinking that? Couldn't it happen?"

"Could, but it's not likely. And besides, it's not like we're prosecuting the crimes. We'd just give people a place to recount their experiences, as a warning to others."

Gould nodded. "And each dom would, hopefully, have a collection of ratings. So you'd get a variety of opinions on whether they're safe or not."

"A human being is not a restaurant you rate on Yelp," Miles argued. "Would you go on the internet and rate people you'd dated? Or had sex with?"

I looked at him strangely. "Totally."

"Dude, there's tons of sites like that," Kamen pointed out.

Miles shook his head. "And they're *horrible*. What, like Rate My Ex Girlfriend dot com? That's . . . revenge porn."

I opened a doc on my computer and started making notes, talking as I typed. "I'm pretty sure people tell stories about their former partners all the time in memoirs and essays and articles or whatever." I was bullshitting. But Gould's idea really did sound awesome to me, and I wanted Miles to come around to it. "We play the same way we normally would. And when we're done, we give the dom a rating. Four stars for how they negotiate limits. Three for competence with equipment. Five for attitude. Or whatever."

"I like it," Gould said.

Kamen grinned. "Yeah, I'd be down."

"It's like Dave said—" Gould nudged Miles "—more than anything, we get people talking about what makes a good dom."

Miles still looked unhappy. "We're going to have a very small reach. We're all queer. And we've all incestuously scened with the—what, six queer male doms in the community?"

I shrugged. "I've played with a shitload of guys who say they're straight. But in the event that our reach seems too limited, we could invite members to suggest doms to rate. Then we post the doms' screen names, and the members who've played with them can review them."

"And I can be flexible with who I play with," Gould mumbled.

I cocked my head, about to pursue that. But Miles broke in. "This is not what Hal would have wanted."

Gould glanced sharply at Miles.

"Oh really?" I spoke cautiously, keeping an eye on Gould.

Miles was bouncing like he had a violet wand up his ass. Which, knowing him, was a distinct possibility. "Hal didn't play safe, not by a long shot. He played like an idiot most of the time, and I doubt he'd have wanted to see us turn our sex lives into some kind of safety school special, or—"

"Stop it." Gould was half out of his chair. "Just shut up right now."

"Dude, Miles, that's *all* you do!" I said. "Anytime we're at the club, you lecture us on what the different pieces of equipment are called and how to use them properly, and—"

"Hal didn't die because he was an idiot!" Gould's voice was shaking. "He died because some jackass who called himself a dom broke the most basic fucking safety rules. He damn well would have wanted the community to be safer for other people."

"You don't know everything about him just because you fucked him!" Miles shot back.

"Whoa, guys, guys." I looked from one to the other, not sure how we'd gotten here. "Calm down."

Miles sniffed. Gould was still hovering just above his seat. He slowly sat back down.

"This isn't revenge porn, or a safety special, or whatever," I promised. "It's just a forum where we talk about the issues submissives face in this community. And where subs can point out the strengths and weaknesses in the doms they play with. We have a chance to do something good here." I turned to Miles. "You're our best writer. And you're so organized. I feel like you'll do a great job. Not just writing articles, but moderating reviews and discussions. We *need* you."

I could see flattery take hold. Miles straightened his cardigan. "All right," he said at last. "I'll try it. But if this looks like it's going to blow up in our faces, I shall exit the aircraft. With or without the rest of you."

"So we're agreed?" I asked. "The Subs Club is a thing? And we'll have a review blog as part of the site?"

Gould was looking at the table and not at any of us, which worried me a little.

"I'll get Ricky to help set up the review portion," I went on. "He can be our IT guy." I looked at each of them in turn. "Hey, guys? Welcome to the Subs Club."

Kamen shook his head. "Every time you say it, man. Sandwiches."

CHAPTER
SEVEN

I spent the week working with Ricky on setting up the website and taking it for a test drive. We had a log-in system where people could register to join the club by filling out a short application and choosing a username and password. They had to give us a valid email and tell us why they wanted to join. I recruited our first members—subs I knew from Riddle and from other kink events. I tried to get a wide variety of genders and orientations, and I encouraged them to list the Fet names of doms they'd played with so I could post those names and make them available to rate. Meanwhile I put up the names of a few doms I'd played with over the years and started rating them. Ricky had designed a cute little flogger icon in place of stars, and we'd established a one to five flogger rating system.

I didn't go out all weekend. On Sunday morning Miles came over.

"I was involved in a certain amount of carnal jollification last night." He dropped his messenger bag on one of the kitchen chairs and took out his tablet.

"Dude, you can just say you got laid."

"Someone I met on Fet."

I passed him the bag of Hershey's Kisses I was eating from. "And? How was it?"

"I guess you'll find out when you see my . . . *rating*." He unwrapped a Kiss and stuck it in his mouth, then fired up his tablet and logged in to the site to show me. "See? Five floggers for safety—he was a skilled negotiator who sterilized his toys like nobody's business. Four for competence—he pushed a needle too deep a couple of times, but nothing heinous."

"Gross. I don't want to hear about needle play. Ever."

Miles ignored me. "And five for attitude. He was polite, let me set the limits, and he gave me snacks afterward."

"Aww, snack doms are the best!" I slapped his shoulder. "See, this is fun, right?"

Miles shrugged. "It is gratifying, in a way."

"And did you see, we have fifteen members already? They've been rating some of the doms whose names I posted. And so far, nobody's been uncivil."

Miles nodded. "I was looking at it earlier. People do sound surprisingly intelligent and respectful."

"I mean, there's this one guy, Tito Blacksaw." I pointed to Tito's name, which had a two-flogger average. "Three women rated him low on attitude, and their comments are negative but not, like, hostile."

I hadn't put up the Disciplinarian's name yet. But I'd made up my mind I was going to ask him for another session. A full session. And then I was going to rate him honestly.

I couldn't stop thinking about him. I'd been half-hard all day at work on Friday, remembering sitting at that school desk, watching him take the paddle down from the wall. The way he'd touched me as I'd stood in my underwear in his den of horrors. His blue eyes and his stupid haircut, which I really could have fixed in five minutes.

The more I thought about him, the more I realized that the issue had mostly been on my end. I'd freaked out about Hal, and that had kept me from talking to D man to man. Right now, I needed to figure out how to get D to agree to a second meeting with me. Which would mean apologizing. Something I didn't typically do well unless I believed I'd been totally in the wrong.

Still, I could fake it. For the sake of the review blog.

So I messaged D after Miles left.

Hey D—
I just wanted to say sorry for the other night. I think I overreacted.
—d

I had my response two hours later.

David,
A shame it didn't work out.
—Sir

I hadn't exactly expected a *No problem, wanna have another go?* But his curtness was unfortunate.

Maybe it could work if we try again. I promise to be more respectful.
—d

David,
I'm not sure that's a good idea.
—Sir

Not sure it was a good idea? I'd show him a good idea. I ate five more Kisses, then tried again.

D,
I apologize for my actions Thursday night. You have no idea how tempting it is to try to justify them. But I want to say sorry and not make excuses. I'll never apologize for standing up for myself, but I am sorry for the way I talked to you. If you are willing to give me another chance, I can't promise I'll be a choirboy, but I will behave better. I'll take whatever punishment you see fit, minus mouth-peeing, which you have already stated you don't do, so that's good. We agree on something.
You have many admirable qualities, and while I stand by what I said about your haircut, I retract what I said about you not treating me like a human being. You're actually one of the better guys I've met.
I hope we can try again.
Respectfully,
—d

David,
You have until Thursday to write up a detailed, coherent apology for your behavior. 500-600 words. Double spaced with 1" margins. Bring it to my house at 7:30. Wear white briefs.
—Sir

D—

What are you, my freshman comp teacher? And what is your thing with white briefs? Did your mother accidentally bleach all your underwear when you were a kid?

P.S. Should I also staple it and include my name and class period in the upper right-hand corner?

—d

David—

Of course you should staple it. And proofread. If you can't obey a request as simple as wearing white briefs, I shudder to think how the rest of our scene will go.

Please address me as Sir if you intend to continue our correspondence.

—Sir

Dear Sir,

How about this? You discipline me for how I behave, not what I wear or who I am. I'll try to be respectful to you, and you can punish me if I'm not, but I don't own tighty-whities and have no desire to.

Shudder away.

P.S. "Proofread" is amusing coming from a guy who misspelled "obedience" in his profile.

—d

David,

Consider the white briefs part of your punishment, as well as a test to see if you can follow directions—a test you failed last week. No tighties, no deal.

—Sir

P.S. Who are you, my freshman comp teacher?

Sir,

See you then. Maybe we can spend all night proofreading each other. If you know what I mean.

—d

David,
I don't.
—Sir

D,
I mean sex.
—d

d,
I see.
—D

CHAPTER

EIGHT

"**O**h my God." Ricky's voice was approaching squeak territory as he followed Miles and me through Cobalt. "Are those . . . Nazis?"

He was pointing at the far end of the room. Unlike Riddle, Cobalt was just one long, L-shaped space with different stations. The name of each station was painted on the wall above it, along with dirty, comic-book-style illustrations. There was Spank Central, Bondage Boudoir, Wax Warehouse, Interrogation Alley . . .

Over by Interrogation Alley, a man wearing a very authentic-looking Nazi uniform—complete with swastika armband—stood on a plastic sheet, staring at a red Nazi flag on the wall. There was a bucket beside him, and a woman in uniform with a matching swastika armband circled him with a riding crop.

My eyebrows shot up. "Uh, yes. That is some . . . Nazi role-play."

"Is that legal?" Ricky couldn't tear his gaze away.

"Sure." Miles led the way toward the other end of the L. "Just maybe not very tasteful in a public space."

"We used to see the weirdest shit here," I told Ricky. "Miles, were you there for the John and Yoko scene?"

"John and Yoko?" Miles frowned.

"That must have been Kamen."

"That certainly wasn't me. But you and I watched the human chess pieces." Miles headed for the ancient leather sofa in the social area.

"Don't you want to see what the bucket's for?" I asked.

"Not particularly. I'd like to sit down and scope out who's here."

"Holy cow!" Ricky said. "Look!"

I turned to him. "I'm really hoping to get laid here tonight, and your Anastasia Steele act is not helping."

"I just . . . What *is* that?" He pointed to a man wearing a police jacket who carried a thick, menacing-looking whip, about three feet long.

"I think that's a sjambok. Miles would know more, but they're . . . Hey, Miles?" I caught up with him and tugged his sleeve. "Is a sjambok made out of hippo or buffalo or something?"

"Traditionally hippo or rhino. But now mostly plastic." Miles glanced back at Ricky. "Believe me, you're not ready for one."

Ricky looked horrified. "I wasn't saying I wanted to try it! I just wondered what it was."

I put an arm around him. "Did you ever read the Roald Dahl story about the elephant with his insatiable curiosity? And all his relatives spanked him for asking too many questions, and then he was eaten by a crocodile?"

"He was not eaten by a crocodile." Miles sat stiffly on the couch, flinching slightly. Still sore from his hot night with the snack dom, apparently. "The crocodile pulls his nose, and that's how he gets a trunk. And that's not Roald Dahl; that's Rudyard Kipling."

"Whatever. I only read it for the spanking."

I didn't sit right away. I didn't trust the furniture here. It felt like there was a fine layer of grime on everything. Plus, Nazis.

I was so glad Gould wasn't here.

"Hey, can I ask you something?" Ricky leaned closer to me.

"Go for it." I slowly sat beside Miles, my nose wrinkling as the ragged leather creaked under me.

"You know when Hal, um . . . died?"

"I vaguely recall."

"Like, how often do you think that happens in BDSM? That someone dies, I mean. Like, how many people a year, or what are the odds or whatever?"

"I have no idea," I said shortly.

Miles spoke more gently. "Depends on how you play."

"Yeah." I leaned back, spreading my arms over the tops of the cushions, ignoring the stickiness. "If you're into the kind of stuff Miles likes, you're lucky if you survive a night."

"What kind of stuff?" Ricky sounded like a little kid pressing for a scary campfire story.

"We'll tell you when you're older." Miles scanned the place. "No Kamen's mom so far. That's a plus."

"Ooh!" Ricky clapped his hands. "Are you guys gonna invite her to join the Subs Club?"

"Uh . . ." Miles looked at me. "Probably not."

"That would be so awkward," I agreed.

"The club's such a great idea," Ricky gushed. "I love it. I really want to contribute some reviews. I just have to find guys to play with first."

"Slow down there, Tiger." I tugged his wrist until he sat beside me. "Someday, you can make poor choices with lots of strange men and then write about it on the internet. For now, let's concentrate on finding you someone safe and awesome to mentor you."

"But it's crazy!" Ricky went on. "It's like, I've wanted to get into this stuff for *years*, but now I'm like, 'What if I *die*?'"

I rolled my eyes. "You're not going to die."

"Yeah, that's, like, why I'm glad you started the club. It makes me feel safer." Ricky had gotten distracted watching one of the Nazis carry a second bucket into the scene area. Water sloshed over the bucket's rim as the Nazi walked. "What's that water for?"

"Uh . . . not sure," I said.

A guy in a leather vest stumbled past us, slurring the song "Friday." I looked around to see where the DMs were, but nobody seemed to pay him any mind. So Cobalt would let a drunk guy in, and Riddle wouldn't kick a murderer out. I was starting to get seriously disenchanted with the club scene. But then, how many times had I played drunk at the leather bar years ago? When had I become such a *mom*?

The bucket of water turned out to be for a Nazi waterboarding scene. Ricky watched, enthralled. Even Miles stood to get a better look. Waterboarding was probably right up Miles's alley. I tried to watch, but as the woman put a hood over the man's head, I started to feel queasy. And when she dunked his head into the bucket, my own lungs went tight.

"I'm not gonna watch," I told Miles. "I'll be right over there." I motioned to the other side of the L and headed off to sit as far from the waterboarding as possible.

The toxicology report had showed amyl nitrite in Hal's bloodstream. Poppers were something I'd outgrown a couple of years before, but Hal had remained a fan. A lot of the victim-blaming morons had used that against Hal. *He shouldn't have been playing if he was drugged.* Others cited the inherent danger in edge play—apparently when Hal signed on for a breath-play scene, he'd agreed to the risks, so it was his fault he was dead.

The way I understood it, Hal had been tied faceup on the bench in Tranquility. He'd been gagged, but Bill had left one of Hal's arms free so Hal could safe signal. He'd tied a thin rope around Hal's neck, and was using it to choke Hal as he jacked him off. Cinnamon had been on the other side of the room, waiting for her handler to return. The sole witness to Hal and Bill's scene, she had testified in court that she never saw Hal struggle or signal. But partway into the scene, Bill had left the room. Had *left* Hal tied up alone. Any top with half a brain knew better than that.

I sat on a metal chair, clenching and unclenching my fists, digging my nails into my palms to keep myself grounded in the present. A voice behind me said, "Hey, hon."

I turned. Kamen's mom stood there in a midnight-blue corset with silver stars on it. Black ruffled bloomers and fishnet stockings, stiletto boots. Her dyed blond hair was piled high on her head, and her face was coated in makeup. When I'd first met Mrs. Pell, I'd thought she was the ultimate dominatrix stereotype, but now I was convinced she was one of a kind. Like her son, she wasn't the brightest bulb in the sconce, but she was a lot of fun. If she hadn't been my friend's mom, I'd probably have enjoyed hanging out with her. But if seeing her in a BDSM club was weird for me, I could only imagine how weird it must be for Kamen.

"Hey, Mrs. P." I tried to pull myself together, but I was still shaking.

"Where's your crew?" She had a funny, strained-sounding voice, like she was always in the process of trying to lift something heavy.

"Miles is watching the Nazi waterboarding. And Kamen and Gould couldn't make it."

She put a hand on my shoulder. Her nails were bright-blue talons. "Is my boy doing okay?"

"He is. We're looking after him."

She smiled. Her teeth were blindingly white, like Kamen's. "I know you are, honey. I appreciate it. Tell him hi for me. Tell him to *call me* once in a while."

"Will do."

"You and Gouldie enjoying the slow cooker?"

"Oh my God. We make so much barbeque chicken."

She grinned again. "You're so sweet, David." She cocked her head, studying me more closely. "You okay, babe?"

"Oh, yeah." I glanced toward the bend in the L. "I just wasn't into the waterboarding."

"I know, honey. Makes me think about Guantanamo. Not my thing."

I almost asked what her thing was, but decided I never wanted to know.

"It's hard for me to watch stuff with breath control, after Hal," I confessed.

"Ohhh." She clucked softly, then came around the chair and crouched beside me. "Wasn't that just horrible? Kamen still has nightmares about it."

I looked at her, surprised. "He does? He hasn't said anything."

She patted my knee. "Well, I don't think he likes anyone to know how much it shook him up. Such a sad thing. But, you know, this is a dangerous game. No matter how carefully we play it."

I squeezed my eyes shut. I was so fucking sick of people making it sound like Hal's death was inevitable. It would never have happened if Bill hadn't left Hal alone with a fucking rope around his neck. There were ways to be kinky without killing someone. There were ways to play hard without *dying*.

I'd seen Bill that night. After the ambulance crew took Hal away. After they'd said I couldn't ride with him, and I'd told GK I had to get to the hospital. He'd said I wasn't in any state to drive, and that there was no point anyway. I hadn't understood at first, because I'd thought the ambulance was taking Hal to the hospital to *save* him.

I'd seen Bill crying. On his knees, elbows propped on the padded bench, sobbing into his hands. I think I knew then. But I hadn't been able to say it to myself.

"Well, hey." Mrs. Pell stroked my hair back from my forehead. "If you ever need to talk, I'm happy to listen."

I tried to smile. "Thanks." I stood. "I guess I'd better, um . . ."

Be anywhere but here.

I said good-bye to her and went to get Miles and Ricky.

"Hey," Gould said from my doorway. "You're still up."

It was two in the morning, and I was lying on my bed. I'd opened and shut all my desk drawers loudly when I'd heard him get up to use the bathroom, hoping he'd take the hint and come in.

"Working on a post for the site," I lied.

I wished I could tell Gould about the apology to D. Wished I could have him read it over for me. But for some reason, I wanted to keep D a secret for the time being. I rolled from my stomach onto my side as he came over and sat on the bed.

I traced the plaid on his pajama pants. "Do you, um . . . Is it ever hard for you, when you're subbing, to, like . . . take a dom seriously? Like, if their rules seem really arbitrary, do you just want to *not* obey them?"

"Hmm. Even if I'm not crazy about what someone's telling me to do, I like to see if I can do it. And I like to see where they're going with it."

"I know." I rested my chin on his thigh. "I'm asking the wrong person. You're, like, supersub."

"No . . ." But it was a halfhearted no. He knew he was perfect— quiet and obedient and thoughtful. He wouldn't even have needed to be transformed through D's tutelage. "I'm not like you. I don't fight. But I'm still more . . . careful now."

"Me too." I glanced at my Warwick Rowers wall calendar and wished I could bang November. "Do you think we're ruining the spontaneity or whatever of what we do? Making it a safety school special, like Miles said?"

"Maybe a little. But I think we're doing a good thing."

I stretched. "I don't even know what I'm looking for anymore. It's like, I want someone to take control, but I don't want to have to *give up* control. So maybe I want someone to force me to give it up. But also I don't want anyone to force me to do anything. Ever." I groaned and went limp.

Gould laughed softly. "You're a mess."

"I know! Fix me."

He pulled me up until I was sitting and hugged me. I liked the feeling of being trapped against him. We were almost the same size. He was just a little taller and rounder, which made him perfect to hug. He scrubbed my back with his fingertips and grunted as I squeezed him. My cock was still kind of hard from thinking about D while I wrote my apology, and I could tell he noticed.

"I'm just happy to see you," I told him.

He laughed, his breath warm against my hair.

"There was this waterboarding scene at Cobalt tonight, and I couldn't even watch it . . ." My throat was too tight to continue.

He was quiet for a moment. "I know."

Suddenly I ached. I didn't want to be alone. It felt more difficult, the older I got, to connect with others. People didn't seem as wonderful and amazing and unique as they had when I was in college. And being around the kind of people who didn't seem to care who I was or what I wanted out of life, like my coworkers, made me feel lonelier than actually being alone. But Gould always made me feel valued. Necessary.

I pressed my hips closer to his and felt his dick stiffening too. "Hmmm." I glanced at him questioningly.

We used to do it, occasionally—jerk each other off. Then we'd stopped when he'd officially gotten together with Hal. It wasn't like we wanted to be anything more than friends, but we loved each other so much, and sometimes I wished we could fool around a little without it getting complicated. I placed a hand on his thigh with exaggerated casualness, like he was my poodle-skirted date at a fifties' drive-in.

He stared at my hand. "I don't think it's a good idea. Do you?"

"Right now I do."

"But afterward . . ."

"Yeah." Touching each other's dicks definitely did something weird to our friendship. And the friendship mattered a lot more than my hard-on.

"How about this?" he asked. I let him push me down on the mattress. He rolled on top of me, crushing me for a minute, and then he was on my other side, one arm slung over me. He gave me an affectionate kiss on the side of the neck, and I snuggled closer to him. "A bed party."

I smiled. I used to host bed parties sometimes when the whole group was over, insisting that Miles, Gould, Kamen, Hal, and I all pile on my bed so we could lie there and talk. It had been a long time since the last bed party.

He stroked my ribs, and I closed my eyes. "Too tired to party," I murmured.

"Then just sleep."

I woke up again at 5 a.m. to find Gould gone and my apology unfinished. I lay there a long time, not even sure what I was thinking about. Just drifting.

CHAPTER
NINE

I had the same smattering of nerves Thursday night that I felt each time I knocked on a dom's door. I had my apology stapled, folded, and stuffed in my pocket. And my fly was undone.

D opened the door, wearing jeans and a burgundy sweater. He'd gotten, if possible, more pornstachily handsome over the last week. I stepped into the house and immediately dropped trou.

"There ya go." I spread my arms. "White briefs. Happy?"

He stared at me levelly. Then headed toward the kitchen. "'I am no man's man,'" he said. "'I bark at no man's bid.'"

"What?"

"Davy Crockett." He turned back to me. "Are you coming?"

Probably not anytime soon if you're gonna quote Davy Crockett at me.

All right, to be honest, I'd been hoping for more of a reaction. A *What do you think you're doing?* and perhaps a mortified reaching out to close the front door before the neighbors saw. But now my back was exposed to the cold night air and to anyone who might pass by and see my pants-less silhouette. My face heated as I turned and shut the door myself. When I faced him again he was still watching me, looking mildly amused, like I was a dog trying fruitlessly to reach an itch at the base of its tail. "Are you a Davy Crockett fan?" I asked.

"Yes. Why don't you pull your pants up and come have something to eat?"

Snacks *before* a scene? This was some new level of snack dom.

I yanked up my pants, and followed him to the kitchen.

He had a buffet set out on the table. Sausage. Bacon. Potatoes. Eggs. A whiskey decanter was on the counter next to two glasses. He didn't say anything.

"What is this?" I asked.

"Breakfast for dinner." He picked up a knife.

"That's not breakfast. That's like you went Zodiac on Old MacDonald's entire farm."

"You—" he spread a giant chunk of butter all over a sausage patty "—do not have to eat it. The grass out back is getting long, if you'd like to graze like a goat."

"No, this looks great. I just . . . Do you ever think about kale chips or anything?"

"Whatever kale chips are, I cannot imagine they would improve my life."

"I hear Davy Crockett was a big fan."

"You heard no such thing."

"And what's the whiskey for? Are we planning some Twain/Faulkner role-play?"

He didn't even glance at me. "The whiskey is because I enjoy it. If you also enjoy it, you may have a small amount."

"I'm good, thanks. How was your week?"

No answer.

"Are you silent because you don't know where to begin, or because you're rejecting my effort to be friendly?"

"Small talk is the last refuge of the insecure." He took a bite of sausage and chewed for a moment. "Scratch that. Marriage is last. But small talk is close."

I stared at him. "My God. What happened in your life to make you this way?"

"Nothing. I enjoy my life."

"If you say so." I grabbed some bacon and put it on a plate. "What would you do if I made small talk without you?"

"I suppose I'd listen."

I leaned back. "Gee, D," I said with exaggerated enthusiasm. "I had a pretty hectic week. I'm looking forward to the weekend, especially Sunday, because that's when my friends come over and we order sandwiches and milkshakes from Mel's Sandwich Shop and watch *Space Camp*."

He took another bite of sausage. "What's *Space Camp*?"

"A reality show about a group of wannabe astronauts fighting for a position at NISS. That's the National Institute for Space Studies. It's the poor man's NASA. Our favorite contestant is this super bitchy astrophysicist named Mandy. If she doesn't win the show, I'll be devastated."

"Why would her fate matter to you? You don't know her."

"She brings me joy."

He shook his head.

"Now you try."

He wiped his fingers on a grease-stained napkin, still chewing. "Try what?"

"Small talk."

I thought he wasn't going to do it. But then he swallowed and straightened, looking me in the eye. "Hi, David. Today I took a walk around the metro parks. I came back and made lunch. Steak and bacon on processed white. I worked on braiding the handle of a new flogger. Now it is dinnertime."

"Not bad."

He poured us each a glass of water. I drank mine greedily, since I was starting to feel a little unsettled. Nothing I did made this man react the way I wanted him to.

"Where do you work?" I asked him.

"The Tent Pole."

"Pretty sure I used to go to a gay bar by the same name."

His mustache twitched slightly in what apparently passed for a smile. "It's an outdoor shop."

"I know." I grinned. "So, you're into . . . outdoor stuff?"

He leaned back, splaying his hands on his thighs. "Yes."

"Where's your favorite place to walk, D?"

"Please don't call me that. I hate nicknames."

"Yet you want me to call you 'Sir.'"

"That is an honorific, not a nickname."

"And 'the Disciplinarian'?"

"An alias. Name your child what you intend to call him, or do not become a parent."

I laughed. "I don't think you're for real."

"I am at least sixty percent for real."

I nodded. "So you hate nicknames. And small talk. And the death of the American man. What do you *like*?"

He breathed in deeply and closed his eyes for a second. "Woodworking."

"Is that all?"

"No. Bacon."

"And...?"

"Silence."

"Wow."

"I also enjoy Olympic track and field events, and competently distilled whiskey."

"Do you look like Teddy Roosevelt on purpose?"

"That was God's fine doing." Silence. And then, tentatively, he asked, "What do *you* like?"

"Hmm. Being difficult."

"But that's not 'for real,' is it?"

"It's about sixty percent for real."

"I can live with that."

I hesitated. "I love my friends. They are . . . the *most* important thing in my life. I'm terrible at remembering to do shit like pay bills and get my oil changed. I can be self-centered, and I like to argue. But if one of them needs me, I'm there. I'd do fucking anything for them."

"Job?"

"Teamendous. In the mall. It's a store that sells tea by the ounce, and tea equipment. We provide samples. That's what I do all day—try to lure people in, load them up with samples, then hope they'll buy a couple of ounces of oolong."

He nodded. "You'd be good at that."

"I do okay. I don't really like it. I'm gonna try to go to hair school someday."

"Hair school," he repeated, as though the words were foreign.

"I want to style hair for a living. The American man is dead and his corpse maimed beyond all recognition, huh?"

"I didn't say that. Where do you want to go to school?"

"I don't know." I hadn't given it much thought recently. "My progress isn't great because I can't motivate myself to do the research and fill out the damn applications. I'm twenty-six. You'd think I'd have my shit together by now."

"Son, a modern-day twenty-six-year-old is the equivalent of a 1940s twelve-year-old."

"What does that mean?"

"You're still a child."

I gave a mock-affronted gasp, though the words actually did sting. "I'm not, though. I just feel like one because I work in a mall. All the other mall workers are between fifteen and seventeen. Except at the Verizon store. Those are some sad, sad thirty-five-year-olds."

He wiped away some water that had dribbled down his finely stubbled chin. "I am thirty-eight. I had a job where I wore a tie. Last year I quit and climbed Katahdin."

"Is that a mountain?"

"In Maine. Then I came back here and started working at the Tent Pole."

"That's cool."

"I was told it was a foolish choice. But I am happy."

I shook my head and snorted. "I've never heard anyone who talks like you."

"What do you mean?" He reached for another piece of bacon. Stopped. Took a swig of his coffee instead.

"You speak really slowly. You enunciate your words. You don't use contractions much. It's just . . . funny."

He didn't answer. I sensed our small talk was at an end.

"So you want to get to it?" I asked.

He nodded. "Let's get to it."

I hesitated. "I'm sorry about last time. Seriously. I brought the written apology and everything, but I feel more comfortable talking than writing, so I want to say even if you don't like what I wrote, I am sorry—not about what I said, exactly. But how I said it. Uncalled for."

A prickling heat started in my spine and crept around my body, making me feel light-headed.

"I'm glad you decided to try again," he said. "And I'm sorry too, for any misunderstanding. Your limits will be respected."

I half smiled. "So what happens now?"

"Why don't you read me your apology?"

That didn't sound like fun at all. "Here?"

"Unless you'd rather go to the den."

"No, thanks." I was genuinely self-conscious about my apology, and I didn't want to stare at a wall of paddles while I delivered it.

He sighed as he watched me pull the square of paper out of my pocket and unfold it.

"What? It's stapled." I showed him.

He shook his head. "Go on."

"Was I supposed to show up with it in a leather portfolio?"

"David."

I studied the paper. The words swam, and the ones I could make out looked stupid and inadequate. "*Self-conscious posturing,*" he'd said last time. Maybe he was right. I began to read. Quickly, before I could change my mind.

"Dear Sir, on Thursday I came over here assuming you thought you were entitled to my obedience just because you're a dom and I'm a sub. I assumed you didn't care about getting to know me and you just wanted to order me around."

I paused. D didn't say anything.

"I actually thought you seemed like a cool guy, and like we could probably do a hot scene together. But I have some serious feelings against people walking all over me. I feel like humiliation is part of a punishment, but I don't like when doms make me feel genuinely stupid."

I stopped. "There's a typo here." I wasn't sure why D needed to know this. "I left the second *e* out of genuinely."

He didn't answer, so I went on. "I just didn't know what to expect from you. I'm sorry for getting mad. I'm really good at overreacting. I like talking, but sometimes I don't know how to calm the fuck down and have a *conversation.* I shouldn't have assumed things about you. I shouldn't have blown off the list you told me to make.

"I appreciate you giving me another chance. I wouldn't ask for one if I didn't think you were worth getting to know better. Sincerely, David."

He nodded when I was done. "Apology accepted. And I apologize too, for making you feel uncomfortable."

"Thank you." I meant it.

He glanced at the pages. "How long is that?"

"Five hundred and five words. But the last two hundred are just the lyrics to 'Sorry Seems to Be the Hardest Word,'" I admitted.

He stood. "Come with me."

"No. I mean, um— Wait." I had a feeling we were headed for the Den of Horrors. And it just seemed like there had to be a way to chloroform him and bolt before we got there. "Let me— I'm not doing a good job of showing you I'm sorry. I could—"

He took me by the arm and pulled me out of my seat as easily as if he were Mandy lifting weights in one-sixth gravity on *Space Camp*. Then he tugged me against his hip and walloped the seat of my jeans twice.

I tried to squirm out of his grasp, but he propped one foot on the rung of the chair and slung me over his thigh. I grunted as I slid forward toward the floor, but his arm was instantly around me, holding me in place. He was five swats in before I could draw a breath. Once I got the breath, I yelled.

I struggled and kicked, slapping at his leg with both hands. D stopped short of a dozen whacks, but it still stung like hell. I scrambled to my feet as soon as he released me, rubbing my ass.

"You don't know how good it feels to do that." It was the first genuine grin I'd seen from him.

"You're a *monster*."

He took my arm and sent me toward the den with another swat.

It was cooler in the Den of Horrors. He sat in the chair behind the big desk and spread his thighs. Then he snapped his fingers and made me hand over the apology, which he set on the floor by the chair. "Stand in front of me. Hands behind your head."

I obeyed.

"Let's see those tighty-whities." He undid my fly and tugged my pants down to my thighs. My ass still prickled, and I flexed it, trying to get rid of the smart. He patted my ass. "Turn around."

My cock was half up and sticking through the slit in the briefs. He ran his fingertips down my cotton-clad left cheek, and I let out a shaky breath. When I faced him again, he told me to take off my shoes and socks and step out of my jeans. I did, and then he took my wrist and drew me over his lap.

I'd been in this position many times before, and it always unnerved me. My fingers brushed the floor. My hips were balanced on his thighs, my dick between his legs. His hand rested on my ass. I curled my toes against the floorboards and tried to breathe.

"Read the rest of the apology." He was stroking my ass, and I shifted uncomfortably as the blood rushed to my head.

"The . . . the song lyrics?"

"Yes, David. The song lyrics."

"That seems—"

He delivered a full-force swat to the center of my ass.

I worked my mouth silently for a few seconds, unable to make a sound. Then I cleared my throat and started reading. I'd gotten about five words in when his hand connected with the seat of my briefs again, making me wince. I kept reading, and he swatted me once more, the sound muffled slightly by the cotton.

I blew out a breath and went on.

He spanked firmly but not viciously, alternating sides, occasionally catching the bare skin around my briefs. I spread my legs, trying to wiggle into a more comfortable position, but he slapped the backs of my thighs so quickly and forcefully it stole my breath for a moment.

"Ow! Ow, D, no. Please—"

He pulled me closer against his stomach. "Hold still."

"Shit."

He stopped. "Keep talking like that and you'll take the rest of this spanking with a bar of soap in your mouth."

"You're—"

He grabbed the back of my briefs and pulled them up into my crack. I yelped and twisted, trying to roll away. He held my back end up by a fistful of underwear and spanked the exposed skin until I was gasping steadily.

He stopped and started to edge my briefs down. I reached back and grabbed the waistband, desperate to keep them up, and there was a short tug of war before he caught my wrist and positioned my hand palm out against my left cheek. Then he started spanking again, striking my hand *and* my ass with each swat.

"Ow! *No!*" I shouted.

"You keep using that word." He spoke calmly. "I'm not a fan."

My palm was throbbing by the time he released my wrist and yanked my briefs down to my knees. I didn't fight him this time, and when his hand started cracking against my bare skin, I shut my eyes and tried to breathe. When I finally did draw a breath it sounded ragged, dangerously close to a sob.

He was good. Maybe not quite the master of discipline he'd made himself out to be on Fet, but pretty damn good. "Stop!" I said, just to see what he'd do.

He was alternating cheeks again, sometimes using a flat hand for maximum impact, other times cupping it to make my ass bounce. "You're getting exactly what you asked for, David," he replied. "Now hold still and take it."

"Go to hell!" It felt so good, just for a second, to say it.

Just for a second.

He stood, pulling me with him over to the cabinet. I lost my briefs in the relocation. I was shaking with adrenaline, my cock still hard, my ass hot and smarting. He yanked open the cabinet and pulled out the decanter, bowl, and a bar of soap. He handed me the bar. "Unwrap this."

Ooh, I could so play this game. I threw the bar across the room.

He turned me toward him, bent me against his hip again, and dealt twenty sound smacks. My cock and balls swung, and I skinned the tops of my toes trying to kick the floor. Tears leaked from my eyes. I felt incredible—free and turned on and terrified. He put me on my feet, pointed me toward the bar of soap, and told me to go pick it up.

Not sure what else to do, I started to cry. I was pleased when he didn't seem at all fazed by the intensity of my reaction. He just waited. I crossed the room and retrieved the soap, trying not to think about the show I was giving him as I bent over. My whole ass burned, and my eyes stung like crazy. I brought the soap back and handed it to him, still choking back sobs. But he shook his head. "I told you to unwrap it."

I flushed, embarrassed that I'd actually forgotten. I fumbled with the wrapper, unable to see through my tears. But he didn't snap at me. Just waited.

Finally I stood there with the bar in one hand and the wrapper in the other. He took the paper from me and pointed at the bowl, which he'd filled with water. "Wet it and lather it up."

I wiped my face on my sleeve and dipped the soap in the water. Rubbed it halfheartedly.

"Use both hands."

I rolled my eyes and got a slap to my right thigh that made me jump. I used both hands, creating bubbly foam that made my stomach turn just looking at it.

He took the bar from me. "Open up."

Hells no.

He gave me a couple of seconds before he pinched my nose with his left hand. I opened my mouth for air, and he stuck the soap in. I started to panic, but he released my nose almost immediately and cupped my face.

"Bite down." His voice was gentler than it had been so far, and I found myself pathetically desperate to keep it that way. I wanted him to know I could do this. I wanted, bizarrely, to make him happy. I bit down, my eyes wide. I hoped my face was nine-cents-a-day-to-feed-an-orphan heartbreaking.

"Hands behind your head. Stand there for three minutes."

He stared at me while I stood. I tried to stare back but ended up looking at the floor. The soap was bitter and slick, and I hated the way it gummed up on my teeth. I'd calmed down, though—if only to stop myself from choking on soap bubbles. I eventually met his gaze again, more hesitantly this time.

I flinched when he extended his hand, but he only placed it on my shoulder and squeezed lightly. I closed my eyes and gave a resigned sigh. He took his hand away, but he remained standing in front of me, which was both reassuring and intimidating. I spent a lot of time staring at his feet. He had on well-worn leather hiking shoes. When the time was up, he slid the soap out of my mouth and placed it in the bowl. "Spit in here."

I didn't want to spit in front of him, but the foamy mess in my mouth wasn't something I wanted to swallow, so I leaned over and spat into the water, trying unsuccessfully to prevent the soap and saliva from coming out in long, unattractive strings. I did take some satisfaction in getting to spit *on* the bar of soap. Globs slid down the tooth-marked bar and mixed with the film in the water.

It was gross. So, so fucking gross. I spit for what seemed like ages, and couldn't get rid of even half of it.

He pointed to the cabinet. "There's a hairbrush on the middle shelf. Take it out and hand it to me."

"I don't . . ." I trailed off.

"Do you really want to finish that thought? Or do you want to reach into the cabinet and get the hairbrush?"

I walked over to the cabinet and retrieved the heavy wooden brush. My stomach clenched as I offered it to him. He took it, sat in the chair again, and patted his knee. "Back over my lap."

I stared at the brush in his hand. I felt like a contestant on a game show, stuck on an obvious question.

The correct answer is, Yes, Sir.

The correct answer is, At what degree angle to one decimal place would you like me bent over, Sir?

The correct answer is silent and immediate compliance.

"No," I blurted.

Wrong, Dave. A, B, and C, but definitely not D.

"I don't fucking *want* to!" I took a step back as he rose. "No! D—"

He took me by the ear, grabbed the soap in his other hand, and led me out of the den and into a bathroom off of the front hall. He turned on the tap and ran the bar under it.

I tried to pull away, but he held me in place. My cock and I were definitely not on the same page here, because it was hard as hell. "Please don't," I begged. "I hate it. I *hate* it!"

He guided my head forward, but instead of trying to stick the soap in my mouth, he swiped it across the left side of my face. I twisted, sputtering and genuinely shocked. "What're you *doing*?"

He rubbed the soap all around my mouth, despite my squirming. Stuck the bar under the faucet and lathered it again, then smeared it over my lips and chin. The bar and his hand were both dripping, and cold water drenched my shirt. I sucked my stomach in, gasping. Heat unfurled somewhere deep inside me, and my balls tightened.

He let go of my ear and took my wrist instead. His grip was surprisingly gentle, if unshakeable.

"I could put this in your mouth," he said conversationally, swiping my cheek. "But you know what I'm doing instead?"

"Missing?"

He let go of my arm. I tried to tuck my ass forward so my shirt covered it, but he swatted me anyway. "I'm exercising *restraint*."

Restraint? If this was restraint, I'd hate to see what hog wild looked like. He cupped the back of my head and brought the bar to my face once more, pushing soap into my hairline and over my ears. I hunched my shoulders as foamy water dribbled down my chest.

"I expect you to show similar restraint with your language."

"That's like, the most cliché dom thing ever," I protested, shivering. Soap bubbles were popping in my nose, and I was miserable and wildly excited at the same time. "'Lose the attitude.' 'Stop swearing.' It's all in the dom handbook, huh?"

D rubbed the bar over my forehead. He leveled his other hand over my eyes to keep soap from dripping into them. I could have run away, but I stayed where I was. "You," he said quietly, "are welcome to think I'm a cliché. But I'm the cliché you decided to mouth off to, so you will accept the consequences." He ran the bar in quick rings around my mouth. "Do you understand?"

I was drenched, sticky, humiliated, and—suddenly—exhausted. I didn't even have it in me to protest when he calmly bent me over the edge of the sink and flipped my shirt up. I heard the jingle as he undid his belt, and the whoosh as he pulled it through the loops. I looked up in time to watch through the mirror as he doubled it. He whacked me hard, and I yelped.

"I said, 'Do you understand?'" Still calm and quiet.

"Yes, Sir," I choked.

He whipped me again. I hissed and bounced on the balls of my feet.

"Good. The next time you swear at me, you'll get a two-quart soap-and-water enema. Are we clear?"

Next time? Part of me wanted to tell him no way in hell would there be a next time.

Most of me would have paid him in gold bars to ensure there was a next time.

Another crack of the belt. I flexed my ass and gripped the counter. "Yes, Sir. Yes. Please, D . . ."

Two more, low down. Almost on my thighs. My cock rubbed the edge of the counter, and I moaned softly. That seemed to make him pause. I watched him through the mirror as he gazed at my ass. My legs quivered. I made that soft sound again.

His shoulders jerked slightly, and he closed his eyes for a second. He put out his free hand as if to touch me, then let it drop.

I barely hid a grin. He was *into* this.

He placed the belt beside the sink and helped me up. Handed me a towel and let me wipe my face. He also let me rinse my mouth.

Then he led me back into the Den of Horrors, where the hairbrush lay on the desk.

"D?" My heart really was pounding now. Most guys didn't punish me this long. They either relented under my histrionics or they got bored and wanted to move on to sex. But D seemed like he could keep this up all night.

"Yes, David?" Nothing sardonic or annoyed in his tone. I had no idea what I wanted to say to him. I knew I had a punishment coming. But I really was hurting, and whatever moment we'd shared by the sink was over now. I couldn't tell anymore who was in control of this game.

"I'm so sore," I mumbled. I didn't expect—or want—him to take pity on me, exactly. But this was one of my favorite parts of discipline role-play, when I started to feel genuinely contrite. I chanced a look at him.

He didn't appear angry, but he wasn't softening either. "The sooner you come over here, the sooner we can finish this."

I nodded, surrendering to the inevitable.

He sat in the headmaster chair. When he motioned me forward, I draped myself over his knee without a word of protest. He gave me a few brisk but not terribly hard swats with his hand, and then picked up the brush.

He popped me twice, right on top of the stripes left by his belt. My head snapped up and I crossed my ankles, trying to stay in position.

Then he went to work.

Turned out I still had energy enough to howl like a dog at every blow. He covered already blazing territory quickly and efficiently. I tuned out what he was saying at first—couldn't think about anything but the pain, truly shocking amounts of it. There was no rhythm, no pattern, just crack after crack of wood on skin, landing anywhere between the crest of my ass to midway down my thighs. But eventually I realized he was asking me questions, and that he expected answers. Well, he could ask all night, and I wasn't going to do anything but cry pathetically and curse whatever circle of Hell had spawned him. Silently, of course.

"David?" He turned the brush over and pressed the bristles against my flaming skin. I jerked, whimpering. "I'd like you to answer me."

I answered by kicking, amazed by how good it felt to struggle with this kind of abandon and know that he could deal with it. He scrubbed me with the bristles, then flipped the brush over and started spanking again. I kicked until I got my left leg off his lap and between his legs, where it dangled, my knee almost touching the floor. My right leg remained over his thighs, and he paddled that sit spot until I let out a scream of rage through gritted teeth.

"Settle down," he said, "and this will go much faster."

Not a chance.

He pulled my left cheek to the side and spanked the skin along my crack quickly and sharply. I twisted again and managed to slide off him and into a heap on the floor. Before I could scramble away, he crouched, picked me up, and placed me on my back on the desk. Then he slung an arm around both of my legs and held them straight up.

I hated this position more than anything on the planet, and made that known.

He told me I could end this anytime.

When I called him a gorgon, he scooped some water out of the little soap dish and splashed it on my ass, then spanked the wet skin with the brush. I lost myself in the pain and the embarrassment. The position didn't allow me any modesty; my dick and balls bounced with each swat. My wet T-shirt clung to my chest, and my nipples, stiff from cold, chafed against the fabric.

He stopped for a moment. "Hold your knees as close to your shoulders as you can."

Was he crazy? Did he really think I was going to *help* him spank me?

A sharp swat to the lower curve of my ass, and I obliged. This arrangement forced my cheeks apart, and blows started landing directly on my crack, dangerously close to my asshole and balls. I closed my eyes, gulping, and tried to remember how words worked.

"I'm sorry. D, I'm sorry. Please! I'm so sorry."

He popped my left thigh. "What are you sorry for?"

"Disobeying you. Being disrespectful. Not meeting the word count." He popped my right thigh. "Ow! Please!"

"How do you address me?" Left thigh.

"Sir! I call you Sir. I *did* call you S—" Right. "Oh, God."

"How are you going to speak to me from now on?"

"Respectfully." I clenched my ass, waiting for a blow that didn't come.

He patted me with the brush. "If I give you an instruction in the future, what will you do?"

"Listen! I'll listen." I dug my nails into my shins, wanting so badly for this to be over.

Two more pops to the crease where my ass met my thigh.

My voice stuck in my throat. I wanted to believe I was staging my desperation, my capitulation, but I knew I wasn't. I needed him to stop. I was ready to end this. "I really will be better. Please—*Sir*—I'll behave."

He set the brush down, stroking the backs of my legs with his fingertips. The skin throbbed under his touch. I shuddered, and then I really let go. My head lolled on the desk, and the sobs wracked my whole body.

"All right." He eased my legs down. "Here now—come on."

He helped me sit. I flinched as my ass met the surface of the desk. There was always an inner battle after a punishment. I felt too embarrassed and messy to want to be comforted, but I craved contact so badly. In this case, I felt disgusting. My face was covered in soap residue and snot and tears, my body was wet and sweaty, and my ass was thoroughly bruised. But the second D's arm slid around me to help me up, I was clinging to him.

"Okay." He rubbed my back. "You're all right."

"I'm sorry," I repeated as he guided my head onto his shoulder. I was surprised—I wouldn't have pegged him for a hugger, but he was good at this.

"It's over." His voice was slightly hoarse.

Shit. Shit, I'd been punished a million times before. I knew how it worked, but this was . . .

I leaned back a little, meeting his gaze, trying to keep still. There was nothing hard or angry in his expression. I swear I saw something change in his eyes as he looked at me. He seemed softer, and genuinely sympathetic. I wanted to kiss him, I fucking wanted to, but he turned away.

I refused to let on how much that hurt.

"Come on." He squeezed me briefly. "Let's get you cleaned up."

He lent me a sweatshirt and let me wash my face again in the bathroom. I took the opportunity to inspect the damage—which, while not as impressive as I would have thought, was nothing to sneeze at. I was bright red from the top of my ass to halfway down my thighs, with a couple of darker patches of bruising on my right cheek. Those bruises went deep into the muscle. I put my underwear and jeans on, wincing, then staggered out to meet D in the kitchen. I flinched as I sat, hoping he'd notice and feel guilty. He'd gotten me a glass of water, and I drained the whole thing.

He was having coffee. "How do you feel?"

I made a face. "Ow."

"You can take a pretty good spanking."

"You call that a 'pretty good' spanking?"

"What do you call it?"

I gripped my water glass. "Gitmo's alternative to blaring AC/DC."

His mouth twitched again. "More water?"

"Please."

He stood and took my glass to the sink. He was definitely trying not to smile.

Actually, now that the pain had become manageable, my most pressing concern was my erection. Sitting at D's table, wearing his shirt, my ass aching from his hand . . . I wasn't sure what I wanted more from him—sympathy or a hard fuck.

"How am I gonna get the shirt back to you?" I asked.

"Good question." He returned to the table and set a full glass in front of me. "I suppose you could come back next week. If you're interested."

"That depends. Do I get beaten with a hairbrush?"

"That depends. Do you behave yourself?"

"Very rarely."

He sat, leaning back slowly. "If I take on a sub, it's usually for six sessions. Once a week. Thursday nights. You agree to submit to whatever discipline I choose. I agree to make sure it falls within your limits."

I took a few gulps of water. Six sessions of enemas, figging, thermometers, and whatever other fun ideas he had up his long polo sleeve. My dick was trying to answer this for me, but I reminded myself to be careful. What about the review blog? Hadn't I come here tonight so I could rate and then be done with him?

Well, hey. I'd be able to give him a more accurate rating if I did more sessions with him. If six weeks was his thing, I ought to review him on how he delivered the whole package. Right? "What if I'm really good? Do I still get punished?"

"Your job throughout each week will be to keep a running list of your missteps."

"Missteps?"

"Anything you do that you feel guilty about. Or that you know you *should* feel guilty about. You'll bring that list to me each week, and I'll decide on your punishment. In addition to the list you provide, any failure to cooperate during a session will result in further punishment."

"Sounds like buckets of fun."

"You can, of course, back out at any time."

"Duh."

He raised an eyebrow at me.

"What? I'm not signing a slave contract here."

"I realize that."

"Do you fuck your subs?" I asked, hoping to startle a reaction onto that stoic face.

"Sometimes."

Well, that wasn't much of a reaction. Or an answer. I thought about how he'd turned away from me back in the den, and stared at him coolly. "I don't think that should be part of discipline."

He waited.

"I want punishment—spankings and corner time and all that. Sex is a different thing. I don't want to have to blow you as punishment. Or have you fuck me. As punishment," I clarified.

Fucking me for other reasons is totally fine.

He nodded. "I do sometimes require sexual service as part of a punishment. But if that's a hard limit for you—"

"Not a hard limit. Just something I'd only do for someone I know."

"All right." He stood and went to the cupboard. "What about punishments that involve penetration? Dildos, plugs? Enema nozzles? Figging?"

How did he say all that as easily as a doctor asking if I'd experienced any dizziness, nausea, or shortness of breath? "Fine."

"Clamps?"

"Balls or nips?"

"Either."

"Uhhh . . . warn me first."

"Okay." He returned to the table and handed me a bag of mini pretzels. "Here."

I stared at the bag. "Are you going to thank me for flying United?"

He ignored me. "I'll give you my number in case you need it. But unless something comes up, I'll expect to see you next Thursday night at 7:30 p.m."

"Do you also have the dom don't-be-late fetish?"

"I'm seldom on time myself, so if it's a couple minutes after seven thirty, I'll live."

I grinned wickedly.

"Don't smile like that. It makes me nervous."

"It's cute, though. Right?"

"Unlikely animal friends are cute. You are terrifying."

I laughed. "Really?"

"Yes."

He put his number in my phone, telling me it was for emergencies only, and reminded me to keep track of my punishable offenses this week. Then he walked me to the door, where he explained entrance protocol to me. When I entered his house each week I was supposed to stand on the welcome mat just inside the door, clasp my hands behind my back, bow my head, and wait for him to address me. He made me practice.

"Does tonight count as week one?" I asked.

"It does."

I didn't know whether to hug him good-bye or thank him or shake his hand or what. He didn't move, so I just gave him a nod. "Cool."

As I turned for the door, he slapped my ass lightly, making me yelp. "Congrats on surviving."

I walked to my car half in love with him and half wishing he'd go climb Katahdin again and fall off.

CHAPTER

TEN

"It's your turn to go first," I said.

Gould shook his head. "Pretty sure it's yours."

We were in the laundry area in the basement of the duplex. It was a really nice room with a tiled floor, potted plants, and a large table with plenty of books and magazines.

It also had the Change Machine of Darkness.

I sighed. "All right." I took a dollar out of my wallet. "If you feel okay about making me do this . . ."

Gould and I usually did our laundry together on Saturday afternoons. We took turns being the first one to try the change machine and risk losing a dollar when it turned out to be empty of quarters.

I fed my bill into the machine. Nothing happened. "We really should just go to a bank sometime and take out, like, eight hundred dollars in quarters."

Gould stepped forward and slapped the machine, which did nothing. "But banks are so far away. The change machine is right here. And *sometimes* it works."

The machine clicked suddenly, then spat out four quarters. "Well, hallelujah!" I added the quarters to the two I already had.

"It's our lucky day." Gould put in his dollar next. Nothing. He jammed the button, but the machine didn't spit the dollar back out. "Oh, come on."

I clapped him on the shoulder. "You shoulda gone first." I opened a washer and drizzled some detergent in.

He let out a long sigh and started searching his wallet for quarters.

"So." I tried to keep my voice casual. "You were out awfully late last night." I'd noticed because I'd spent last night at home, watching TV, not doing my hair school applications, and wishing it were Thursday so I could go back to D's.

"I was trying some stuff with a rope guy."

I dumped my clothes into the machine. "Who?" Gould had taken a strange interest in rope after Hal died. I wasn't a therapist or anything, but it kind of bothered me.

He fished three quarters out of his wallet, then started checking his pockets. "You don't know him. Found him on Fet. He lives like two hours away."

I raised my eyebrows. "Had you *met* him?"

Gould became really interested in the quest for quarters.

"Gould."

"We'd chatted on Fet for a long time. He's not weird."

"Gould."

"What?" He set two more quarters on the top of the machine. He was one short.

"You didn't even fucking tell me where you were!"

"I left the address on the back of a receipt in my room."

"Who do you think I am, noted symbologist Robert Langdon? If you go missing, I'm supposed to crack your fucking da Vinci code?"

Gould patted his pockets, looking annoyed. "It wasn't a code. It was the address written on a piece of paper. Are you going to lecture me, or are you going to ask how it went?"

"Lecture you," I growled in his ear as I passed. I set my laundry basket on the table. I placed one of my quarters next to his. "How did it go?"

He scooped up the quarters and went to the machine beside mine. "Wasn't the greatest."

"You gonna tell me why?"

He loaded the coins into the slots. "You know how I'm pretty quiet. In scenes?"

Gould could disappear into subspace in a second. He'd do everything a dom told him to without protest, unless the dom asked for something that was a Gould Hard Limit, and then Gould would safeword. Actually, when I'd first met Gould, he wouldn't safeword.

He wasn't even half the pain slut Miles was, and he'd still take anything he was given, just to avoid speaking up. Some of his stories had scared me.

"Yeah?"

Gould shrugged. "He just wasn't super into it. Like, he wanted more reactions."

"Why are your reactions his business?"

"I dunno. I mean, lots of doms get freaked out by how quiet I am. Just, this guy was really . . ." He met my gaze for a second, then looked away, shrugging again.

"Really what?"

"Critical, I guess." Gould piled his clothes into the machine. "Like, he said I was hard to read and that was making it difficult for him to get into his headspace. Which is fine, it was just the way he said it. Then he said something about how he knew how to get me to scream, and I told him I wanted to stop for a minute. Then he turned out to be one of those '*I want to stop* is not the safeword' guys. Which is true, but we weren't doing the kind of scene where 'I want to stop for a minute' would have meant anything else, you know? So I just left."

I could tell the whole thing was really bothering Gould. "Hey. You know you didn't do anything wrong, right?"

He spent a few minutes shaking out his balled-up socks. "I used to wish Hal was a dom."

I didn't say anything. He didn't usually talk about Hal unless he *needed* to, so I tried to just shut up and listen when he did.

Gould threw the socks into the machine. "I know he wasn't the most responsible guy in a lot of ways, but when he and I used to do scenes together, he was great. I mean, he wasn't a dom, and that was obvious. But he was really good at reading me."

Keep going. Tell me.

He slammed the lid shut and turned to me. "I know doms aren't mind readers, and I know it's my responsibility to communicate and whatever Kink 101 shit, but sometimes I wish doms wouldn't *talk*. And I wish they wouldn't try to make *me* talk. I wish they'd just magically do what I want."

I held out my arms. "C'mere."

He glanced around. "There's cameras."

"You think the security cameras have never seen a hug before?"

He smiled, and his shoulders relaxed a little as he stepped forward. I hugged him hard.

"We have the review blog now," I said. "Give him a lousy rating, then let him have it in the comments."

He shook his head and pulled away. "No. If he heard about it, he'd know it was me."

"Who cares? You're not gonna play with him again. And he's not local."

"I'm making a big deal out of nothing. It's just frustrating to play with people like that."

"It's not nothing."

"Whatever." He put the detergent in his empty basket and picked the basket up.

I dug my nails into my palms, still, for some reason, nervous as hell about sharing this. "I had a situation kind of like that too."

"Yeah?" Gould picked up my basket too, and we headed out of the laundry room and up the stairs.

"I met with the Disciplinarian."

Gould stopped and stared at me. "What?"

"C'mon." I urged him up the rest of the steps and into our apartment.

"Yeah," I continued once we were inside. "The first time we didn't get along. But the second time—"

"The *second* time?" He dropped the baskets on the kitchen floor, and we went to the living room. Collapsed on the couch.

"I agreed to six sessions with him. One per week."

"So you're giving me shit about not telling you when I play . . ."

"Because the whole thing's so weird. I don't *like* him."

"Doesn't he have that thing about how safewords are chickening out?"

"Exactly. He's a total I-don't-know-what. But he's hot. And I don't actually think he's a bad guy."

"So you *do* like him?"

I rolled my eyes. "No. Yes. I don't know." I remembered being in D's arms after the punishment. Remembered how fucking hard I'd been. How I'd gone home and spent most of the night jacking off to the memory of his voice, his hands on me. Rubbing my bruised ass against the sheets to get the pain back again. "He's, like, some cliché manly man from the early twentieth century. Eats nothing but meat, framed a piece of hide he tanned himself. Makes all his own paddles. Drinks whiskey straight. Has that mustache."

"Does he have a name? Besides 'the Disciplinarian'?"

I sighed. "His name's David."

"Destiny."

"Yep. But I call him D."

"Nicknames already?"

I slumped. "He's, like, the exact opposite of everything I ever thought I wanted. It's infuriating."

"Let's just insert that sound bite into a preview for a Katherine Heigl romcom..."

"Shut up."

He grinned. "I'm glad you like him."

I sighed. "Six weeks."

"Kim Basinger did nine and a half."

"And didn't that end really badly?"

"Yeah, but you'll be fine."

"Thanks."

Gould picked at his thumbnail for a moment. "You're sure he's safe?"

I nodded, my stomach tightening. *No one's safe. Maybe. I don't know. Maybe I like not knowing.* "Yeah."

He nodded. "Hey, I'd kill to find someone I wanted to play with more than once."

"Poor Gould." I leaned back, resting my head against the cushion and staring up at him. "You'll find someone who wants a quiet boy."

"I guess." Gould snorted. "Even my parents think I'm like, autistic or something. I really need to learn how to talk to people who aren't you."

Gould's parents were like Scooby Doo villains. They weren't mean, exactly, but you could totally picture them haunting an amusement park in order to get ahold of an inheritance. They seemed kind of ruthless, but in an almost comic way. Like they could easily be thwarted by an unkempt pothead and his intensely phobic Great Dane. I was half-repulsed by them and half-amused, which seemed to be how Gould felt too. "They love you."

He turned that crooked smile on me again. "I don't think anyone else really shares your high opinion of me."

"Then they're stupid." I poked him in the side.

He jerked away. "Daaave. I know I'm starting to look like the Pillsbury Doughboy, but—"

"Hey," I interrupted firmly. "None of that."

"I have gained weight, though."

"No one cares but you."

He didn't answer. His weight had always been a sensitive issue. His mother had taken him to tons of fitness classes as a kid, because apparently having a stocky child was some kind of tragedy in Mr.-and-Mrs.-Gould world. Gould had carried that self-consciousness with him into adulthood. I tried to keep an eye on him to make sure he wasn't trying any weird diets or obsessing too much about it.

I remembered hearing a fight between Hal and Gould years ago. I'd watched through a half-open door as Hal pinched Gould's side and shouted, "You think I care about this? Nobody cares but you. You need to *get over it*."

I hadn't meant to use the same words Hal had. I glanced at Gould, but I couldn't read his expression. I wondered if he was remembering the same thing.

"The Subs Club is up to thirty-two members," Miles announced at our second official meeting. We'd decided since we spent every Sunday at my place anyway, we would also hold club meetings during that time. At our first meeting last week we'd talked briefly about how to recruit more members. This had led to a lot of jokes about "members," which had resulted in Kamen picking up his guitar and composing an impromptu song called "All My Members." Then we'd ordered massive sandwiches and milkshakes from Mel's Sandwich Shop down the street and watched *Space Camp*.

Today, we'd resolved to get more serious.

We sat around the kitchen table. Gould was eating string cheese. Kamen was tuning his guitar, oblivious to the rest of us. He'd taken to keeping one of his two guitars at my place, so he could play when we were all hanging out.

Miles continued, "This week we had a great article by Gould about how to communicate during a CNC scene without breaking character. Lots of discussion on that one. A couple of people have commented that what we're doing is a violation of privacy, but many more support us." He adjusted his glasses and studied his tablet. "An interesting thread on why BDSM discourse is always so D/s oriented when a huge contingent of kinksters don't do D/s . . . It was started by GretaHan. She's in a domestic-discipline relationship and says she gets tired of DD being lumped in with D/s." He glanced at me.

"Why are you looking at me?"

He shook his head. "No reason."

A couple of years ago I'd gotten semidrunk and confessed to Miles I was interested in domestic discipline. He'd never let me forget it, even though I most *definitely* wasn't interested in it anymore. Because DD was weird and Hal was dead, and just . . . no. I would never give up that level of control.

Miles cleared his throat. "So we could maybe be more inclusive in our language. Some people in the Subs Club are bottoms but not subs. And they face some of the same safety issues as subs."

"Well we're not calling this the Bottoms Club," I said. "It doesn't rhyme."

"The word 'bottom' weirds me out," Gould agreed.

Miles set the tablet down. "We don't have to change the name. But maybe a subheading under the site title that's like, 'A discussion group for submissives and bottoms' or something?"

Gould and I agreed this would be fine.

Kamen looked up suddenly, focusing on Miles. "Dude, I sent you a post I wrote about people who don't wanna do BDSM full-time and don't go to clubs, but they like just doing a little bit of freaky stuff at home. Can we use that?"

Miles nodded. "I've only had a chance to look at it briefly. It'll need some work before it can go up on the site."

Kamen looked a little hurt. "Okay, sweet."

"And it doesn't really deal with safety concerns," Miles continued. "So if you can find a way to tie it to the Subs Club's core values, that would be better."

Kamen didn't answer.

"It's a cool idea, though," I offered, not wanting Kamen to be bummed. "I mean, not everyone's like us and spends too much time obsessing about kinky shit. So people who aren't full-time players might have specific safety concerns."

Miles nodded again. "True. They don't necessarily have established roles or specialized equipment, and might be getting their information from Wikipedia instead of from more experienced players. I'll have another look at the article, Kamen."

Gould peeled off a string of cheese. "One other thing. I posted a warning on our main site and the review blog—but Bill Henson has a new username and a new profile on Fet. No pictures of his face, no mention of who he is. He's SayImADreamer. I thought people should know."

Kamen looked concerned. "How do you know that, dude? Are you still stalking him?"

Miles and I were quiet.

"I don't stalk him." Gould spoke softly, without looking at Kamen.

"No, it's good to warn people," I jumped in. "I'll change his name and profile link on our site."

"He's getting slaughtered on the review blog," Miles said. "Lots of past subs coming out of the woodwork."

I'd noticed. Actually, while Bill's overall rating was low, he did have a fair number of defenders. His thread was by far the most heated on the blog. Several members thought it was cruel to even have his name up—*shooting ducks in a barrel*, someone had said.

Whatever. I was thrilled with the horrible things people were saying about him. I hoped Bill would hear about the blog and know there was some secret society where his sins were routinely dragged up and rehashed.

Miles scrolled down. "Also a stay-at-home mom in Kansas makes thirty thousand a month working from home and wants us to ask her how."

"Oh man, that would be amazing!" Kamen tightened a string on his guitar. "Let's ask her how."

"Kamen, buddy." I winced. "That's a scam."

He looked up and grinned. "I know. Do you guys really think I'm that stupid?"

Well . . .

"Of course not," Gould said quickly.

"Do you ever think about that, though?" Kamen put the guitar strap over his shoulder. "Like, what if some of those things that look like scams are the real deal? What if every once in a while, a legit Nigerian prince needs help, but he can't get it because all those fake princes have cried wolf?"

I shook my head. "I have never once thought about that."

"Well. Now you have." He started strumming and singing:

"I'm the crown prince of Nigeria, and I own an oil well.

"I'm making tons of money, but I need your help.

"Just wire twenty grand into this private account.

"Give it a month, and I swear, you'll make ten times that amount . . ."

"Wow. You've got a solid-gold hit there."

Kamen beamed. And kept going: "I'm contacting you as a foreigner because—"

"So how many doms do we have on the review blog?" Gould interrupted.

"Thirty-nine," I replied.

"I'll tell you who we should put up for people to rate," Miles said. "You know that bastard on Fet who calls himself the Disciplinarian?"

My stomach plummeted.

"Hell, yeah." Kamen stopped playing. "My friend Pete said that guy's *insane.*"

Fuck, fuck, fuck.

Miles raised his brows. "Can Pete rate him?"

"Naw." Kamen shook his head. "Pete never had a session with him. Didn't get through the application thingy." He grinned at me. "Dave tried to get a date with him."

Miles turned to me. "Really?"

I shook my head. "Just . . . I thought about it. I thought about it . . . and then I . . . didn't."

I could feel Gould's gaze on me.

Miles sighed. "Well, maybe I'll try to get a session with him, then. I'm really not big on discipline, but I could take one for the team."

I sat there sweating for a moment, and then I blurted: "I'm seeing him!"

They all looked at me.

"I mean, I saw him. I played with him."

Miles tilted his head. "*Oh*?"

"Whoa, dude!" Kamen looked perplexed. "He took you? You're, like, way worse than Pete at following directions."

"It just sort of . . . happened," I mumbled.

Gould was focused on the table, doing a terrible job of not looking guilty. Miles followed my gaze.

"Did you know, Gould?" Miles asked.

Gould nodded.

Miles shook his head, then turned to me again.

"Yeah, he's, um, interesting," I said in a rush. "He requires six sessions with subs as part of his training program. So I'm just gonna complete the program and then rate him at the end."

I tried to sound casual, but they were all still staring at me. Like they knew. Like they fucking knew I was hard for danger.

"Is he, like, a dick?" Kamen asked.

"Definitely. I mean, no. He's interesting. But weird. He looks like a combination of that guy from *The Hunger Games* and—wait, not *The Hunger Games*. What are those other games? *Games of Thrones*."

"There's only one," Gould said.

"What?"

"Game."

"Huh?"

"Of thrones. Game *of Thrones*."

"Oh. Well, there's like six seasons based on twenty books; how was I supposed to know they're all about one game? Anyway, he looks like a young Davos Seaworth mixed with Teddy Roosevelt from the Night at the Museum movies."

"And from history," Gould said quietly.

"Right."

Miles set his tablet aside. "So he's a bear?"

I shook my head. "He's definitely not a bear. If he encountered a bear—human or animal—he would skin it and turn it into a rug. He's like . . . a man's man. I mean, he's a total asshole. But he's kind of sweet."

Miles looked too shrewd for my liking. "So how many weeks do you have left with him?"

"Five."

"If at any point during those five weeks you eat squirrel gravy, you're kicked out of the club," Gould warned.

Kamen laughed. "Squirrel gravy." He started strumming the guitar again.

"Saw a squirrel the other day,

"But I couldn't hit the brakes.

"So I cooked it into gravy,

"And then I poured it on a steak . . ."

Gould cleared his throat. "So. This seems like a good place to end this meeting. If nobody has further discussion points, maybe we could move on to *Space Camp*?"

We made popcorn and then gathered in the living room to stream the previous night's episode of *Space Camp*. Miles sat in the armchair, his back straight. He had a way of looking rigid during even the most relaxed of activities. Gould and Kamen took the couch, and I sat on the floor leaning against Gould's legs.

"Man-dy, Man-dy, Man-dy . . ." Kamen and I chanted when she came on screen.

Mandy flicked her dark braid over the shoulder of her space suit and looked at the camera. A voice-over from last week's episode: "I came to *Space Camp* 'cause it's my dream to work for NISS. And I'm warning y'all I'm about to explode like *The Challenger* in here."

"God, she's ridiculous." I reached up to grab a handful of popcorn from the bowl on Gould's lap. "I love her so much."

Miles gave his obligatory sigh to let us know he'd never partake in such lowbrow entertainment if we three plebeians didn't insist. "I can't believe I'm watching this."

"Shut up; you love it."

"Has any astrophysicist in history ever said 'y'all'?" Gould asked.

We were treated to clips from last week's episode, where the contestants had competed in the one-sixth gravity chair. Mandy turned to Parker, the nasal mathematician from Michigan. "Even in one-sixth gravity, you're still fat."

I spat an unpopped kernel into my palm. "She is the worst."

"But, like, the *best*," Kamen added.

"I know. How can you be the worst and the best at the same time?"

I thought about D. D was the worst and the best at the same time.

I couldn't fucking wait for Thursday.

CHAPTER
ELEVEN

"**D**o you have your list?" D asked. We were sitting at his kitchen table. He had set out a package of Oreos.

Fucking snack doms, man.

"Yeah." I pulled it out of my pocket, my stomach fluttering. Noticed his look of disapproval. "What, do you want me to get a Trapper Keeper?"

"Proceed with caution."

"Sorry." I left off the "Sir." It felt more natural.

He had me read each item. Then we talked about it. That seemed weird at first. Did I really have to turn "Tripped Steve at work" into the Gettysburg Address? I hadn't done too much this week that I felt guilty about, but I hadn't wanted my list to be too short, so I'd put a lot of dumb stuff on it, just to give him things to punish me for.

But what surprised me was that talking about the list was *fun*. In order for D to understand the significance of each transgression, he had to ask me about the context. When I got to "Teased Miles about dressing like the girl from the old *Footloose* before she gets slutty," he asked me about my friends.

I looked up from the paper. "What about them?"

"You say you're close with them. What are they like?"

I was sort of touched that he wanted to know. "Uh, well. Miles is incredibly smart. He's sexy in a kind of Amish way, and he knows everything about kink. If you're a dom you probably couldn't wish for a more awesome sub to do a scene with—except it would be like having sex with Wikipedia."

D laughed, a sharp bark that startled me. I grinned too.

"He's older than the rest of us," I went on. "And has a really involved work life. He runs his own T-shirt–design company." I paused. "Sometimes I wonder if he thinks the rest of us are too immature for him."

I grabbed another Oreo. Popped it in my mouth and chewed.

"And Kamen's the nicest guy you'll ever meet. Total doofus, but I mean, like, helps old people cross the street, the whole deal. He's a musician. Works as a cook at the Green Kitchen. We went to high school together."

"And you both ended up in the scene?"

"Yeah." I brushed crumbs off my shirt and into my hand. Then I wasn't sure where to throw them, so I just held on. "His mom's in the scene too."

"His *mom*?"

"I know." I very subtly emptied my fistful of crumbs onto the floor. "They mostly stick to different clubs, but it's still crazy. He's from, like, BDSM royalty. His grandma helped found one of the first women's leather groups in the country."

"So it runs in the family?"

"Apparently. I like his mom. She's nice. Just a little intense."

"And . . . Gould, is it?"

I hesitated, smiling. "Have you ever had someone you're—you're not in love with *that way*, but they're still your soul mate?"

"Can't say I have."

I shook my head. "That's Gould. I adore him. I live with him. I want him to plan all my birthday parties. I want his face on a fucking calendar. I love *hearing* him in the house, making sandwiches or watching *Bloodline* or whatever. But I'm not . . . I don't want him to be my boyfriend."

"You just love him."

"Exactly. I just want to squeeze his adorable-ass guts out in a way that doesn't hurt him and then have him reconstitute so I can do it again."

"That is not a type of relationship I'm familiar with. But okay."

He took an Oreo. Twisted it apart and licked the frosting out of the middle. It got in his mustache. So, I mean . . . there was cream in his mustache, and I was super mature about it.

"I recommend it," I said. "Everyone should have a Gould."

We moved on to talking about how I'd wanted to start applying to hair schools but instead had spent the week killing time on Facebook. I didn't mention to him how truly guilty I felt about that particular item. It just seemed too complicated to get into the whole issue of how I was incapable of doing anything to advance myself career-wise.

"All right." He rose when I was done. "Let's go upstairs."

I was really happy to go somewhere *not* the Den of Horrors, until it occurred to me that the upstairs might be worse.

It wasn't. Two bedrooms, framed posters of national parks on the hallway wall. No pictures of family.

We went into the first bedroom, where a brief but potent fantasy of D throwing me down on the bed and fucking me dissolved as he ushered me toward the bathroom. The bathroom needed a serious makeover. There was some mildew around the ceiling, and the walls were done in 1950s Awkward Sea Foam and white. D rummaged in the linen closet and pulled out a child's yellow plastic potty-chair and two thick but faded towels. He set the potty-chair next to the toilet and the towels on top of a rack by the door.

I was liking this less and less. "Oh, I forgot to tell you, Sir. I am actually potty trained."

He stopped and stared at me for longer than I could hold my winning smile.

"Anyway. Uh, carry on."

He stared a moment longer, and I looked down at the floor, pretending to be interested in the tiles. He reached back into the closet and pulled out a box that, unfortunately, I recognized.

A red bag enema kit.

"Sir?"

He looked at me. "Yes, David?"

I suspected pointing out that I didn't want an enema would do little to discourage him from administering it. "Nothing."

"You said you've had enemas before." D opened the box. "Any reactions I should know about?"

"I whine a lot. And yell that the agony of a thousand plagues is inside me. I sometimes also beg for the mercy of a swift death."

"I meant reactions to the enema's contents. I'll use soap and water, which shouldn't cause anything but cramps. Has an enema ever made you sick or dizzy?"

"Sometimes I get a little dizzy when I expel, but not bad. I do get . . . um, never mind."

"What?"

I sighed, my face heating. "One time I shit in a guy's wastebasket because I couldn't make it to the bathroom. So maybe my self-control's not as good as some people's. Fair warning."

"Well, the good news . . ." D turned his attention back to the enema. My stomach dropped as he removed the red water bottle from its packaging, then pulled out the length of ribbed tubing. "Is that you get to decide when to expel. If you need to go before the eight-minute mark, you'll use this." He kicked the potty-chair. "If you can hold it eight minutes or more, you can use the toilet. Like a big boy."

I flushed from my ears all the way down to my chest.

He looked at me. "How does that sound?"

"Uh . . . fine."

He turned and took a large plastic cup off the closet shelf and filled it with water, then set it on the counter by the sink. Reached into the closet again and snagged a bar of soap, which he handed to me. "Unwrap that and run it under the tap, please. Get it good and lathered, then set it in the cup."

Lathering the soap brought back unpleasant memories of last week. I set the bar in the cup and watched it cloud the water. Out of the corner of my eye I saw him screwing the nozzle onto the tube.

"We'll let that sit for a while." D set the bag on the sink counter and grabbed a towel off the rack. "Come on."

I didn't fight.

We returned to the bedroom. Now that I got a better look at it, I wondered if it was even his bedroom. It didn't look used. And there was a photograph on the wall of a large black horse with a thick neck and a long, flowing mane and tail.

"Is this your room?" I asked.

"Guest room." He spread the towel on the bed.

"You have a framed picture of a horse in your guest room. Do you secretly have an eleven-year-old daughter?"

He glanced at the wall, then over at me. "That, David, is a Friesian. A medieval war horse known for its grace and beauty, courage in battle, and immense strength."

"And you're a fan, huh?"

He stepped beside me and put his hands on his hips. "I am indeed an admirer. I should very much like to own a baroque-style gelding someday."

"I don't even know where to begin with that."

"I wanted to offer guests something pleasing to the eye."

"Do you also subject all your guests to bowel cleansing?"

He squeezed my shoulder. "Strip."

I did. Slowly. Kicked my clothes away when I was done. He gave no indication he was particularly aroused by the sight of my naked body, but I went ahead and imagined a raging erection in his pants.

"Come on over here." He walked back to the bed and patted the towel. "Knees and elbows. Ass up as high as you can get it. Legs spread."

I took up the position on the bed, hoping my ass looked incredible. I rested my forehead on my folded arms.

"Higher."

I stuck my ass up a couple of inches higher.

"Who do you think invented enemas?" I asked. "Like, who thinks, 'You know what would be a great idea—'"

His hand connected with my ass so hard my forehead slid off my arms and onto the towel, and I got towel burn. "Ow! What was that for?"

"For fun."

I turned my head to the side, waiting for the sting to fade. He placed his hand on the burning spot, and I jumped. Relaxed gradually as he soothed away the worst of the smart with his thumb. I blinked at the wall, hardly daring to breathe. He had some calluses along the top of his palm. I loved the feeling of the rough skin against the heat of where he'd swatted me.

"Do you notice a pattern in things you wrote on your list?" he asked.

"Uh . . . they're all things I did?"

He swatted me again. "More specific."

I thought about it. "It's all stuff I said without thinking. Or did without thinking. Impulse, I guess."

"Very good." He ran his nails lightly over the little bumps he'd raised on my skin. Pleasure spread from the back of my neck down my spine. The burn from the swats had faded into an almost pleasant prickling, and I shoved my ass toward his hand. "Holding two quarts of soap and water requires self-control. So while you're holding your enema, I want you to think about specific ways you can implement self-control day to day."

"I love your life-lessons approach to discipline." I tensed in anticipation of a third swat, but it didn't come. "I can't usually think about much when I'm holding an enema," I confessed eventually.

He pinched me. "Try."

I heard him go back to the bathroom and run water.

Fuck. I didn't want to think about trying to hold two quarts of water for eight minutes. And I definitely didn't want to think about using the potty-chair. I pressed my legs together.

He came back into the room, and I turned my head to the other side to watch him approach. The red bag was bulging, and he'd put the nozzle designed for vaginal douching on the end of the tube, rather than the small, tapered anal nozzle. The vaginal nozzle had a thicker, bulbed head and multiple holes. I briefly considered telling him I couldn't do this—that I'd take an extra spanking or something. I'd been glib with D about my past enemas, but in truth, I hated them. Hated the complete loss of control over my body. Hated the cramps, hated the mess of expelling—worse if the dom was watching.

But afterwards I usually felt better. Physically and, sometimes, emotionally.

There was a small hook on the wall about six feet from the floor. D hung the bag from it and pulled a small bottle of lube out of his pocket. He slicked the nozzle generously. Then he reached over and tapped my ass. "Legs open. Ass up."

I moved my legs apart again, arched my back, and thrust my ass up as high as I could. He spread my cheeks and smeared some lube around my hole. It was cold. He started to push the nozzle in, and I clenched without meaning to.

"Relax." He gave me a warning pat.

I gritted my teeth. "Easy for you to say."

He slipped the nozzle in despite my hiss of resistance.

I shifted as he forced it deeper.

"Do we have to do this?" I mumbled, turning my face against my arms again. I was curious about what he'd say.

"No. We don't."

Part of me was disappointed. Wanted him to say yes. Wanted him to tell me to keep my mouth shut—that this was my punishment and I was going to take it.

He put a hand on the small of my back. "But I think this will be a good way to practice doing what you're told instead of getting what you want."

I hesitated, then nodded into my arms. *Fair enough.*

"Hold still. I'm going to start the solution flowing. Once it's in, you'll stay in this position and hold it as long as you can. Fight me, and I'll be happy to spank you while you're holding it."

I nodded again, my voice AWOL, my stomach tight.

"David?"

"Yes, Sir."

He hesitated a moment, then gave my lower back a brief rub. "You'll be all right."

"I know." I barely got the words out.

He reached over and unclamped the tube. There was a gurgling sound, and a few seconds later, several tiny streams of warm water hit my insides. The solution continued to burble as it filled me. At times I swore there wasn't even any water coming out, just soap bubbles. I tensed as my stomach began to distend and the pressure on my bladder grew.

I buried my face deeper in my arms, trying not to think about what was inside me and how it was going to feel coming out. My gut cramped, and soon I ached from my chest down to my hips. I set my jaw and swayed gently back and forth. I was *not* going to lose control.

"Why don't you tell me what you are, David?" D suggested quietly.

"Huh?" I managed.

He stroked my ass with his free hand and started fucking me slowly with the nozzle.

I grunted. "Don't . . ."

My cock stiffened in spite of my discomfort, and my breathing grew rougher. I whimpered in panic as the round head of the nozzle brushed my prostate, and my back arched up like a cat's. If he kept this up, no way would I be able to hold it.

"What are you?" he asked.

I let out a long sigh and got back in position. "A human. Twenty-six years old. About six one—"

He fucked me faster. I moaned and clenched around the nozzle.

"You really want to play this game?" he asked.

I clenched harder, trying to stop the nozzle moving in and out. But he didn't let up. "Ow. No. This is the worst game. I give up. What am I?"

"You're a naughty little boy."

I froze. My cock hardened considerably. "*What?*"

"You heard me."

"Gross."

"Oh. So it doesn't do anything for you, to think of yourself that way?" His voice was different—softer, raw. "As a bad little boy who needs to be punished?"

OMG, stern seventies dad. All the nasty and all the hot.

I struggled to breathe. "N-no." A drop of pre-cum slid from the head of my dick.

The red bag gurgled. He patted my thigh, jamming the nozzle deep inside me. He pulled it all the way out, so that water fountained onto the towel and my legs—then speared it in again.

I groaned.

"Say it, and I'll give you a break."

The cramps were excruciating. My guts roiled, and the more I tensed my stomach, the worse it got. But I didn't know how to relax without ejecting everything, nozzle included. "I'm not going to say it."

"No?" He spanked me once. Hard.

I gasped and curled my hands into fists.

Again. My throat tightened. "N-no."

Another swat so hard it took my breath away. "Why not say it? You know it's what you are."

I squeezed my eyes shut. "I'm a—I'm a naughty . . . little boy." I wished the bed would fucking swallow me up.

"You are." He placed a hand gently on my stomach. I winced, trying to pull away, but he rubbed careful circles until I exhaled. He didn't say anything else.

I wriggled against the towel, my cock painfully swollen, my face flaming.

There was a click, and the solution stopped flowing. D stroked my hair back from my forehead, tugging it lightly. "Halfway there."

"Ughhh . . ." It was a weak protest. I thought about the potty-chair, and shame made the heat spread through my entire body. I wasn't going to be able to hold this for eight minutes. I wouldn't even be able to hold it until the bag was fully emptied. I closed my eyes, on the verge of a freak-out.

D petted me for a few seconds, and I held myself rigid, determined not to make a sound. Another click, and water rushed into me again.

I opened my eyes. "I have to go."

"David."

That was all he said, but it was enough. I shut up. I stayed still and quiet until the bag hissed and bubbled and finally emptied. D clamped the tube shut again.

He pulled the nozzle out of my ass. A little water spilled onto the towel, but he didn't scold me. He held my ass cheeks together for a moment, as though to help me keep it all in. Then he stood and took the enema equipment into the bathroom. I used his absence to groan into the towel. Another cramp hit, and I fought it even though I knew that only made it worse. What I needed to do was breathe through it, but I was afraid of losing control. I rolled my face against the towel and kicked the bed.

D came back, and I froze, remembering that I'd promised I'd stay still. I couldn't take a spanking with my stomach hurting like this. Absolutely couldn't. Keeping my face buried seemed like a good option—if I couldn't see him, maybe he couldn't see me.

He sat beside me, and he smelled like the woods. I focused on that.

"Five more minutes."

I nodded.

"You all right?" he asked.

"Cramps," I muttered. Another one hit. I let out a shuddering breath and crossed my ankles, holding position as best I could.

If I shit on his towel, D would probably never fuck me. I would cease to be a sexual being in his eyes and would instead become an un-housebroken puppy, or an incontinent old man.

A bad little boy.

The words seemed silly, and yet they gave me a jolt of heat every time.

D reached under me and rubbed my stomach again. I closed my eyes and sighed unhappily. By the time he took his hand away, I didn't hurt anymore. I started to think maybe I could last the full eight minutes.

"I can make this feel good, you know." His voice was very soft.

"What, Sir?"

"An enema."

I snorted, still refusing to look at him. "I doubt that."

"An erotic enema can be—"

"Oxymoron."

He ran his hand lightly over my ass, and I shivered. "If the receiver is completely relaxed, and herbal tea is used as a solution . . ."

"Whoa, whoa, whoa. Hold up." I turned my face toward him, forgetting, for a second, about the chaos within. "You want to put *tea* up my ass?"

"It's incredibly soothing."

"You're incredibly psychotic. I work with tea. I don't want to think about it that way."

"Coffee enemas too. Very cleansing, and the caffeine kick is intense."

"That's weird as f . . . It's weird." Another cramp. I sucked in a breath.

"You know, enemas might be my favorite punishment," he said. "I love spanking, but giving an enema is . . ."

"Better than bacon?" I ground out.

"Nothing is better than bacon. But ripping the last ounce of control from someone is as close to bacon as you can get."

I managed one deep breath. "You've got a long way to go if you want to rip all my control from me."

"Really?" He drew his finger lightly down my crack, and my balls tightened. I lost all ability to think or speak or move. "You feel in control right now?"

I felt like my ass was up in the air, my bowels were full of soap, and that the dude from the Saw franchise was standing over me. "Totally."

He patted my ass. "Okay, little boy."

Nooooo.

Why? Why every fucking time he said it, did I want to come?

Humiliated as I was, there was something about this I liked. I liked being here with him. I liked his attention on me.

"Would you touch me?" I whispered.

"Hmm?"

I lifted my face from the towel. Stared at the blue-and-gray striped pillows. "If you were giving me a, uh, an erotic enema? Would you touch my cock?"

"Your cock, your ass. I'd run my nails up and down your thighs until you spread your legs for me."

My breath caught, and my dick touched my belly, leaving a damp smear. And I wasn't the only one into this fantasy. His voice and breathing were ragged.

"Two minutes," he whispered.

The cramps wouldn't let up. I twisted the comforter in both hands and moaned. Everything hurt. My head, my stomach, my knees . . .

Fuck, I was gonna go. I was gonna go *right the hell now.*

I sprang to my feet and rushed for the bathroom. I looked at the potty-chair and realized in an instant there was no way I could use it. It would be a mess, and humiliating, and just . . . no. I sat on the toilet.

D came into the bathroom a few seconds later. Getting rid of the enema felt too good for me to worry about what D was seeing or hearing, or the fact that I was disobeying him.

I just sat there helplessly until I was almost empty. When I could think clearly again, I looked up and caught his expression, which was . . . not as ominous as I'd expected.

"Sorry." I covered my face with my hands.

"David."

I moaned. "This is so *embarrassing*."

"You do realize you're very appealing when you're not performing?"

I lifted my head. "What?"

He had a hint of a smile on his face. "The brat is fun. But this is better."

I went back to staring at the floor. "I'm shitting my brains out. This is *not* sexy. And it would be awesome if you'd leave."

He didn't.

I closed my eyes and tried to pretend it wasn't me making these sounds. "Please leave?" I asked softly, sincerely.

"All right. You can shower when you're done. I'll be downstairs."

As soon as he left I finished up, flushed, washed my hands, and started looking for towels so I could build a towel ladder and escape through the bathroom window. When I couldn't find enough towels, I contemplated just throwing myself out the window. But this was only the second floor, and I was pretty sure the fall wouldn't kill me. So I got in his goddamn shower, cleaned up, then went out to the guest room to get dressed.

I stood there for a moment, holding my clothes and staring at the picture of the Friesian. "Who *are* you?" I asked it in a harsh whisper. "Who the *fuck* loves horses and watching people shit and tighty-whities and Davy Crockett? A fucking psycho, that's who."

"David?" D said behind me. I closed my eyes and let out a long hiss of breath through my teeth.

Shoulda jumped out the window.

"Of course you're standing right there." I spoke as calmly as I could, without turning around.

"Tea or coffee?"

"Cyanide, please."

He laughed, low at first, and then heartier than I felt the situation warranted. In spite of myself, I started laughing too.

I heard him sit on the bed. "Come on over here."

"I'm good here." I kept my gaze on the Friesian. Majestic. Regal. Strong. *You are the Friesian, Dave. Be the Friesian.*

"I can get a paddle," he offered.

"You're such an ass." I walked over to the bed and plopped down beside him. Glanced at my soft cock, still red from the shower. I

THE SUBS CLUB

wanted to ask if I could put my clothes on, but maybe . . . maybe I was okay like this.

After a long silence I said, "The brat thing—that's not just an act. It's me."

"Partly," he agreed. "But I think a lot of it's nerves."

I stared at my hands. "Could be," I conceded.

"I do the same thing." One side of his mouth quirked when I looked at him. "My act is just different from yours."

I studied him. I had suspected since our first meeting that there was more to him than bacon and silence. I wanted him to tell me who he was. Where he'd grown up and what his favorite holiday was and what songs he sang when no one was around.

I shook my head slightly. "I don't know how to stop. I've always played like this—the arguing and the never shutting up. I don't know how to stop," I repeated, more urgently. I was asking him for something, but I wasn't sure what. "You're right. I don't know how to submit."

"Maybe you need to be pushed."

Yes.

No.

Fuck.

"I know a lot of subs who've gotten 'pushed,'" I told him bitterly.

"Not forced," he clarified. "Pushed."

I knew what he meant. And it was exactly what I wanted. Except how was I supposed to say yes when every day on the review blog more subs came forward with stories about a time when some dom had justified throwing consent out the fucking window by saying they needed to have their limits stretched?

"It happened tonight," he continued quietly. "We went past the point where you could control your reactions. And now you're talking to me as David. Not as . . ."

"Superbrat?"

His mustache twitched. "If what you want is a game, that's one thing. But if you want real discipline—where you are held accountable for your actions and where the consequences to bad behavior are truly unpleasant—"

"This was unpleasant."

115

"You have to trust me."

"Why should I?" The question was sincere. I didn't know him. I didn't know how much of his interest in my life was real, and how much was just him needing intel in order to concoct devious punishments.

"Do I make you nervous?"

I gave my head a quick shake. He didn't. Or not any more than any other dom. In fact, he made me less nervous than most.

"What's so hard about obeying me?" His voice was somehow rough and gentle at the same time.

I opened my mouth, not sure how to put it. "I don't want you to take advantage."

"Take advantage how?"

"I don't want to say 'You get to decide what I need,' and then have you turn it into some kind of free-for-all. Or have you make me feel guilty if I don't want what you want."

"I wouldn't do that," he said simply.

I knew he wouldn't.

I tried to figure out what to do with the mess of feelings inside me. "I'm . . . Maybe you don't know this, since you don't hang out at the club much. But last year, my friend Hal . . ." I broke off.

"Ah." D shifted back a few inches. "That kid who died? I didn't realize he was your friend."

"A really good friend. Part of my group."

"I'm very sorry."

My chest clamped tight. "Me too."

Hal would have been the bad boy of our nineties band. The one in the black jeans and leather jacket. The one all the tween girls would try to redeem in fanfiction.

After a minute, D spoke again. "I knew him. Or, I did a scene with him once."

I stared at him. *No way. Hal would never have . . .*

No, Hal definitely would have. Would have played with anyone strange and demanding and be-stached. Would have found D funny, just as he'd found Bill funny.

"You did?"

"Nice guy. We weren't a great match. But he was something different."

I laughed. "That's one way of putting it."

"Must've been hard to lose him." D sounded gruff.

I nodded, digging my nails into the comforter. "For so many months, my friends were . . . not themselves, and I hated it. But I knew if I could just keep them laughing, or keep them annoyed with me—anything to distract them, basically. So I kind of learned to be a real brat, instead of just playing one on TV."

I paused.

"I get so tired of being that guy. I don't want everything to be a joke. I don't want to annoy the shit out of you. I mean, sometimes I do. But not all the time."

"What if I said I thought I could handle it all? The brat, and everything else you are?"

I looked at him again, and he looked back at me. I saw a Crockett-esque determination in his gaze. I saw how close his hand was to mine on the comforter, and there was something like the strike of a match—a flare of warmth and fear and hope.

I smiled tentatively. "I would say be careful what you wish for."

We leaned toward each other. His lips brushed mine, and his mustache scratched me, and I sank into the kiss, letting it slow my mind and quicken my heartbeat. Some people got kissed under fireworks or on Ferris wheels or by rivers. I got kissed on a bed under the watchful gaze of a warhorse while I was still damp from the shower I'd had to take to clean up after an enema.

Roll with it.

His mustache rasped once more against my upper lip and the underside of my nose. I murmured and let him lead, heat winding from my chest down to my groin.

We pulled away, both of us suddenly awkward.

"That's, um . . ." He turned away.

"Yeah." I scratched the back of my neck.

"That's all I had planned for your punishment, so . . ."

"I should get home." I stood and started dressing. I was so fucking confused. He was supposed to be my experiment for the review blog. And I was supposed to be his project of the month. So why did I feel so . . . *urrrrrrghhhhhhhhh*?

"David?" He was still looking at me.

"Hmm?" I couldn't get my zipper up.

"Maybe we could help each other lose the act? What do you think?" He sounded tentative.

I grinned slowly. "We can try."

He reached out and zipped my fly. I stared down at his hand, which lingered at my crotch.

He could do it, couldn't he—take control of all the little things? All I had to do was stop resisting, and he'd . . . he'd help me, right? Help me hold an enema, help me not panic over a spanking. Help me zip my goddamn jeans. He'd help.

I glanced up at him. He pulled his arm back to his side.

"I'll, uh, see you next week." I offered him a handshake.

He accepted. I felt those calluses again along his palm. He met my gaze briefly, and I couldn't help it—I wanted to kiss him again. Then we both turned away.

"See you next week," he said.

CHAPTER
TWELVE

I got as far as my name and address on an application to the Paul Mitchell School. And then I stopped, the same old fears rolling through me. What if I got into a school that was far away? What if I had hours' worth of commuting, or worse—had to move?

I wanted to stay here. In the town where I was comfortable, in the job where I was comfortable—if not exactly happy. With the friends I couldn't live without. Why couldn't I do that?

Because you can't work in a mall forever. Because your life isn't going to stay the same.

I sighed and put my head on the desk.

I imagined doing that thing from movies and TV where I'd turn and Hal would be sitting next to me. He'd be a snarky ghost, commenting on my application fails; picking up random objects in my room and being like, *Wow, you haven't changed at all, have you?* And I'd be all, *What's it like being dead?* And he'd say something bittersweet and ghostly like, *Well, Dave, you ain't lived until you've died.*

But when I turned he wasn't there. I tried talking to a photo of him on my desk, but it just felt awkward. So I settled for remembering how the five of us used to go to Mel's every Friday afternoon for milkshakes. How the milkshakes always cost three twenty-nine, unless you got mint chocolate chip or peppermint twist. Those cost three eighty-seven.

Hal was the first close friend I'd ever lost, and grief was relatively new to me. Miles, who had taken like five classes on death and grief and whatever in college, had helped me a lot with what he called "processing." But I still had trouble understanding my own brain. Some days Hal's death was the first thing I thought about. But some days I hardly thought about it at all, and then I ended up with guilt worse than grief. Life really did go on. Someone died and, in the same fucking instant, was replaced by a hundred new babies. The world had never felt Hal's loss like I did.

Sometimes I wanted to tell my friends what it was like to love them. See if they experienced it the same way—like it was something rare and ridiculous and amazing and terrifying. I was always wondering if they were happy, or if they felt lonely. If there were things each of them couldn't share, even with the rest of the group.

After Hal died, we'd seemed so scattered. Aside from the funeral, we hadn't spent time together for weeks afterward. Miles had turned to his family, and Gould wanted to be alone, but I'd needed company. So I'd started inviting everyone over. I'd lived in the duplex with a girl named Cara at the time, but she was gone a lot, so I'd make excuses to have the guys over. *"Oh, hey, Super Bowl's this weekend."* As though anyone but Kamen cared about sports. An Oscars party, a St. Patrick's Day dinner; it didn't matter. And when they were here, I'd act like nothing had changed. As though I could override our mutual grief by being some exaggerated version of myself. I ragged on them relentlessly, joked about everything. And to an extent, it had worked. They'd needed to engage with me, even if it was to tell me to shut up.

I'd tried other tacks too—made it clear I was always willing to talk, that I was there whenever they needed me. But nothing worked as well to hold us together as being a bit of a bastard.

Maybe the Subs Club was me finally stepping up. Using my experiences to do something good for others. Maybe my destiny was to guide people through the process of establishing safe kinky relationships and also give them awesome haircuts.

Inspired, I logged into the Subs Club admin page. Ricky had submitted a nauseatingly cute article about navigating the scene as a newbie. I posted it and kicked off a discussion in the comments section.

We had a slew of new comments on the review blog. Most of them were contributions to ongoing discussions, but a few were by someone called "Anonymous"—weird, because the application required you to register with a non-"Anonymous" username. They were posted on various review threads:

You ought to be ashamed of what you're doing. You are trying to create a war in this community. You ought to be the ones kicked out of any group, organization, party, anything!!!

So just because doms aren't up to YOUR standards, you have to write a blog liballing them all? Get a life.

If I got a hold of you I'd whip you until you couldn't stand up. You'd all run with your tails tucked pathetic little cowards. You just need a real dom to teach you a lesson about respect.

You are all so f%#@ing stupid its like you don't know anything about BDSM. Why would any dom even want your sorry asses?

I scrolled back through the posts, deleting each Anonymous comment. My heart was pounding. I'd get Ricky to help me figure out who this person was and block them from the site. No big deal.

But the good feeling I'd had minutes ago dissolved. Maybe I was an idiot. An instigator and a coward. I wasn't a vigilante, I was a kid in a Halloween costume—and not a very good costume either.

I took my phone out of my pocket and dialed without thinking about it.

D picked up on the fifth ring. "Hello?"

"I know I'm not supposed to call outside of sessions unless it's an emergency, but this day sucks."

He hesitated. "What's the trouble?"

"Oh, you know." I tried to laugh.

I couldn't talk to him about club stuff. What had I been thinking? If he knew I was reviewing his fellow doms, that I planned to review *him* . . .

He'd probably agree with everything Anonymous had said. I put my elbows on the desk and leaned forward, feeling like a dumbass. "I've been bad all weekend. Hung up on my mom. Kicked a puppy. Totaled a car. Slashed some kid's trampoline. Shoplifted."

"You've had a busy two days."

"Yep."

"Do you want to come over?"

I gasped. "It's not even Thursday!"

"I'm aware of that."

"Are you saying you *want* me to come over?"

"David."

"Yes?"

"Do not tempt me to retract my offer."

"I'm totally coming over."

"Please do. We have a lot to address. The puppy you kicked. The trampoline you slashed."

"We're not really gonna 'address' anything, right? I didn't really kick a puppy. I just, um . . . I can't make myself work on these applications, and—"

"David. Just come over."

CHAPTER

THIRTEEN

D answered the door in sweatpants and a T-shirt.

I stared for a moment. "Sweatpants?"

"Is that a problem?"

"No, it's great. Sweatpants are what everyone should wear at home. Just never in public."

"Good to know." He closed the door behind me.

I followed him into the living room. The TV was on, and whatever he was watching involved terrible special effects and a young woman in a very tight and artfully sullied tank top aiming a flamethrower at two battling monsters.

He settled on the couch. Patted the seat next to him.

"What are you *watching*?"

"A Syfy channel original movie. Come over here."

I didn't move. "Who are you, and where is D?"

His eyes didn't leave the screen. "A friend and I often watch these movies and bet on the outcome. In humans versus creature movies, we bet on which humans get killed. In creature versus creature movies, we bet on which creature will emerge victorious." He picked up his phone. "Today it's *Pteranosquid vs. Pegasaurus*. It looks like . . ." He typed into the phone. "I'm set to win twenty dollars. Pteranosquid appears to be a sure thing."

Of course. Bacon, whiskey, silence, Friesians, and Syfy original movies. Why not?

I cautiously slunk over and sat beside him. "Is a pteranosquid . . . ?"

"A pteranodon with gills and tentacles that terrorizes both air and sea, yes." He didn't look up from his phone.

"And a pegasaurus is . . ."

J.A. ROCK

"A Pegasus that is part dinosaur. These things, David, are often exactly what they sound like."

"Just making sure." On screen, a white winged creature with a horse's body and a reptilian head took flight, making straight for a tentacled pteranodon that was dive-bombing a seaside tourist town. "This really doesn't seem like something you'd be into."

He set the phone aside. "I have many secrets, David."

I laughed. "I'd noticed, *David*."

He gazed at me sideways, and I had just enough time to see a tiny smirk before he grabbed me and pulled me over his lap. I grunted and struggled, and he rubbed one giant hand over my ass. "You're wearing ridiculous jeans again." He hooked a finger in my back pocket and tugged. When I glanced up, Pegasaurus had taken a chunk out of Pteranosquid's wing.

"Take 'em off, why don't you?" I squirmed as he rubbed. My cock was already hard, and my jeans were ridiculous, I agreed. Tight enough to be a second skin, and keeping me from feeling the warmth of his palm. They needed to come off.

"No," he said slowly. "No, I don't think I will." He slid his hand over the curve of my ass and down between my legs, where he grabbed my balls through the denim. I bit my lip and rocked against his hand. "Be still now. I'm trying to enjoy my movie."

I was not still. He swatted me hard three times. I flexed my thighs and curled my toes and panted through the sting. He went back to rubbing circles on the denim, and I went back to trying to push my cock against his thigh. He held me down with one arm, and let the other hand alternate between rubbing my ass, rubbing my dick, and spanking me.

By the time Pegasaurus was killed by a jet missile and plummeted, flaming, into the sea, I was a mess. Sweating, breathless, unable to keep my hips still. D's hand roamed my body, pushing up my shirt, twisting my nipples, tickling my stomach . . . I moaned and spread my legs, silently begging for him to take my jeans off. My one attempt to remove them myself resulted in D resting his arm across my back to keep my upper body in place and then using his other arm to pull my knees forward until my ass stuck straight up. Then he spanked

124

me so hard and so fast I couldn't do anything but clench my fists and move my mouth wordlessly.

Finally he stopped. The room was silent except for my gasps. "Please?" I whispered, not daring to move. "Please?"

Slowly he pushed his hand under my shirt again. Stroked the sweaty skin between my pecs, then tweaked my nipple again. I flinched, my breath catching, but I didn't squirm.

"Good," he said quietly.

I got even harder at the praise.

He undid my fly. It took a few seconds of struggling to get my pants off. I lay in my T-shirt and underwear over his thighs, licking my lips between soft gasps. He slid his hand up my right thigh, under my briefs, and squeezed my ass cheek. My legs trembled. He reached around and stroked my balls, and I jerked, drawing one knee under me.

Finally his hand closed around my cock.

He started slow, then stroked me faster and harder as onscreen the monster screams escalated and something exploded.

"Oh God," I said between breaths. "Okay, okay . . ." I arched my shoulders upward, and I came, soaking my underwear.

I collapsed. I couldn't believe it. I'd gotten him to make me come, and all was right with the world.

"Damn it." He abruptly released my cock.

"What?" I struggled to see what was going on.

"The fucking pegasaurus came back to life. Now it's killing the pteranosquid, and I'm going to lose twenty bucks."

Once the movie was over we had a quiet lunch of deli meat and white bread.

I folded a slice of roast beef carefully on my bread. "So do you watch monster movies for the money? Or the love?"

He poured barbeque sauce on his turkey slices. "I suppose there is some love. I am . . ." He paused and sighed. "Attempting to write a screenplay."

"A screenplay." I wanted to make sure I'd heard right.

"For a Syfy movie. About a creature called a crocopython—"

"Shut up."

"—which terrorizes a group of people on a small island designated for scientific research."

"Oh. My. God. Where is the screenplay?"

"Where you will never find it."

"You have to show it to me."

"I will do no such thing."

"You wouldn't tell me about it if you didn't want me to read it," I pointed out.

"It is simply an exercise in personal betterment. It is not fit for your eyes." He stood and headed for the counter. I followed, scooting in front of him and going to my knees.

"D. I'll do anything."

He looked down and lifted one eyebrow. "Anything?"

I gazed up at him. "Yes, anything. Please? I let you fill my ass with soap. You can let me read your screenplay."

He tugged my hair. "Hmm. I'll have to think about this." He stepped past me and poured himself a whiskey. "Sit at the table and be silent for five minutes. If you can do that, I'll show you the screenplay."

I got to my feet. Went to the table, sat, folded my hands, and waited patiently. He knocked back the whiskey, keeping a wary eye on me.

What? You don't think I can do this?

I really, really wanted to talk. But not as much as I wanted to read the screenplay.

Eventually he retrieved his laptop. Opened the screenplay and set the computer in front of me. "So you *can* be still and quiet." He gave my hair another tug. "I'll remember that."

"'Crocopython,'" I read from the title page.

"If you read it out loud, I will—"

"Oh, I'm reading it out loud. This is not up for discussion."

He stood there, his arms crossed, sandwich forgotten. "A lot of the early scenes aren't written yet. Just so you know. It sort of . . . starts in the middle."

I scrolled to a scene that looked juicy and read: "'Jon: What is that?' 'Tom: A crocopython.' 'Alice: It's huge.'" I glanced up. "D, none of your characters say more than three words at a time."

He nodded once, a look of supreme peace and satisfaction on his face.

I refocused on the screen. "This is a Syfy movie. There needs to be tons of ridiculous expository dialogue. Like . . . Okay, like, 'Tom: That snake's the size of the cement mixer that killed my mother. Back when she built this lab, she swore she'd never try to play God. But now . . . we've unleashed hell.'"

D gazed over my shoulder at the screen. "That sounds terrible."

"But that's how low-budget monster movies work. Also, you can't name your characters Tom, Alice, and Frank. What is this, *See Spot Run*? They need crazy names. Who's the main character?"

"Tom."

"Okay, he's now Jake Mandragon. Frank is Tank Kevlar. And Alice is Dr. Brittany Sands. Who's your wild card?"

"What?"

"The bad boy who never plays by the rules and is going to appear to get eaten but then blasts his way out of the crocopython's belly at the end."

"Oh. Jon."

"He needs a single name that's not really a name, like Twix. Okay, look, I'm opening a duplicate document, and I'm gonna help you."

I went to work, changing names and dialogue and reading it aloud to him as I worked. "'Jake Mandragon: Dr. Sands, head to the back shed, where my uncle kept all his banned firearms back before he died in a freak explosion, leaving me in charge of the lab. Grab the freeze gun. Tank Kevlar, you—'"

"Why would Tank Kevlar's friend call him by his full name?"

"It doesn't matter! His name's Tank Kevlar; you have to say the whole thing. 'Tank Kevlar, you start the Humvee.'" I turned to an imaginary camera and raised a brow. "'This Amazonian repto-mutt is about to experience the Ice Age.'" I turned back to D. "See what I did there?"

He sighed again.

"You love these movies! So don't pretend you're not grateful to me for turning your screenplay into something that will actually sell."

"Love is such a strong word."

"D, come here. Sit with me."

He pulled up a chair and sat next to me, still holding his empty whiskey glass.

"You don't have to accept my changes," I said. "I respect your work as is."

"Keep going."

I slumped back, my fingers brushing the floor. "I'll have to think some more. You should put this in a Google Doc so I can read it as you work."

He shot me a glare that didn't look too serious.

I nudged his foot with mine under the table. "When you live in Hollywood, can I come to your penthouse apartment to get spanked in an opulent setting?"

"I will never live in Hollywood."

"Yeah, it doesn't seem like it would be a good fit for you. But it's fun to dream, right?"

"I suppose."

I softened my voice. "What did you want to be as a kid?"

"A park ranger."

"Aww."

"But money was tight, and I saw how much my mom struggled. I figured it was best to get a cubicle job."

"Well, hey. At least you never worked at a mall."

He toyed with the glass. "I sometimes think, now that I'm older, that I may have let certain opportunities pass me by. There are things I didn't want ten years ago, and convinced myself I'd never want. But now . . ."

"Dude, it's not like you're ancient. You can still go out there and live your life and do whatever you want."

"I don't have much interest in 'going out there.'" He looked up. "I envy what you have with your friends. I don't have anything like that."

I felt a pang of sympathy. "What about your monster-movie-betting friend?"

"He's a good guy. But we don't have much in common beyond a love of hybrid creatures."

I hesitated. "Well, if you don't feel like you have enough friends, you're welcome to hang out with mine."

He chuckled. He ought to do that more often—it did great crinkling things to his eyes, and made him look . . . sweet.

"I'm serious. We should all get together." Possibly this was the worst idea ever. But there was only one way to find out.

He hesitated, the smile slipping from his face.

"Relax." I was suddenly nervous. "I'm not proposing to you. I just mean group dinner or something."

He nodded slowly. "If you think they can tolerate me, I'm willing."

I tried to hide how excited I was about this. No need to scare him.

But then I rested my head on his shoulder, and it totally did scare him. His whole body jerked. He relaxed in gradual increments.

I patted his arm. "Oh, D. Just you wait. We're gonna have a good time. You, me, and all my friends."

I met with GK and Kel again at Finer Things. This time it was on their invitation, and this time they didn't make small talk.

"David." GK looked tired. "We wanted to discuss your club."

Well, fuck.

"Club. What club?" I wasn't sure how far playing dumb would get me. But I had to try. I'd had a feeling this was what they wanted to talk about. Miles, Kamen, Gould, and I had read through over forty applications last week. We were even getting applicants from out of state—and from Canada. And we'd recruited almost every sub we knew from Riddle to join our site.

"The Subs Club." GK had a *giant* coffee in front of him. "You've heard of it?"

I nodded cautiously. "Heard of it. Sure. Who hasn't?"

Kel had papers with her. She put an arm over them when I tried to see what they were. "We have reason to believe you're behind it."

"Whaaaaaaa . . . ?" I trailed off at her glare, looked down, and took a sip of my tea.

"Are you?"

I shrugged. "Maybe, maybe not."

Kel turned to GK. "He totally is."

"I'm right here," I said. "And yes, I'm involved with it. Proudly."

Kel sighed. "It's really causing some problems within Riddle. We've had four people cancel their memberships this month."

"Doms?" I asked.

"I'm not at liberty to say. But believe me, it's not just doms you guys are alienating."

I knew that. Some of the worst comments we got on the blog were from angry subs who shared Anonymous's opinions.

Just because a dom doesn't play how you want . . .

You have no right to criticize someone's style . . .

You're a sub, but you get mad if a dom tries to take control? Sounds like you're the one who doesn't belong in the scene . . .

"We're not trying to alienate anyone," I said. "We just want to provide honest feedback about local doms."

"Privacy is a *huge* concern for people in the scene."

"The blog is private. You have to be a member to view the site. And it has nothing to do with you or with Riddle."

Kel rubbed her temple. "Riddle *is* the scene in this city. I mean, there's Cobalt, but what does Cobalt have?"

"Just a couple of waterboarding Nazis," I agreed.

"Maybe the blog is private." GK turned the giant coffee mug around and around. "But everyone knows about it. And it's mainly Riddle members who are being reviewed."

I stared at my tea, wondering why I insisted on drinking this shit outside of work. "Look, we don't give out emails, addresses, or phone numbers. We use scene names. Or first names."

"It's still risky."

"What's risky is that there are rapists and abusers posing as doms. And they almost always get away with it, because no one fucking speaks up."

"I agree with you there," Kel said. "But I'm not sure this is the best way to go about—"

"How else are we gonna do it?" I looked back and forth between them. "Fetmatch won't let people talk, and the cops don't do a damn thing when kink goes awry, as we've seen. And you two care more about Bill's right to *heal*, or whatever, than ours, so we can't use Riddle as a safe space."

"We do *not* care more about Bill's rights than yours."

I played my ace card. "What about Gould? Even if he *wanted* to come back to Riddle, he couldn't. Because you chose Bill for your rehabilitation project."

Oh, I could see it in their eyes—the idea of hurting Gould ripped at their souls. Kel's jaw was clenched, and even GK looked like he was watching a movie where a dog died trying to save a child.

I continued. "We *need* a place that's just ours. And where doms don't get to tell us we're wrong for having concerns."

"Nobody thinks you're wrong." Kel's voice was firm. "But these are concerns we can all talk about *together*. We have the roundtables for discussions like this."

"Who comes to the roundtables? The same twelve people every month, telling their 'One time, at band camp' stories. The discussions never get heated, and nothing changes."

Kel looked affronted. "You haven't come to a discussion in years."

GK leaned forward. "What happens if someone tries to retaliate? If you end up in a scene with a dom who's not a fan of your club?"

I raised my eyebrows. "If you have to worry that doms are going to get violent because someone expressed an opinion about them, then we do have a problem."

Kel shook her head. "Most wouldn't. Some would."

"The guys who dropped their Riddle memberships want your head on a platter, that's for sure," GK said.

I stared at him evenly. "And what about what they did to earn their bad reviews? Huh?"

"From what I understand, they might just as easily have worn chaps that didn't fit as violated somebody."

"Oh, please." I waved him off. "We're not that bad."

Kel picked up one of the papers. "'MidwestMaster's tits are so big it's no wonder he can't swing a flogger properly. All that wobbling must really throw off his aim. And mock necks are for Sunday school teachers and aging queens.'" She set the sheet down. "From your blog."

"How did you get that?" I demanded.

She ignored me and jabbed at the paper. "This isn't useful information. It's cruel."

"That . . . should have been better moderated," I admitted. "It's true, though. You can't get into subspace if your dom's man boobs are making little smiles in his preacher turtleneck."

"You're undermining your own cause," GK said. "There is nothing *dangerous* about a mock neck."

"I beg to differ."

He tapped Kel's papers. "People are going to get hurt through this."

"No. We're going to stop people from getting hurt. Some of the people we're calling out on our site are big shots. Jimmy X, for instance." Jimmy X regularly participated in Riddle workshops and had even served as DM at play parties. "He told one woman if she was really submissive, she'd let him touch her breasts."

No response.

"This guy's a member of Riddle." I looked at them. "What are you gonna do about it?"

GK shook his head. "I've known Jim for years. He doesn't think like that. Maybe he needs a reminder about respecting limits, sure, but it's very possible that what he said was acceptable in the context of a scene."

"'Very possible?' That's what you want to assume—that it was all in good fun? Because she didn't think it was, and she shredded him in her review."

"Then she needed to communicate with him that he was going too far."

"Noooo, dude. He needed to not go too far. End of story."

"I'll talk to him."

"Yeah, because a man who thinks he can manipulate women into letting him take what he wants—you tell him he shouldn't do that, and suddenly he's like, 'Oh, what an overbearing, misogynistic fool I've been . . .'"

Kel put a hand on GK's arm, but addressed me. "We're not going to pretend abuse doesn't happen. But Jesus, David, the media's been painting our community as a bunch of dangerous freaks since Hal's death. We *have* to stick together."

I could see how hard GK was gripping his coffee cup, could suddenly see what looked like *tears* in Kel's eyes.

"Why is this so threatening to you?" I was genuinely confused. "You're a woman. Most abuse victims in this community are women. Shouldn't you want—"

"Don't you *dare* tell me what I 'should' want as a woman."

I took a breath. "I just want to understand why something that's *my* project, that has nothing to do with you, bothers you so much."

"Because!" Kel snapped, her eyes definitely watering now. She dashed the tears away. "Fuck." She dabbed at her eyes with a napkin and sighed.

GK looked at me wearily. "Because we built Riddle. From the ground up. And we don't want to lose it."

Kel nodded, expression almost pleading. "We saved up for *years*. Did the floor plan. Figured out all the permits we'd need. Decorated, bought the furniture. There were months of legal nightmares. The downstairs neighbors protested, the fucking Family Values Association said we couldn't put a club like this so close to a Chuck E. Cheese's ..."

"That is kind of fucked up," I agreed.

She crumpled the napkin in her hand. "I just don't want to see it fall apart."

I almost pitied her. Almost. "You act like we're trying to sabotage you. That's not what we're doing at all."

GK let go of his mug. "You've seen what's happening as a result of this club. Doms are hurt, subs are paranoid ... You're not bringing people together. You're creating deeper and more permanent divisions."

For a second, I almost relented. Almost said, *Okay, then let's talk about how we can work together to fix this.*

I remembered going to the roundtables at Riddle each month for the first year I was a member. A group moderator would ask questions, and we'd have a discussion about whatever that month's topic was. Safe play, aftercare, poly scenes, edge play ... I remembered how fun it had been, how nerdy I'd gotten about my newfound BDSM knowledge. For someone like me who'd grown up without siblings, with distant parents, Riddle had seemed like a miracle. A place I finally *fit*.

But all I had to do was think about Hal, and my anger rose again. "You took a place that submissives and bottoms thought was safe, and you let someone die there. And now we can't trust that it won't happen again."

They looked genuinely horrified. Maybe I was going too far, and maybe I didn't care.

I pushed my chair back and stood. Pointed to Kel's papers. "And now you're invading a private space we tried to create. *You're* the ones turning this into a confrontation. Not me. If you'll excuse me, I've got to go."

They watched me struggle to get the lid on my to-go cup. Finally I threw the cup and the lid in the trash, and walked away.

CHAPTER

FOURTEEN

I put off telling the others about my run-in with GK and Kel. At the next club meeting we talked about moderating the site and reviewed some of the comments that had made it through. On one ongoing discussion about when a DM should intervene in a public scene, for instance, we'd had a comment from someone called "Fucktopus" that was less of a contribution, and more of a personal ad.

"Seriously, who moderated this?" I asked.

No one answered.

I read it aloud.

"'I am eight kinds of fun. A tentacle furry with a big heart.'" I gasped. "A tentacle furry! Nooooo!"

Kamen looked up from his sandwich. "Tentacles aren't furry."

I continued. "'I have had eight mechanical tentacles built, each of which is robotically controlled and has dildo attachments. So if you are interested in being penetrated multiple places by my tentacles of fun . . .' Oh my God. Miles!" I called. "Didn't you use to want to have tentacle sex?"

"What?" he called back from the bathroom. The toilet flushed and the sink went on and then off. He returned to the kitchen, shaking his hands dry. "What's going on?"

"This guy's a *tentacle* furry. He has robotic dildo tentacles."

"Why on earth you'd think that would interest me . . ." Miles stepped closer and peered at the screen, looking more than a little interested. He shook his head. "Honestly, David." He was in full British-aunt mode. But if anyone in this room wanted to be penetrated multiple places by tentacles of fun, it was Miles.

"Kamen's right, though. He wouldn't be a furry, would he?"

"There are non-furry furries." Miles took his seat. "There are dragons, which are called scalies. Cetaceans. Avians, or featheries. And lizards, which are herps."

"Shouldn't they be called herpes?" Kamen asked. And then he laughed. Oh, how he laughed.

"How do you know all this shit?" I asked Miles. "And an octopus isn't any of those things, right?"

"It's a cephalopod," Miles confirmed. "I'm not aware of a term for cephalopod furries."

"How about 'freaks'?" I muttered, and then continued reading Fucktopus's ad. "'I am interested in doing a Moby Dick–style role-play, where you would hunt me in the ocean, and I would become your primary maritime nemesis representing all evil and glory in your life.'"

"Wow," Gould said. "I feel like we have to delete it . . . but I don't want to."

"We're leaving it to see what kind of responses he gets." I scrolled through some of the messages in the admin box. "Waaaiit. Did you guys see this one?"

"You'll have to be more specific." Miles opened his sandwich and began stacking the ingredients neatly.

"'I have a question for you guys. My friend is in a D/s relationship, she's a sub. And the guy is like older than her and pretty creepy. One time he locked her in the closet for three days as a punishment. Like he let her have her laptop but she wasn't allowed to be online and like he'd only open the closet to feed her. Another time he dislocated all her fingers on one hand as a punishment. He popped them back in right away but she said it was the most pain she's felt in her whole life. And like those were not punishments they'd talked about beforehand, that was just what he did because he was mad at her.

"'They have like a really screwed-up codependent relationship where they can't live without each other. She says she wants an intense relationship. But I think it's abusive. But I don't know how to tell her, or if I should. Does anyone have any advice?'"

"Oh, shit." Miles made a face. "That's fucked up." You knew it was fucked up when Miles used the phrase "fucked up" instead of something like "highly unpalatable."

I read it over again, feeling sick. "What the hell are we supposed to tell her?"

"We should tell her to talk to her friend," Kamen suggested.

I ignored him. "Do we go to the police?"

"No." Gould's mouth twisted to the side. "*We* don't. I mean, what about that woman who used to play at Riddle who'd pancaked her breast in a scene? What about all the people who have burns or brands or spikes through their lips? Some people do play really rough."

"Gould, you can't seriously think this is okay."

"Of course not! I'm just saying, if she insists this is the relationship she wants, what can the police do?" He paused. "What if we talk to GK and Kel?"

"No," I said immediately.

"Why not?"

"Let's see if the girl who wrote this will give us a name for the guy—if he's on Fet, or just a first name, or whatever—and ask her to rate and review him, using what she just told us."

"Are you *crazy*?" Miles demanded. "If he is abusive, and somebody tells him he's been reviewed here, he's going to assume she went behind his back. He could seriously hurt her, or *kill* her."

"I want to know what's wrong with talking to GK and Kel." Gould was still staring at me.

I sighed. "Because they don't support us, okay?"

"What do you mean?"

"They know about the club, they know we're behind it, and they don't approve."

The others were silent a moment.

"I met with them the other day," I went on. "First they let Bill back in, and now they're trying to get us to take down our site because it's causing too much of a stir in the community or whatever."

Miles frowned. "How do they know about the site?"

"Not sure." I shook my head. "But if they know, probably other doms do too."

Gould looked at me. Hesitated. "Yeah, I played with a woman last night at Cobalt who definitely knew I was involved."

I opened my mouth, then paused. *Woman?* I exchanged a glance with Miles. I knew Gould had played with a woman years ago, but I was pretty sure he'd gotten real gay since then.

I decided to ignore it and focus on the important part. "What'd she say?"

"She made a lot of sandwich jokes."

"Told you." Kamen seemed unfazed by the idea of Gould with a woman. "Everyone thinks sandwiches."

Gould scratched the back of his neck. "She asked if she could punch my rewards card."

"What . . . does that mean?" I asked.

"Apparently it just meant pegging."

"But she didn't seem to mind?" I kept thinking about what GK had said about retaliation. Maybe it was more important than I'd thought that we remain anonymous. "That you were part of the club, I mean?"

"No. When we were done she asked how I was gonna rate her. She seemed really excited about it."

Miles was staring at Gould. "This *is not* good. This was supposed to be anonymous."

"Well, it is the internet." I tried to hide my discomfort. I really, *really* didn't want to deal with anything that would prove GK and Kel right. That made the Subs Club seem like a bad idea. "And it's not like we're doing anything wrong."

Kamen licked mayo off his hand. "Why don't we ask this girl if her friend in the abusive relationship would talk to us? And maybe we could find out more and, like, convince her that her relationship's bad."

"Buddy, I don't think that would work."

Kamen slapped the table. We all jumped.

"Why not?" He glared at us. "I know I don't phrase my ideas as good as you guys. But you act like everything I say isn't a realistic possibility."

"We don't—" I started.

"You do. If I suggest stuff for the club, you never think it's good enough." He cast a particularly dark look at Miles. "And you all think I was fine with what happened to Hal. Like it just rolled off me, but it didn't. I was as upset as you guys!"

I remembered Kamen at Kink by Candlelight saying he didn't like Bill. And his mom telling me that Kamen still had nightmares.

But with the other two so much more volatile than Kamen, it had been easy for me to assume Kamen was—not *okay*, but more resilient, maybe?

Gould reached across the table, wiggling his fingers at Kamen. Kamen reluctantly took Gould's hand. "That's *not* what we think," Gould said. "Your ideas are good. And we know how much you loved Hal. He'd be really proud of you."

I caught Miles rolling his eyes, and I kicked him under the table.

Kamen still wasn't looking at Gould.

Gould stood, pulling on Kamen's hand. "Come with me a minute."

Slowly, Kamen got up and followed Gould to the living room. I turned to Miles. "What's your problem?"

Miles adjusted his glasses. "He always does this. Says what Hal would think, like he's some sort of diviner who speaks to Hal from beyond."

"*You're* the one who told us weeks ago that the review blog isn't what Hal would have wanted. And who the fuck cares; don't we all think about Hal and how he'd feel?"

Miles looked at the floor. "I know."

"And can't you just let Kamen post what he wants on the blog?"

Miles's jaw tightened. "My apologies. I've just been . . . out of sorts, lately."

"Well, shape up, okay? Because the four of us *have* to stick together." I winced inwardly as I echoed Kel's words.

He nodded. "I know."

Gould and Kamen returned a few minutes later. Kamen looked slightly happier. I didn't ask them what they'd talked about, but I apologized to Kamen for not listening to him, and he waved it off. Miles, however, made some bullshit excuse and left.

Space Camp was a subdued affair. Even Mandy's assertion to Parker that "Houston, we got a problem, and it's your bleepin' attitude," couldn't break the tension.

I stood on D's doorstep, exhilarated and nervous. More than anything, I was ready for a break from this shitty past few days. I didn't

want to think about GK and Kel, or the Subs Club. I just wanted to raise a little hell with D. I was wearing mesh athletic shorts, as per some cryptic instructions he'd sent me, and I had a bunch of flowers my coworker Helen had gotten from a guy she didn't like and then given to me.

Shut up, behave, and show him you can be good. No, wait, what the fuck, don't change for him. Be who you are. Be a mouthy little cockwad. Give it to him. Challenge him. Make him sorry he signed on for six weeks of you.

But we'd bonded further since our impromptu screenwriting session. He'd shared his script with me as a Google Doc—he had changed all the names to the ones I'd suggested—and I'd read the whole thing and pointed out places where he could add more ridiculous exposition. Maybe, just maybe, I ought to let my affection for him carry over to these weekly sessions.

He opened the door.

I grinned. Partly because I was delighted to see him. And partly because I'd just decided there was no way I'd stop on his welcome mat and wait for him to address me.

"David." He held the door for me. The house smelled like coffee.

"How are you?" I thrust the flowers at him. "These are for you. Actually, they're for Helen, but she doesn't want them." I walked past him, heading toward the kitchen. I didn't make it more than a few steps before he caught my arm and tugged me around. He set the flowers on the hall table and swatted me back toward the mat.

"Ow."

That got me another swat.

"Sorry."

"Stop talking. Wait to be addressed."

I stood on the mat, put my hands behind my back, and looked at D. He was wearing a casual sweater and khakis, looking like Daniel Boone had discovered a sale at L.L.Bean. He was so handsome. Just so fucking handsome. I didn't think the pornstache was weird at all anymore. Everybody should have one.

He sighed and stepped beside me just as I remembered I was supposed to bow my head. I started to do it, but he laced his fingers through my hair and forced my head down. Heat and resentment ripped through me simultaneously. He trailed his hand down my back and stopped just before he reached my ass.

"Thank you for the flowers," he said.

I inhaled sharply as he slid his hand a couple of inches lower and squeezed. I pushed back into his hand. "No probs."

He leaned close to me. "Are you sucking up?"

"Well, I'd rather suck *you*, Sir. But I'll take what I can get."

"Come on." He sounded like he was trying not to laugh, and my mood lifted for the first time in days.

He had me follow him into the kitchen, where he got me a glass of water and offered me deer jerky. I stared at it. It was only a step or two away from squirrel gravy, but I accepted it. I had said I wanted him to teach me about venison.

"Did you dry this meat yourself?" I asked. "Wait, did you shoot the deer?"

"I bought it at a gas station."

"The deer?"

"The jerky."

I tried it. Nope, nope. Disgusting. I spit it into a napkin.

He pretended not to notice.

I balled up the napkin and pushed it behind his saltshaker. "Did you pay up for the bet you lost?"

"I did. But I hope to win my twenty back next week with the world premiere of *Sharkigator*."

"I'll be rooting for you."

"You know . . . " He went to the counter and poured himself a mug of coffee. Held the carafe up inquiringly, but I shook my head, and he replaced it. "It was said, back in the days of yore, that Davy Crockett was half horse, half alligator. I've often wondered if that contributed to my love of hybrid monsters."

"And horses?"

"Possibly."

"You know Davy Crockett was a total racist, right?" I nodded smugly when he looked at me. "That's right, I've been on Wikipedia."

He leaned against the counter. "There were two men: David Crockett, the politician, and Davy Crockett, the folk hero. One was a product of his time, the other is a product of ours. People are flawed, multifaceted, and I choose to admire the legend, not the bigot."

"D?"

"Yes."

"I want you to be an internet meme."

"I don't know what that means."

"I don't expect you to."

We moved on to the reading of the list. Everything I fessed up to made my cock a little harder as I imagined him slapping my ass, his voice low and rough as he scolded me. God, I just wanted to be close to him. If he put me over his lap, I'd spread my legs for him, I'd tell him how sorry I was. I'd do fucking anything he wanted.

The trouble with these lists was, I didn't really connect with them. We both knew D was going to punish me, and he probably spent the week planning what he was going to do, same as I spent the week wondering what he had in store. It was a fun game, but no matter what I'd done—whether I'd rolled through a stop sign or made fun of Miles's cardigans or ignored my mother's calls—the results would be the same. D would use whatever I put on my list as an excuse to do what he'd intended to do all along.

But then were things I felt legitimately guilty about. My utter inability to take responsibility for my future, for instance. I still hadn't completed a single application to styling school. These were things I wanted to fix, things I wanted someone to get after me for. But I didn't think tighty-whities and an enema were going to do the trick. I wondered how to talk to him about that.

I took a deep breath, pushing those thoughts aside, and read the last item on my list. "I'm sorry I called you the other day and bothered you outside of a session time."

He came around to stand by my chair. I tensed. He threaded his fingers through my hair, then pulled my head back so that our eyes met. "That," he said firmly, "you do not have to apologize for."

I tried not to smile.

He released me. "And I would not be opposed to you coming by on other days that are not Thursdays."

Now I smiled. "Reeeeeeaaaalllllyyyyy?"

He crossed around the table and sat in front of me. Folded his hands. "Are you wearing white underwear?"

I snorted. "Dude, what is your *thing* about underwear? Seriously, the tighty-whities, the potty-chair, the 'bad little boy' stuff... Are you allowed within five hundred feet of playgrounds?"

"I just like humiliating adult men in tight white underwear."

"Fair enough. How do you feel about manties?"

"I do not know what you're talking about, nor do I care to find out."

"They're panties for men. Lingerie."

He reached for his mug and took a sip of coffee, never breaking eye contact with me. Then he got up, went to the counter and poured himself a whiskey. Knocked it back and stared at me once more. "I have erased your last words from my memory. Let's go to the den."

"Uh-uh. I don't care if you think you're goddamn John Wayne. You are a modern man, living in the here and now, and you will accept that men sometimes wear panties and it's awesome."

"Stop saying 'panties.' Please."

"Women are real, D. And so are men who wear their clothes."

D grunted. "Are you telling me you want to wear... manties?"

"Nope." I grinned. "Just wanted you to know they exist. Also, kale chips. And participation awards."

He shut his eyes briefly and spoke in that dry, inflectionless tone. "I would like you to join me in the den for your punishment. If you're finished with your water."

"Sure. No problem." I spread my arms. "Have your way with me, Sir."

He led me to the Den of Horrors and had me stand by the school desk. I noticed there was an extra chair by the wall, but I didn't comment. He took a small package out of the cabinet and unwrapped it. Tossed the wrapper onto the desk. I studied it. A cheerful-looking model in baseball pants with a white pad over his torso stared back at me. *Body Wellness Disposable Heating Pads.*

D snapped his fingers. "Take your underwear off. Then put the shorts back on."

"Wait. I wore tighty-whities just for you and you want me to—"

"If you don't take your underwear off right this second, I will beat you with everything on this wall." He indicated the wall of implements.

I stifled a laugh and stripped my shorts and underwear off. Yanked my shorts back on, a little apprehensive. He got a piece of paper and a pencil out of the big desk, walked over to the school desk and put the heating pad on the chair. "Sit," he ordered.

I did. He set the paper in front of me.

It was a crossword.

He placed the pencil on top of it.

"I'll be in the living room. You'll stay here until you've completed this. It is a lesson in silence, stillness, and concentration."

I started to feel strange, but I wasn't sure why. I raised my eyebrows. "A crossword. Really?"

"Really."

"Okay. Cool. I'll sit here in my shorts and Shortz it up."

"Quietly."

I hated stillness and silence. "Can I come into the living room and do it?"

"No."

"Do you do this to all your boys?" I asked, hoping to goad him into a punishment that was more my style. "Force them to play pseudo-intellectuals in your schoolroom dungeon?"

He just ruffled my hair and left the room.

The pad got hot fast, but the heat was a lousy substitute for the burn of a spanking. I was surprised by how much I wanted *him*— wanted his contact, his closeness, wanted him to be irrefutably the cause of my discomfort.

Screw him, if he was gonna leave me here. If he was gonna refuse to talk to me and go do whatever the hell he did when he wasn't torturing adult men in tight white underwear or eating dried Bambi—watch *The Adventures of the Wilderness Family* or *Sharknado*? I didn't know.

All right, Dave. 1 Down. You got this.

I sat back, fidgeting. My stomach fluttered with nerves, and I wasn't sure why. All D was asking me to do was sit here, unsupervised, and do a puzzle. Wasn't like I was tied to a bench with a rope around my neck.

One of Hal's arms had been free. That was what Cinnamon had said at the trial. Confirmed by the paramedics. Supposedly he could have loosened the cord around his neck. Could have gotten out.

If I hadn't been outside smoking, would I have noticed what was going on?

Maybe not. Because I'd been angry with him. I could have been right there in the club, and my stupid pride would have kept me from checking in with him.

I felt the same wash of guilt I'd been torturing myself with for a year and a half. I hadn't followed the trial. I'd let people give me updates, and I hadn't stopped thinking about it the entire time it was going on. But I hadn't sought out information. I wasn't even called as a witness, since I'd been outside when Hal had died. I'd had to give a statement right afterward, because I was the one he'd come to the club with, but other than that the law wasn't much interested in me.

I knew jack shit about legal matters, so all I really took away from the whole disaster was the bottom line: Bill Henson had been found innocent of second-degree murder. I'd listened to Miles rant afterward about how they should have tried him for manslaughter instead, how that would have increased the chance of conviction. But I'd barely paid attention. I'd thought about going to Bill's house, had fantasized about killing him. But I knew I wasn't any kind of avenger.

The only one of us who'd had that in him was Gould. I'd been so confused when I'd gotten the call from the police to come pick Gould up. I thought there'd been a mix-up—Gould? Assault someone? Never. Bill hadn't pressed charges, but a few days later he'd taken out the restraining order. I'd kept Gould at my place for a few days, even though he'd insisted he was fine, that he'd just temporarily lost control. But he hadn't wanted to talk about the incident, and even once I'd stopped keeping such a close eye on him, he'd wanted to stick around. Cara was getting ready to move out, so I'd asked Gould if he wanted to move in.

Maybe there'd been just a tiny, selfish part of me that had wondered if *now*—now that Hal was completely out of the picture, Gould and I would . . .

The memory hurt too much to finish.

I stood up, making the school desk creak. I walked across the room and started playing around in the headmaster desk, opening and closing drawers. Nothing inside but an empty notebook and a heavy wooden ruler. I went to the wall of implements, took down the nightstick, and tried to twirl it. It fell to the floor with a thud. I took a bunch of stuff off the wall and started arranging the implements in a sort of kinky Stonehenge.

D still didn't come in.

I started to feel shitty. I wanted to show him the real me—the guy who'd taken control after Hal's death. Who was there for his friends and showed up for work every day on time and actually could conceive of a world beyond *I want*. Instead I was showing him a child. A spoiled brat. And it was his own goddamn fault, for making me feel like it was safe to show him that.

I strode back to the school desk and sat down, grinding my ass against the heating pad until I was good and sore. I took off my shoe and threw it against the wall.

He did come in then, and my relief at seeing him was short-lived.

"What is going on in here?" he asked.

Big manly man. No kale chips, no crying, no manties. I tried to imagine him when he was a baby, sucking stones in his crib when his stomach was empty rather than bother his mother with a basic human need like hunger. But that wasn't him at all, was it? He wrote terrible screenplays and wanted to have friends and liked spending time with me. He'd started to drop the act. Why hadn't I?

Because I couldn't tell right now whether I was acting.

He glanced across the room at what I'd done with his implements. Then he turned to me. "Do not get up again." His voice was brusque but steady. "Are we clear?"

I glared at him.

He smacked the desk and leaned down in my face. "*Do* you understand me?" he demanded. I flinched and opened my mouth, shocked. I suddenly fucking hated him. No, I didn't. I wanted more of this, more of the man who forced me to obey. It was what I needed, what I couldn't ask for. I just—resented him. So much.

"Yes, Sir," I spat.

He pointed at the crossword. "Sit there. And finish that. You have fifteen minutes."

He left.

I started filling in all the crossword spaces with FUCK OFF—even if it didn't fit. 13 Down: *FUCK OFF*. 5 Across *FUCK OFF*. *FUCK OFF FUCK OFF FUCK OFF . . .*

I looked at the paper when I was done. *Shit*. It was like those movies where a kid gets possessed and writes stuff on the windows like *HE'S COMING* and the next day has no memory of doing it. I was seriously *gross* with sweat.

My hand started to shake. I crumpled the paper, and, not sure how to dispose of it without disobeying my order not to get up, sat on it.

It crinkled under my ass. The whole situation was ridiculous.

I'd let Hal get hurt. Because of this part of me. The part that was childish and spiteful and needed to push back when someone pushed me. Hal had wanted to annoy me by playing with Bill, and he had, so I'd left him.

I'd left him, and he'd died alone, and maybe he'd been scared. I'd never fucking know.

I grabbed the paper out from under me, un-balled it, and wrote at the bottom *I'M SORRY*.

The most pathetic bit of emotional manipulation ever, except I meant it. It wasn't that I wanted D to go easy on me, exactly. I just didn't want him to be angry. I'd never felt more deserving of a punishment than I did right now, and yet I wasn't sure I could handle anything tonight.

I crumpled the paper again and held it in my hand.

And waited.

By the time D came into the room, I'd swallowed the lump in my throat and forced my expression defiantly blank.

"How's it coming?" He pulled up the other chair and sat beside me.

"Fine," I muttered. A muscle was twitching in my right temple.

"Where's the puzzle?"

Numbly, I held out the ball of paper. Listened to him uncrumple it. He was quiet as he looked it over. I felt the tightness in my throat again.

Fuck this. I just wanted to go home. Watch a stupid movie with Gould. Go to sleep.

He asked, without concern or accusation, as though he were only mildly interested in the answer: "Do you really want me to fuck off?"

I shook my head. The room was blurry. I stared straight in front of me.

He crumpled the paper and tossed it on the floor. "I don't know what to do when you act like this."

I shrugged.

"What is this, David? A game?"

Fuck if I knew.

He shifted, and his chair creaked. "Tell me what's going on."

What was going on was that I wanted comfort from a man whose only interest was in punishing me. He wasn't my friend, wasn't my boyfriend. He wasn't going to stay with me forever. I was scared of how *much* I felt. What if Bill really was sorry? What if he'd screwed up because of some impulsive decision, like I did every fucking day, except there was no forgiveness for him? He just had to live with what he'd done forever.

I don't care. I don't fucking care.

A dark, savage fear broke over me and slipped down my body. "I—" My voice cracked.

"David." He seemed wary. "Come on into the kitchen. We'll get some water."

I shook my head. "What if I could have stopped it?"

"Stopped what?" His voice was soft and sounded close, but I felt disoriented, like I wasn't sure where in the room he was.

"That night, with Hal; I was there. I let him play with Bill. I was pissed at him, and I didn't—didn't keep an eye on him."

"That is not your fault." He said it so firmly I almost believed him.

"I could have. I could definitely have stopped it."

"You—"

I leaned out from the desk and kissed him. He kissed me back, just for a second. Hungrily enough that I didn't think he was just being nice. He pulled gently away. He looked at me, and for once he didn't seem to know what to do or say.

I wanted more. I wanted my tongue deep in his mouth, I wanted to feel that pull in my body from throat to groin, wanted him to slide a hand between my legs, strip me down. Open me up and shove his cock inside me. Sex would help. More than punishment. It would get me out of my head, make me feel good again.

I reached for him, but he didn't move.

"This isn't a good idea right now," he said.

"Why not?"

"Because I don't think you're feeling well."

"I'm the one who knows how I'm feeling. And I'm fine."

He stood. "Come on. Let's take a walk."

"God, you're so . . ." I stood and followed him as he headed out of the room. "You obviously feel something for me. So why not just fuck me?"

He turned back to me. "Because we do things on my terms, not yours."

"I'm not talking about fucking as part of our Sir/boy game or whatever! I mean as two human beings who are attracted to each other."

"You're welcome to stay here. But we're not having sex tonight. And you will respect my wishes."

"I am respecting your wishes. You *wish* to fuck me. So just do it."

He kept walking.

"Come on!" I shouted. "Was all that stuff in your profile bullshit? You said you could transform me! You said you'd make me obedient." He stopped, and a rush of satisfaction spurred me on. "You're in such high demand; I want to see what you can do. *Make me*! Make me fucking listen to you!"

He turned, his shoulders rigid. Then he said, very clearly, "Red."

I froze. "What?"

"Red. I'm safewording. Session over. Now are you staying or going?"

I continued to gape. It hadn't really occurred to me that he— or any dom—could safeword. That they'd ever need to. D was the one *doing* things in our sessions. If he wanted to stop, he could stop anytime.

Numbly I gathered my things. I wasn't coming back here. No way. I couldn't.

I'd fucked up so badly. And I couldn't use Hal as an excuse. This was all me.

He offered me a ride home, and I pretended I hadn't heard him. I didn't think I could manage an apology or a good-bye. But once I had my shoes back on and my underwear balled in my pocket and was standing by the door, he said, "I'll see you next week."

"You can't mean that." I didn't look at him.

"I do. And I expect to see you here at seven thirty."

"I'm a shithead," I muttered.

"Seven thirty," he repeated.

"No."

He leaned forward and kissed me gently on the lips. The kiss was brief and chaste and left me flushed, confused. "Seven thirty."

I nodded slowly. "I don't . . . Maybe."

I left before he could say anything else.

CHAPTER

FIFTEEN

The next day, Kamen was at my house when I got home from work. He was sitting in the kitchen, sans guitar, looking through one of my hair magazines. "What's payot?" he asked as I walked by him to rummage in the cabinets for snacks.

"Ask Gould." I found an ancient bag of pistachios and sniffed it.

I was still on edge. I hadn't stopped thinking about yesterday with D. I'd sent him several apology messages, and he'd assured me that he wasn't angry. That we'd meet Thursday as usual. But I still felt guilty. Why couldn't I learn to just *shut my mouth*?

He flipped the page. "There's some crazy hair in here."

"Yeah." I sampled a pistachio. Tasted fine to me. "Are you here for the good bread? 'Cause I think we're out."

"Nah." Kamen shut the magazine. "I just wanted to say hey."

I looked at him and got this incredible rush of affection. Kamen liked every movie, every type of food, every style of music. He could find something to admire about any painting in an art museum. Where I hated to go places with Miles because Miles had to find some intellectual way of ripping apart anything I claimed to enjoy, seeing the world through Kamen's eyes was a blast. He was happy when the sun rose. Happy when the twenty-fourth caller on the Q-Hits station won a vacation to the Dominican Republic, because he loved when good things happened to other people. He didn't like Taylor Swift or olives, but that was about it.

I'd once made a list of things I wanted to bring up in front of him, just to see what good he'd find in them: ISIS, Ebola, puppy mills. But anytime I opened my mouth, I realized I couldn't. He was so fucking sweet. If I hadn't known him most of his life, I might not have believed he was for real.

"How are things going at work?" I asked.

"Good. We're changing the menu."

"Again?"

"Yeah, Hannah's crazy. She says we should do more seafood." He leaned back so the chair was balanced on two legs. I didn't even bother warning him not to do it. "How's your applications and whatever?"

I brought the pistachios to the table and sat. "Awful. I suck. I really do wanna do this hair-school thing. I don't know why I'm so hell-bent on self-sabotage."

He nodded, looking dead serious. "Yeah, it's kind of like me and my music. I really want to do it for a living. But I get real busy with work and then I forget to set up times to play in bars, and then it's like, when am I gonna actually make this happen?"

What was sad was that it probably wouldn't ever happen for Kamen. He had a good voice and was decent on the guitar, but he had a lot of work to do if he was going to make a living with music. I didn't even think he realized how much work.

Damn it. I'm such a dick.

Who the fuck cared whether Kamen had what it took to be a rock star? He was my best friend and if that was his dream, then I fucking wanted it for him, eight hundred thousand fucking times over. Why did I never tell them? How could I go around all the time caring about them all this much and never telling them?

I scooted the pistachios so he could reach them. "It'll happen."

He studied me. "Seriously, you okay?"

"Ugh, maybe. I think. I feel like I've been screwing up a lot lately. The thing with GK and Kel. And I was awful to D last night."

"Dude. GK and Kel are just in a weird position. You're not screwing up. You've done so much good stuff. And if you were rude to D or whatever, just be like, 'Hey, man. Sorry. Let's have sex.'"

I winced. Didn't tell him that sentiment was exactly what had gotten me in trouble in the first place.

"I love you, buddy. You know that, right?"

He tilted his head. "Aw, Dave. No one ever says that to me except my family."

I stood and crossed behind him, stooped, and gave him a hug. "I'm saying it."

He turned and hugged me back, and it was, like all of Kamen's hugs, a borderline painful experience.

"Love you too," he said. "You want to hear a new song?"

"Is it about squirrel gravy?"

"No. It's, like, 'Hotel California' if it was played by a mariachi band."

Well. Who could resist that? I brought him his guitar.

On Saturday evening I showed up at D's place unannounced.

"I'm sorry," I told him, standing on the mat even though it wasn't Thursday. "I really am just—incredibly sorry. I'm . . ." I shook my head rapidly. "I'm rusty. It's been a long time since I've done this kind of thing with anyone. And I'm not trying to play the dead-friend card, but I'm doing a terrible job getting back in the game."

"Two things," D said. "One, I *would* like to fuck you."

"Oh, thank God."

"Two, you've apologized. I've accepted. Let's move on."

We moved on to the living room and flopped on the couch side by side.

I stared at his bare mantle. The nearly empty bookshelves. "I'm not usually the kind of person who tries to push someone into having sex."

"I know that."

We sat in silence for several long minutes.

"You're not like anyone I've met before," I went on. "When I read your profile, I thought you'd be a real jerk. But I feel like you . . . You're not what I was afraid you'd be. You do respect me, and I should've respected you."

We both stared at the blank TV screen. I watched the movement of his reflection as he scratched his head. "That profile was written several years ago. Back when I was less sure of myself. Compensating for something, I guess."

I grinned. "You should change your profile."

"I suppose I should. Really, aside from messaging you, I haven't been on that site in ages."

"Really? So you haven't been looking for my replacement?" I said it teasingly, but I was curious—and nervous—about the answer.

"Not yet." He glanced at me. "Have you been looking for my replacement?"

"Not yet." I leaned back, my hands folded on my stomach. Just sitting next to him was making me uncomfortably warm. "Nope, you're a damn good catch. You and your mysterious past and your Den of Horrors."

"I'm not mysterious."

"Will you let me ask you three questions?"

"I suppose."

"Would you rather: Daniel Boone or Davy Crockett?"

"Crockett. No contest."

"What would you name your baroque-style Friesian gelding?"

"Vidar."

"I won't ask."

"Good, because you only have one more question. But I'll tell you it's the Norse god of silence and vengeance."

"Of course. Uh, let's see . . . Where were you born?"

"In the suburbs. My mother raised me. We had to leave our house when I was seven. We had an RV for a while. Camped a lot."

"I'm sorry."

"I liked it. And she was good at making it seem like an adventure."

I leaned closer to him. Stared up at him with my head against the cushion. "Have you ever been in love?"

"That's four questions."

"You're right." I studied him. "I'm gonna go with yes. But you've said before that marriage is the last refuge of the insecure. So I'm gonna say . . . married to a nice woman before you realized you liked guys? Messy divorce?"

He stood. I thought for a second I'd offended him. But he walked to the bookcase and took a small, framed photograph from behind a collection of Ivan Doig novels. "Actually, my first boyfriend was in high school. More recently I dated this gentleman for several years before we parted ways amicably."

He handed me the picture. The man in the frame was a legit human version of a Friesian stallion. Brown skin, wavy black hair, biceps the size of butternut squashes. Thighs like fucking missile cylinders. He was smiling at the camera and dressed like he was ready to lumberjack. Hard. I swallowed. "Amicably?" I repeated tentatively. "But you don't . . . you don't still see each other. Ever. Right?"

"Jake and I talk on occasion."

"Jake? How is his name not Titus Crowsfoot, Esquire? Or something?"

"Because that would be ridiculous. That's like a name from our screenplay."

Awww. Our *screenplay.*

"*He's* ridiculous!" I thrust the photo back. "He's beautiful! Oh my god, D, why would you even let someone like me in your front door if you'd had *that*?"

He didn't answer. Then suddenly he reached down, picked me up off the couch, and slung me over his shoulder.

"Whoa." I clutched at his shirt "Whoa! What are you doing?"

He started toward the stairs. "I'm going to show you why I let you in my front door."

I struggled, still not ready to surrender to the indignity of this position.

"Stay still." He went up the steps unhurriedly and without straining, as though I wasn't any burden at all. This was some serious Rhett Butler shit.

We didn't go to the guest room. We went to *his* bedroom, which looked almost identical to the guest room, sans Friesian wall porn. The bed had a headboard with rungs. That, in my experience, was how you could tell the hard-core doms from the neophytes. It was all about the rungs.

He tossed me gently onto the end of the bed. "You," he said, reaching out to undo my fly, "are going to listen to me for the next—" he checked his watch "—fifteen minutes." I was still too shocked to move. "I'm going to fuck you, and when I'm done, there won't be any doubt in your mind that I want you here." He paused. "I presume you're still interested in fucking?"

"Y-yes."

He yanked my jeans and underwear off and thrust my legs apart. Pushed my knees up toward my chest and smacked my hole with two fingers. I gasped, my head snapping up.

"Stay put," he growled.

I watched him undress. He was all that I'd imagined: hairy, paunchy, and hot as fuck. His dick was kind of small, but I appreciated that. His balls hung low and were covered in long, light brown hair. The left one was decidedly bigger.

He condomed up, doused his cock in lube, then returned to stand at the end of the bed. I reached down and stroked my dick. I didn't give a shit if I had permission or not. He calmly caught my wrist and flung my hand aside.

He spread me again and slapped my crack with his slick cock. Worked two fingers inside me, crooked them, and rubbed my prostate until I was nearly sobbing. Then he took his fingers out and slid his cock in. It burned like hell, but I took it, my head falling back and a deep, guttural moan escaping.

To my surprise, he started slow, one hand tangled in my hair, the other on my hip. He withdrew almost entirely, then eased back in, so the sensation of being gradually filled pushed another moan out of me. He gave me a few more gentle strokes, and then he rammed into me. I twisted as he stayed there, balls-deep, staring down at me. "You want more of that?"

I nodded, panting.

He pulled my hair and started pounding me steadily.

"Oh," I whispered over and over again, writhing under him as his heavy balls slapped my ass. "Oh, oh, oh . . ."

"What do I have to do," he demanded, "to keep you still and quiet? Gag you? Tie you up?"

I smiled. "You could kiss me."

I winced at a particularly hard thrust. But then he stopped, leaned down, and kissed me. I closed my eyes and hummed with pleasure as he pushed his tongue into my mouth, his jaw working gently in time with his slow thrusts, his mustache rubbing the tip of my nose raw. I tilted my head back as he kissed the side of my neck, sucking the skin. I shifted my hips—a hint, an invitation. He ran the backs of his fingers over my nipples, and I exhaled.

His cock slid from my ass. He kissed my forehead, 'stache scratching my hairline. I snickered. Placed my arms above my head and spread my legs wider.

Caught his smile.

He skimmed his hand down my stomach to my waiting cock. Wrapped his fist around the shaft and didn't pump, just held it and stroked his thumb lightly over the slit.

I went rigid with the effort not to come.

"Scoot up." He let go of me.

I scrambled up the bed until my head was on the pillow.

"Hold your legs up higher." He popped open the lube and drizzled some more on his cock.

I brought my knees as close to my chest as they'd go. I heard a strange sound and realized it was me, breathing in a series of strangled, whining huffs. I wanted the burn and stretch of him where I was still sore. I wanted his mouth over mine, his nails raking my skin, him shouting as he drove into me. But mostly, I wanted to know that I was getting exactly what he wanted me to take.

I wanted to be his fucking *boy*.

He picked up his belt. Used his free hand to cross my wrists, and then he looped the belt around them and pulled the tail all the way through the buckle until the edges of the leather dug into my skin. Then he tied the tail around the rungs of the headboard.

"Keep your knees up."

I strained to obey, my thighs quivering with the effort. He climbed onto the bed, and I sighed at the warmth of his body next to mine. "Yes, Sir."

He got between my legs. Pushed my thighs apart, digging his fingertips into the flesh.

I arched my back. "Please . . ."

He positioned his cock. Then he took my dick in his fist, yanked it once, and drove into me at the same time.

I yelped.

"Knock that off." He forced his cock all the way inside me. "You've wanted me to put you in your place since you walked over to my table at Finer Things." He took me in fierce, hungry strokes, occasionally tugging my dick. "And I'm finally going to do it."

The burn finally eased to the point where I could speak. "Is that . . . all . . . you've got?" I asked as the bed creaked under us.

I saw a flicker of a smile before his expression hardened again. He shoved his hips back and then plowed forward, nearly sending my head into the headboard.

I wrapped my legs around him. "I've seen Madonna air hump harder in concert videos from the eighties," I whispered.

His hands came down on the pillow on either side of my head, and he lifted me half off the bed with his next thrust. He hammered me hard and fast, and I couldn't do anything but bounce on the mattress, gripping him with my legs. The belt bit into my wrists, and I was pretty sure my ass was never going to be the same again after this. "Come on," I goaded. "You call—*ah*!—this—fucking? Come on. Come *on*," I chanted, bumping his hip with my heel.

He stopped. "Did you just *kick* me?"

I didn't answer. I was still panting and squirming, trying to fuck myself on his cock. I wouldn't have called it kicking. More like nudging.

He reached out and undid the belt from the headboard and freed my wrists. Before I could say anything, he grabbed me and flipped me onto my stomach, his arms on either side of my shoulders. "You wanna kick me?" he demanded. "You wanna try to ride me like a damn horse?"

"You do love horses."

He yanked my hips up. "I can ride you ten times harder, pony."

I opened my mouth to denounce any and everything that made me think of furries, but then he hauled me up onto my elbows and knees. Got behind me and forced my shoulders down, then shoved his cock back in, and all I could do was grunt. He rode me with one arm around my waist, using his free hand to slap my thigh. And I mean, he *rode* me. My knees and forearms got comforter burns, and my head repeatedly got shoved against the rungs of the headboard. Every few seconds he took a break from whacking me and flicked my balls to make me clench harder.

I grabbed the rungs to steady myself. "What is this, the tiny carousel in front of Kmart? Put some . . . uh . . . uhhhh . . . *effort* into it . . . cowboy."

The headboard knocked against the wall, and the bed groaned as he lifted my back end off the mattress with each thrust. His alarm clock toppled from the nightstand, along with an issue of *Hiker Today*. A tin of Altoids slipped dangerously close to the edge, and I saw D reach for them.

"This is . . . *aghhhh* . . . no time to . . . freshen up," I informed him.

I heard him open the tin. He pulled his cock out of me, and I almost yelled at him. The next thing I knew, he'd popped a 'toid into my ass.

"What the *fuck*," I said. The burn started a moment later, and I arched my back, opening my mouth in a silent cry.

"This'll be fun."

"Those are *mints*! For your *mouth*! They're my favorite kind of mints, and now I'll never be able to enjoy them again because you've *turned them into ass mints*!"

He stroked my cock. The sting from the ass mint mixed with the pleasure spreading up from my groin. I opened my mouth and bit the pillow, the fabric chafing my nose. He leaned forward and pushed two fingers inside me.

"You've needed this—a long time." D cracked his palm against the crest of my ass, driving his fingers in and out of me. "You cocky . . . little . . . *brat*." He brushed my prostate, and my whole body tightened.

I heard a series of wet slaps. He was jerking off while he fingered me. He rubbed circles over the knot of nerves inside me, and I couldn't even cry out. Just clenched around his fingers again and again while he worked that sensitive spot. I came hard.

He finished a few seconds later, streaking my thighs.

"Oh, fuck." He slipped his fingers out and collapsed over my back, running his other hand down my side. "Oh . . . "

I stayed where I was, shuddering and trying to breathe. He kissed my neck, and my knees buckled. I sank onto the mattress. He lowered himself alongside me. My ass throbbed, though the burn from the mint was fading. He turned me to him. His face was red and glistening with sweat, but he looked incredibly satisfied.

I stopped panting and gazed at him. Then I started laughing.

He chuckled too and pulled me close.

"I'm starting to think you could tame me," I said.

"I'm starting to think you were already pretty tame."

"You've had worse brats than me?"

"David, you don't even crack the top six."

"What?"

"I don't think you're as hard-core as you think you are."

"Yeah, well, maybe neither are you."

"Fair enough."

I propped up on one elbow. "I used to be hard-core. I used to go to bars and I'd let guys raise welts and—and—I was fierce." I made claws at him. "Rawr."

"Terrifying."

"I've only met girl brats, though. I never meet other guy brats."

"Well, I've met enough 'guy brats' to last a lifetime."

I was silent a moment. "What time is it?"

He glanced at the clock. "Almost eleven."

"I should go."

"You can stay the night, if you want. If you're tired," he added quickly.

I beamed and rolled onto my back, stretching my arms over my head until I grabbed the rungs. "I'm exhausted."

"I have a nice guest room, as you know."

I released the headboard and kicked at him.

He grinned. "You should see your face."

"You suck! I'm not sleeping with the Friesian!"

"Why not? You make such a good horse."

"Do not even joke about that. I *hate* animal play."

He guffawed. "So you think we should sleep in my bed?"

"I think you should take the couch," I grumbled. "D'you mind if I shower?"

"Be my guest. I could use one too."

"You can join me."

We showered, then settled into bed, where I tried not to wriggle with joy. I was in bed with him. He'd fucked me just how I'd wanted to be fucked, and he'd invited me to stay.

I'm crushing it.

I dozed, but I couldn't quite go to sleep. Mostly because I could sense he wasn't asleep, despite his deep breathing. His muscles were tense, and I was close enough to feel his heart beating too fast. I got the feeling he wasn't used to people in his bed. Part of me wanted to pull him into my arms and show him how awesome it was to spoon. But I wanted to, you know, respect his boundaries. So I passed a fitful night, bothered by his tossing and turning, but keeping admirably quiet.

In the morning he was sleeping beside me, his brow furrowed, the skin under his eyes dark. I kissed him, and he mumbled.

"Hi," I said.

"Mm-hmm." He didn't open his eyes.

I slid off the bed and went to get my things.

"Hey."

I turned. He was watching me.

"Lemme see that ass."

I flushed and went to stand beside the bed, facing away from him. The back of one thigh was still sore, and I wasn't really looking forward to trying to take a shit, but other than that, I felt great. I bent forward slightly, and he brushed the thigh bruise with his fingertips.

"Very nice. Spread 'em."

I bent farther and held my cheeks apart, gritting my teeth.

Not going to say anything. Just going to obey.

He ran a finger lightly down my crack, just barely skimming my hole. I tensed, which made him laugh softly.

"Ohh, yeah. Come here." He hooked an arm around me and pulled me back toward the bed. I collapsed onto the mattress, and he drew the covers over both of us. "You got somewhere to be?"

"Not really." I pressed my face into the crook of his shoulder.

"Then go back to sleep."

I smiled against his skin. "Keep doing this."

"Hmm?"

I looked up. "Keep pushing me. Keep telling me what you want to do to me and then doing it. Every time I argue, push me harder. I like it." I paused. "I feel like I'm close to something. I don't know what, but I want to find out."

He closed his eyes. "Don't worry. I'm not done with you by a long shot."

"Did you ever go to leather bars?" I asked. "Or did you ever play back when . . . I don't know, when there weren't so many rules?"

"What happened to going back to sleep?" he mumbled.

I ignored that. "I didn't always play safe. I definitely didn't play sane. And consensual—yeah, most of the time. But sometimes a guy would start doing something without asking me, and I'd just go along with it to see if I liked it or not. And it didn't feel wrong. You know what I mean?"

He sighed and opened his eyes. "I didn't really do the bar scene. But I know what you mean."

For a second, my whole body ached. I wanted to tell him about the Subs Club. I wanted to tell him I didn't know what was right anymore. That I didn't know how to be a leader, but I didn't want to give up trying. "I'm afraid of getting so caught up in, like . . . kink ethics, or something, that I lose the—whatever you want to call it. Passion." I made a face.

"I think there's a balance."

"I know there is. I had it, before Hal. And now I'm so fucking paranoid."

"You think something's going to happen to you?"

"That's the weird thing. It's not even about me. I don't, like, fear for my own life. I fear for theirs."

"Whose?"

"My friends. I just think, 'What if I lose them too?'"

"How would you lose them?"

"Oh, I don't know." I shrugged. "What if Miles falls down a sewer or Kamen gets hit by a car or Gould gets cancer? Or, you know, what if they play with the wrong partner and end up like Hal? People can get killed so many ways; I don't understand how anyone survives past age three."

He placed his hand on my hip. Then he twitched his mustache back and forth, like some backwoods version of *I Dream of Jeannie*. "I, uh . . . I don't . . ."

I should have known he'd be the worst person ever to talk to about feelings.

But he cleared his throat and spoke more certainly. "Most likely, you and your friends will live long, full, happy lives. But in the event that you lose someone else, I am *certain* that their time on Earth was much better for having had you as a friend."

"Don't." I pulled away from him. "That shit works on me!"

"What shit?"

"When people say nice things about me. I get all emotional. Go away!" I swatted his hand as he reached for me. But when he tried to withdraw, I grabbed his wrist and forced his arm around me. I nestled against his shoulder. "I love them, D. I love them so fucking much."

"I know you do."

"After the funeral, Miles was having trouble at work. He couldn't focus, and he thought his company was going under. So I just . . . I made up a new identity and ordered a hundred shirts. I don't say that as, like, I'm a great friend, because I think I'm probably a shitty friend for deceiving him, but it made him feel better, getting that order. And now I have a hundred Star Wars T-shirts in my closet and a fucking hole in my life where Hal should be and no idea how to have sex with anyone without an instruction manual."

He stroked my hair. "He had a lot of energy. Hal."

I smiled. "I know."

"He told me he didn't want a safeword," D said quietly.

My stomach clenched. "He was such a fucking moron."

"Lot of people don't use them."

"But with someone you don't know? Come on."

"You know what else he said, though?"

"What?"

"That if I was a serial killer I'd better not try anything. Because his friends knew where he was and who he was with and if they didn't get a text by 10 p.m., they'd come looking for him."

I laughed, a lump forming in my throat. "We'd been to a workshop," I explained. "About having a call buddy when you meet with new partners. We kind of did it as a joke at first—any time one of us played, we were all like, 'Who's gonna be your call buddy?' But, I mean . . . it's not such a dumb idea."

It hadn't saved Hal. I could torture myself forever with what could have saved Hal. A word? Probably not. A call buddy? No. I blamed myself, I blamed Bill. And I blamed Hal, for acting like he'd rather have had a short life full of adventure than one that was long, boring, and safe. Everyone wanted to make like Hal was so stupid, but I kind of understood why he'd let someone tie a rope around his neck even though neither of them had done breath play before. Maybe he was caught up in the moment. Maybe he just wanted one fucking experience that was—was raw and wasn't, like, *the safeword is "Kankakee River Basin," and I'm going to need exactly two hugs after this to make me okay again.*

It was sweet, though, that he'd told D about his call buddies. I tried to remember if I'd been on call that night. Probably not. Hal had probably used Gould. I made a note to ask Gould if he remembered.

"It's gonna be okay," D said. I could tell he felt awkward, and I wished I knew how to thank him for what he'd shared.

"I know." I smiled again and kissed him softly. "Keep pushing."

CHAPTER
SIXTEEN

Dear David,

It has come to my attention that this Thursday is Thanksgiving. I will be out of town visiting my mother. I regret that we will miss a session and wondered if you would like to have dinner sometime this week to make up for it. I can make bacon.

Sincerely,

D

Dear D,

I have a better idea if you'll be around the day after T-Give. My friends and I have a tradition known as Black Friday: The Revenge. Because we can't all eat together on Thanksgiving due to family, etc., we pool our accumulated leftovers the next day for a feast like no other. Would you like to join us? I know it would involve a lot of talking, but . . . my friends are pretty cool.

—d

I held my breath for forty minutes straight until he replied.

Yes, I accept.

—D

D,

I am starting to think you really *like me.*

—d

I am starting to think so too.

—D

D,
OMG.
—d

d,
Perhaps we could meet Tuesday night instead for our session.
—D

D,
Just don't be too mean, please, Sir. It's the holidays.
—d

Cool it, Tiny Tim. I'm gonna push.
—D

I met with Ricky at Mel's Sandwich Shop on Sunday to talk to him about how we could improve site security to avoid people like GK and Kel getting ahold of the information on it, and to prevent users like Anonymous from being able to post.

"There *are* ways we could make the site more private," Ricky said as we walked down the street with our milkshakes. "But it's the internet. You can't totally stop the wrong people from seeing it."

"It's frustrating." I sucked until I dislodged a cookie piece from my straw. "I don't want to hide what we're doing. But . . ."

I noticed a stringy-haired woman in a ragged coat and holey Skechers staggering toward us. She looked like she could be anywhere from thirty to fifty, and she clutched a Folgers can. As she neared us, she held it out. "I'm a *vet*!" she shouted. "You got money for a *veteran* of the U-nited States Army?"

I fished in my pocket for some change and tossed it in the can. "There you go."

The woman was staring at Ricky. "Hey, Duck Soup. Back to the rice paddies for ya?"

I stared at her, shocked.

Ricky shook his head. "Fuck off," he said to the woman.

Dear God. There went my impression of Ricky as a charming innocent.

"Whaddya think, can I get my nails done at your salon?" The woman held out a hand brown with sun damage, the nails yellow and ragged.

I gaped.

Ricky rolled his eyes. "Yeah, every Tuesday and Friday, ten percent discount. Fuck-wad!"

He strode forward and I followed. Behind us, the woman shook the can and yelled, "I'm a *vet*!"

I jogged up beside Ricky. "What a racist bitch."

He shrugged. "Eh, it's all right. I've given her money before, and we've talked. She's not really a veteran."

"Why didn't you tell me? I wouldn't have given her money."

"Seriously, it's fine. Maybe she'll actually come to the salon."

"Wait. You don't really work in a nail salon, right?"

"No, Dave, I was just fucking with her. God, you're as racist as she is."

"I'm sorry! I was just asking."

Ricky slurped the last of his milkshake. "Part-time. I work in my mom's salon part-time."

I glanced at him. "Stop fucking with me!"

"What? I love nails. My mom's place is on Wendell. Stop by sometime."

"Are there really discount days?" I thought about this for a moment. "And what's your confidentiality policy?"

"Confidentiality?"

"If the guy I'm seeing knew I liked manicures, it would kill him. I trust you would be . . . discreet?"

"You care what he thinks about you getting manicures?"

"No, not at all. But I've already introduced him to the idea of men conditioning their hair. And to the existence of manties. I have to proceed slowly."

Ricky nodded. "We actually have a special manicure for men where we use bigger clippers and we don't ask what kind of polish you want."

I high-fived him.

Ricky tossed his cup into a trash can. "I didn't know you were seeing someone."

"It's pretty recent. It's like a play-partner thing except I also sort of want to marry him."

He stuffed his hands into his pockets and looked at the ground. "That's cool. I've actually been playing with someone too."

"You are just blowing my mind today."

"Yeah. It's been going pretty well."

"So," I pressed. "Who is he?"

"Uh, he's just some guy I met online."

"Do I know him?" I asked.

Ricky didn't answer.

"I *do* know him! Are you embarrassed to tell me?"

"I just want to see where it goes before I tell anyone."

"Ricky. Ricky, Ricky, Ricky. You can tell me. I promise I won't tell anyone else."

He didn't answer. He seemed genuinely uncomfortable, which surprised me.

"Is he older?" I asked.

Ricky nodded, smiling a little.

"Where'd you meet?"

"At Cobalt." Ricky's grin broadened suddenly. "He treated me like a prince. I didn't want to play in front of people, so he took me home."

My tone immediately sharpened. "He could have been a killer."

Ricky flinched.

I took a deep breath. "It's okay. Sorry. You're alive; clearly he wasn't a killer."

Ricky nodded, but kept his head down. "I was so nervous, and I kept, uh . . . uh, you know." He scratched his nose. "I had bad gas. Which is, like, the least sexy thing, I know. But he was really good at making me feel okay about it. He, like, held my wrists above my head. And he tied them with his belt. And then he made me hold a position with my knees up while he touched me. And he said I wasn't allowed to come."

"How'd that go?" I asked.

"Great! For a few seconds. Then I came."

I grinned. "I would have turned you over and whipped your ass so hard . . ."

"Well he didn't." Ricky sounded a little indignant. "He said this was my warning. But next time he'd put me in a cock cage to make sure I didn't come."

"So there'll be a next time?"

"I hope!"

"Awww." I slung my arm around him. "You're growing up so fast."

"Shut up," he said.

But he sounded pleased.

CHAPTER

SEVENTEEN

"What do you do when you come in?" D asked Tuesday night. He pointed to the mat, which I was now several feet past. I sighed and backed up. I stood straight, clasped my hands behind my back, and bowed my head.

"You look mutinous," he said.

"Huh? I'm not even doing any—"

"I'd like you to count out three minutes, then join me in the kitchen."

I frowned. "Count out?"

"In your head or under your breath. Count out sixty seconds three times. I want you in the kitchen precisely at the end of the third minute. Start . . ." He glanced at his watch. "Now."

He headed to the kitchen.

It took a lot of concentration to keep counting at the same rate. Sometimes I'd get distracted and slow down, then I'd have to speed up to even things out. I heard the squeak of a chair on the kitchen floor, then the *clack* of wood on wood. I realized instead of cutting off at sixty I'd kept counting and was now at eighty-six. Simple enough. I'd just count to one hundred twenty, then start over. Or figure out what one twenty plus sixty was. One eighty, right? But triple digit numbers took longer to say, so my timing might be off. I ought to just start back at one when I hit one twenty. This was so dumb. What was I, a stopwatch?

With an estimated ten seconds left to go, I started toward the kitchen. D was at the table drinking coffee, which smelled good. I thought about asking for some, and then I saw the wooden paddle on the table and reconsidered the wisdom of expressing any desire beyond a will to astonish him with my letter-perfect attention to his instructions.

He checked his watch. "Seven seconds off."

"Not bad, huh?" I did think that was impressive, considering.

"I'd planned to give you ten with the paddle for the entrance you made. So that will be an additional swat for each second."

"That's so subjective, though. I mean, when were we starting—when you said 'now,' or the second after? And when were we ending? When I crossed the threshold into this room, or when I stopped walking? Or when you looked up? We have to clarify these things beforehand."

"Pick up the paddle."

I weighed the fleeting joy I'd get from disobeying him against the pain of additional swats. I picked up the paddle.

"Hand it to me."

Our fingers brushed as he took it from me, and I felt a thrill despite my nervousness.

"Bend over the table."

I stepped to the side of the chair and leaned over, placing my forearms against the table's surface.

He walked behind me, and I willed myself to stay calm, relaxed. I let out a sharp breath as I heard him slap the paddle lightly against his palm.

"Count each swat."

He tapped the paddle against the seat of my pants, and I couldn't help it—I tried to tuck my ass away from it.

"Out," he ordered.

I sighed and pushed my hips back.

He withdrew the paddle. A second later it cracked across the center of my ass.

"Oh!" I squeezed my eyes shut.

"Count," he reminded me.

"One," I said quickly. "Hey, D, I was thinking—"

The paddle connected again—a loud, forceful blow that made my knees buckle. I flexed my fingers against the table, trying not to hiss. "Two."

I reached for the 1970s paddling fantasy I'd had that night at Riddle—the rust-colored bell-bottoms, the shag carpet. But it seemed considerably less sexy now that my ass was actually getting blistered.

"I trust you." I swallowed. "Seriously, I think you're a good guy. And—ow! Jesus, D. *Three*—I really want you to give me what you think I need. So if that means—fuck! Four. Sorry, didn't mean to swear—if that means sex as a punishment, fine. I don't know how much of a punishment sex stuff'll be, though, because honestly, you make me so hard—"

"David?"

"Yeah?"

He delivered number five, hard enough that I shifted my weight back and forth and whimpered.

"We will discuss this later. Right now, you are being punished."

I struggled to regain my breath. "Right. Sorry. Five."

D rubbed the paddle over my ass and gave me a series of taps with it, focusing me. "What are you supposed to do when you enter my house?"

"Stand on the mat. Hands behind my back, head down. Wait for you to address me."

"Very good." He walloped me.

"Ow! Ow, ow, *shit*." I brought one leg up, trying to lessen the sting. "Six. We can stop here. I'm really sorry."

"Can we really? How many swats did I say?"

"See, I still really don't think that's fa—"

He took my shoulders and pulled me upright. He leaned forward and said in my ear, "Go to the den and get the rubber paddle."

"But—"

"You have thirty seconds."

"I don't want—"

He turned me around, bent me over his arm, and gave me a flurry of swats with his hand. "I. Said. Go. Get. Me. That. Paddle. Thirty seconds."

I went to the den, scrubbing my backside with both hands. I paused before pulling the black rubber paddle off the wall.

It was fucking heavy. About seven inches wide, a foot long, and half an inch thick, it would cover pretty much my whole ass with a single swat. I tried it against my palm, and the sound was a solid slap, almost a thud.

I took it back to the kitchen, my cock hard, my stomach churning.

"Here you go." I hoped my tone was so demure he'd feel bad about overreacting. We didn't need the rubber paddle. The wooden one would do the job just fine. We didn't even need the rest of the swats, because I totally got the message.

He took the paddle and used it to point at the table. "Bend over. Ass out. Legs spread."

I swallowed and complied.

"One word out of you that's not the number we're on, and I will take your pants down and paddle your bare ass. Got it?"

I nodded.

"An answer, please."

"You just said—" I paused. Reconsidered. "Yes, Sir."

"Thank you."

He drew the paddle back and struck.

The pain was like a mushroom cloud—so immense and unfamiliar that I didn't recognize it as a disaster at first, not until it bloomed and billowed over me. I couldn't breathe. Couldn't move, couldn't yell, couldn't sink to my knees. My whole body went rigid and I just stayed there, perfectly still.

I curled my fingers against the table and opened my mouth, letting out a very long, silent cry.

The blaze morphed into a steady throb I could feel from my throat all the way down my thighs.

"Count," D said calmly.

"Seven," I choked out.

The next swat was lighter, or maybe I just didn't have much sensation left in my ass. I still hissed and knocked my fists against the table. Swat nine brought on what I hoped would be a sustainable numbness. But as soon as swat ten landed, the pain came shooting back. I gulped several times.

Not gonna cry. Definitely not gonna cry.

D paused and flipped my shirt up. Rubbed my lower back, his callused fingers drifting in serpentines that almost tickled. I gave a small, rough sob.

Take this. Let him break you down. Trust him.

"Stick your butt out."

I tried to obey, but I was no longer sure I could move anything below my waist. He patted my ass. "Out, David."

When I whimpered and didn't move, he pulled my hips away from the table and undid my fly. "No! No, D. I'll listen . . ."

But he yanked my jeans down to my ankles, smacked my legs apart, and then pressed on my lower back so that my ass went out and up.

The cool air hit the backs of my burning thighs, and there was a second of absolute silence.

Then he delivered swat eleven over my underwear, and I pressed my face against the table. My legs were shaking, and I felt nauseated.

D paused. "What number was that?"

"El—eleven." My voice cracked. "D, this hurts so much."

"You're breaking my heart."

Jerk.

He swatted again, and my legs went slack. I held on to the table to keep from sliding to my knees. I shook with silent sobs.

"David? Number?"

"Sixteen," I said, loudly and sarcastically.

He yanked my underwear down and delivered three hard, fast whacks that left me breathless. He placed a hand on my blazing skin. "Assuming those didn't count," he said, "what number are we on?"

My arms were stretched across the table, and I gripped the opposite edge, panting. The waistband of my underwear dug into the tops of my thighs as I struggled to keep my legs apart. I gathered the last of my strength. "Let's assume they did count."

Another hard whack, this time on my thighs. My eyes watered. This felt good. Awful. Crazy.

Push me. Help me give up. Don't let me win. "Twelve," I whispered.

He pulled my underwear to my ankles and swatted my calf to get me to step out of my pants and briefs. Then he lifted my left leg to the side and slapped the paddle against my inner thigh. I shouted. "Thirteen."

"Good."

That word was almost enough to make the next swat survivable. "F-f-fourteen." I burst into tears.

He put my left leg down and picked up my right. Cracked the inside of that thigh just as hard. As soon as he let go, I pressed both legs together as the pain blazed and spread. I coughed, now crying too hard to speak. It scared me for a minute.

He waited. Rubbed the paddle across my ass. I choked on another attempt at *fifteen*. "I c— I ca—" It was too much. Too much, and I'd pushed too hard, and now I couldn't even safeword because I couldn't get anything out except bizarre choking sounds. Fuck my life.

He set the paddle on the table.

"Margin of error," he said gruffly.

I forced myself to take a breath. "What?"

"I'll give you a two-second margin of error for the three minutes you counted." He pried my hands off the table and helped me stand. "We're done."

I staggered as he drew me against him. I gave a series of fast, ugly sobs against his chest, then I closed my eyes and bawled like a *child*.

And I didn't even have strength enough left to be embarrassed.

He held me until I got my crying under control.

"D—did you just go easy on me?" I managed finally.

He chuckled, and I loved the sound of it, the vibrations I could feel in my own body. "Don't expect me to make it a habit."

He led me to the sink and helped me rinse my face, because snot was definitely a thing that was happening. Then he made me drink a glass of water.

He took me to the living room. He covered one of the throw pillows on the sofa with a dish towel, then made me lie facedown on the couch, one pillow under my head and the towel-covered one under my hips. He sat at the end of the couch, my legs in his lap, and spent a good ten minutes rubbing my ass. Distributing the heat, easing the sting and then bringing it back by pinching or kneading too hard. I was exhausted, and eventually I just accepted that I wasn't in control and went limp.

After that, he was nothing but gentle.

"This works too," I ventured at last, my voice croaky.

"What's that?"

"To shut me up." I tried to laugh. "If you're ever looking for an alternative to spanking."

"I'll keep it in mind."

I rolled slightly, trying to see him over my shoulder. "Don't you know anything about training?" I asked. "More with honey than with vinegar, and all that?"

He squeezed my thigh. "I prefer vinegar. I think you do too."

"Ow, *ow* . . . I like both."

"Well," he said softly, running a hand down my back. "There can be some of both."

He eased me up and hauled me into his lap. I groaned as I put weight on my ass again. He stared at me for a moment, and I waited, all but pursing my lips in an effort to cue him. He leaned forward and kissed me. A gentle kiss that grew more forceful, more demanding. I put one hand on the back of his head, and put the other hand on the side of his neck to feel the warmth of his skin, the twitch of his pulse. He wrapped his arms around my waist and pulled until my cock met his hip.

I brought my hands to the front of his shirt and hesitated before undoing the first button. I looked at him for permission. He nodded.

I unbuttoned the shirt, and he slipped out of it.

I let him yank my T-shirt over my head. I kissed down the side of his neck to his shoulder, then pounced on him, trying to push him against the arm of the sofa. My ass still hurt, but it was tough to care when I was this hard. He caught me and held me at arm's length, then eased me back, straddling me.

"The things I'd like to do to you," he whispered.

"Do them," I urged.

"The first thing I'd like to do . . ." He brushed his thumb over my nipple as he leaned to kiss my jaw. Kept his lips close to my ear.

I arched my back and sighed happily, waiting to hear all the dirty things he was gonna do to me.

". . . is see your list for this week."

What?

I sat up. "But I just got punished."

"For refusing to follow protocol. We haven't even covered what you've been up to this week."

"D! Come on."

"Are you refusing?"

"No. God, no. Let me up; I'll get it."

D released me, and I tried to pounce on him again, but I got a very firm reminder to go retrieve the list.

The man was a bastard and a half.

Someone ought to spank him.

Someone ought to do a lot worse than spank him I thought later, as I sat naked on his dryer with clothespins on my nipples.

The dryer was on, and the heat was killing my already bruised ass. The clothespins had been dipped in Vicks VapoRub, and if D got near enough to me, I was definitely going to claw his eyes out.

But he wasn't near enough. He was sitting on the laundry room steps with a small remote control in hand, watching me wince as the dryer shuddered and hummed under me. My nipples burned from the Vicks, but the sharp ache of the clothespins occasionally eclipsed the burn. He had a quirt and a wooden spoon by his side.

You'll get one good shot at his eyes when he comes over here. Claw them out. Claw them and run.

But he didn't come over. So I settled instead for admiring his shirtlessness.

The remote D held controlled the plug up my ass—the plug that was gently fucking me with each rumble of the dryer. It had a thin strip of silicone running the length of my cock, and two loops—one that went around the base of my cock, and another that went under the head. The whole apparatus vibrated. Five speeds.

D was having a field day. He'd start the plug vibrating slowly, and between the buzz from the plug, the tremors and heat from the dryer, and the steady burn in my nipples, he'd get me squirming and moaning. Suddenly he'd bump the plug up to the highest speed, and I wouldn't even be able to speak. I'd just rock back and forth, grinding my battered ass against the machine's hot surface, seconds away from coming . . . and then he'd stop. And I'd complain. Well, the first time I'd complained. But he'd gotten up, walked to me, and flicked the clothespin on my left nipple. Once I'd recovered from that, I'd been super quiet.

"This is fun," he said from the steps.

I clenched my jaw as he bumped the vibrator up to midspeed. "This device seems too complex for a man of your simple tastes."

"Oh, no. Not at all." D turned the vibrator up again, and I snapped my head back, pressing my legs together. I was once again on edge, my balls drawn up tight. I needed someone to fuck me so hard I'd scream.

D didn't slow the vibrator down, and for a second I thought this was it, that he was finally going to let me come. Then he turned it off.

I bit back all the horrible things I wanted to call him.

He got off the step and walked over to me. I tensed, not sure if he intended to do harm. He removed the clothespin from my left nipple. I kept eye contact with him, but let out the most agonized sigh I could muster as sensation came shooting back to the area. He took the clothespin off my right nipple and dug his thumbnail into the swollen flesh.

I bit my lip.

Not a sound. Don't let him see your fear.

"Stand up."

I did. My ass and thighs felt inflamed, the skin too tight, the kind of ache that would last for days. My nipples still tingled from the Vicks.

"I want you to come without using your hands."

"Are you gonna use *your* hands?"

He smacked my ass, which I took as a no.

"Hands behind your head. I want to see you come." He turned the vibrator on to medium speed. My hips started jerking. Horny as I was, it was still difficult to figure out what to do to make myself shoot. I tried clenching around the plug and shifting in an effort to get it to graze my prostate. I tried focusing on the vibrating bands around my cock, but they were too small to do much besides tease.

D picked up the spoon. He told me to take a step back and turn to the side.

This did not bode well. But I did it. Because I was a pleasant and obedient individual who adored a man cloned from Satan.

He began to smack the base of the plug with the spoon, not hard—but with a perfect rhythm. I moaned in time with the blows. He brought each blow farther down between my legs, until the spoon was grazing my balls with each swat. God I was close. And then he wrapped his arms around me, and his hips pressed against my ass.

I whimpered as he rubbed himself against the base of the plug, shifting it inside me. My back, damp with sweat, brushed against the slightly coarse hair of his chest. He pulled back then rocked forward again, hammering the plug deeper into me with each thrust of his hips. I took a quick breath and released the first spurt of cum. He slid his hands up and pinched my nipples, bringing back the pain from the clothespins. I yelped and clenched hard around the plug, coming all over the closet door.

I thought I was done, but he reached down and slowly squeezed the base of my cock, milking more out of me. I moaned, too tired to resist. When he let me go I slumped against him, so ready to be done. But instead of leading me back to the couch in the living room to let me recover, he handed me a rag and pointed to the mess I'd made. "Clean up."

"But I'm—" I started.

"David. Have you ever considered just doing what I tell you?"

"Many times. But I usually decide against it."

"Get me the Vicks." He held out his hand.

I glanced behind me. The Vicks was still on the laundry table where he'd left it after dipping the clothespins. "Why?" I demanded.

"I won't tell you again."

I fetched the tub and handed it to him. He opened it and spread some onto my very sensitive, very tired cock and balls. I squirmed as the menthol started to wake each nerve. He reached around and pulled the plug partway out of my ass and smeared some cream onto the tapered part between the shaft and the base before pushing it back in. Then he told me once more to clean up my mess.

My asshole and cock tingling, I wiped up my cum as quickly as I could. The tingling became an icy burn, and I straightened, my jaw tense. He watched me, occasionally cracking the spoon against his palm, which startled me into tightening around the plug, which in turn made the burn worse. When I was done, I hurried to him. Tried to stand still. He slipped the loops off my cock and removed the plug from my ass, then handed me my clothes.

"All right," he said. "You can get dressed."

"Uh, can I clean up?"

"Nope." He grinned. "I want you thinking about me on your way home. And consider how much more comfortable you'd be if you'd just done what I said the first time."

"You are the purest of evil."

"I recommend washing with milk. It'll get rid of the burn. Water might make it worse."

I dressed quickly, wincing the whole time.

"David?" he said innocently as I stormed from the laundry room. "Are you sure you don't want to stay for coffee?"

"You're dead to me," I called with a wave, as I hobbled toward the front door.

I drove home, reminding myself several times not to speed. I writhed on the seat, trying to find a position that didn't make my ass hurt like hell. I placed my forehead on the wheel at a stoplight and gave a shout of frustration.

At last I reached the duplex. I jumped out of the car and raced up the front steps.

I burst into the house. "Gould! Where are you?"

"Good God, David, what?" he asked from the kitchen.

"I need the antidote!"

"What are you talking about?"

I reached the kitchen and stood in the doorway. "I have Vicks in my ass and all over my cock, and if I don't get it off I'm going to die. I need milk. Milk!"

He appeared to be trying very hard not to laugh. "Okay. Calm down."

"Easy for you to say." I staggered in and clutched the edge of the table. "You don't have Mrs. O'Leary's whole flaming stable up your ass."

"Bathroom. I'll get you the milk."

I shuffled to the bathroom and yanked my pants and underwear down, half expecting to find my dick covered in boils. Everything looked normal, just a little pink. And I smelled like menthol. I turned so I could see my back in the mirror. My ass was spectacularly red, with plenty of dark purple on the sit spots.

"Jesus," Gould said from the doorway.

I whirled.

He was pouring milk onto a dishcloth. "What did you do to earn this?"

"Nothing. D's a monster."

"Uh-huh." He handed me the cloth, and I pressed it to my dick, whimpering. "Come on. Wipe it off."

When I didn't move, he took the cloth and gently cleaned me.

"Better?" he asked.

"Yeah." I took the cloth from him and wiped my crack. I hissed dramatically.

"Turn around."

I obeyed. He clucked again at the sight of my ass. "Dave. Good grief. You're gonna be sore for days."

"I got a little mouthy. Then I got a lot paddled."

I saw him smile in the mirror. "No kidding. Pants up."

I pulled my pants up. "Ohhh my God." I limped to the kitchen, where I ransacked the cupboards until I found a bag of tortilla chips with nothing left but the crumbs. I got a container of salsa from the fridge, opened it, sniffed it, then dumped the chip shards inside. Started eating it with a spoon. "So what've you been up to?" I tried to sound casual, like he hadn't just helped me sponge bathe my dick with milk.

He shrugged. "Answered some work emails. Talked to a dom on Fet for a little bit. She seems awesome, but she's got a couple of meh reviews on our blog, so I don't know. I think I'm still gonna play with her."

"Gould, do you like girls?"

He shrugged again.

"I won't be mad."

He rolled his eyes.

"What? You can tell me!"

"I like girls a little."

I shrieked, clapping my hands over my mouth.

"It's not a big deal," he protested.

"I know, I know." I put my hands down. I took the salsa bowl over to the table and sat across from him. "I'm just trying to understand. Since when?"

"Since always. High school. I went to prom with Kristie Lyons."

"I thought you threw up when she took her top off?"

"Yeah, that was because I'd had a beer, though."

"I think you throwing up after one beer is sadder than you throwing up because of boobs."

He sagged forward, resting his forehead on the table. "After Hal, I played with a couple of women because I just didn't feel like . . . I don't know."

I put a hand on his hair and patted.

He didn't move. "I prefer dudes, okay? I'm just saying I don't mind, once in a while . . ."

"Playing with a lady."

He looked up and snagged a chip shard out of my salsa. "Right."

"It's a little something different. It's your summer home."

"My volunteer job on the weekends." He licked salsa off his thumb.

"It's the expensive restaurant you treat yourself to once in a while."

"Sure."

"Okay. I'm fine with that."

He straightened and shot me a glare. "Of course you are. What is there not to be fine with?"

"You just surprised me is all."

We killed the salsa and went to our rooms, and I spent most of the night texting D. Just little messages. Right when I imagined he was about to fall asleep, I'd text him that my ass still burned—it didn't really—or that I wished that plug had been his cock. I wanted him to feel like I was right there in bed with him, annoying the living fuck out of him. But every time I texted, he texted right back, usually something five times dirtier than what I'd said. I finally fell asleep around two, surprised he'd outlasted me.

CHAPTER
EIGHTEEN

I filled the others in on my latest session with D the next afternoon. We were all off for the rest of the week for the holiday and were celebrating in my living room with a *Law & Order: SVU* marathon.

I didn't typically give them hard-core details about my sessions, but Gould cracked some Vicks joke, and the others wrestled the story out of me.

"You know Vicks isn't for internal use," Miles said disapprovingly.

"Yes, Miles, I know technically it's not for internal use, but we used it internally, and the world didn't end. Also, the cold I was getting is completely gone."

Miles grumbled. "Well, stick to hot sauce or ginger in the future if you're figging."

Kamen strummed his guitar, coming up with the chords for "Killing Me Softly."

"Figgin me softly with hot sauce," he sang over the sounds of justice being served. "figging me so-oftly, with hot sauce."

"Buddy . . ." I warned.

"Filling my whole ass with his burn . . ."

I turned to Gould. "Do you believe this is happening?"

He raised his brows. "Is there anything you wouldn't believe happened in this house?"

"No," I admitted.

I flipped through our unread messages on the Subs Club site on my phone. I had a message from a sub I knew named Josh who proposed putting the Disciplinarian's name up on the review blog.

I hadn't given much thought recently to the prospect of rating D. Now that he and I were making progress as play partners and as— well, friends—I wasn't quite so keen on offering him up for review.

For once in my life, I wanted to keep my opinions private. And I didn't want to see reviews from fawning former boys of his, or from anyone who had something negative to say about him.

Without thinking too hard about it, I deleted Josh's message. Then I deleted it from the Trash, so the others would never see it.

Miles checked his phone. "I might head out. I've got some stuff to take care of."

"Where have you been sneaking off to lately?" I asked. It wasn't the first time over the past couple of weeks that Miles had bailed while we were hanging out.

"Nowhere. I've just been busy with . . . work."

"Why did you hesitate before 'work'?"

"Heavens, Dave. It's not important. I'll see you all on Black Friday."

"Wait," I said as Miles stood. "I have a Subs Club thing."

He waited. "Yes?"

"Um." I glanced at the TV. Was momentarily distracted by the beauty of Benson's hair. I tore my gaze away. "I know I said I was going to rate the Disciplinarian when I was done with the six weeks."

No one spoke. Miles gave me a *go on* look.

"And . . . what if . . . I don't want that?"

"You don't want to rate him?" Miles repeated.

"That's right, I'm not going to rate him!" I announced, as the end credits music played behind me. "I don't care what you all say. I like him, and I think I was wrong about him being an asshole. He's a good dom and I don't want to put him on the blog. I want him to just be *mine*." I paused. "And I invited him to Black Friday: The Revenge. So deal with it!"

I glanced around, waiting for the protests to begin.

"Sweet," Kamen said.

Miles cocked his head. "Yes, Dave, that's splendid."

"Oh." I looked at each of them. "Wow. That was easy. Okay, Miles, you can go." I waved him away.

"Waaaaiiit a minute." Kamen muted the TV. "We get to meet D?"

"Yes. Just be normal," I warned. "All of you. For the love of God. Please. For one evening."

"Us?" Kamen asked innocently.

"Yeah, you think *we* need to be told to be normal?" Gould echoed Kamen's mock incredulity.

Miles widened his eyes. "Are you *embarrassed* by us?"

Kamen nodded. "Yeah. You don't want us to be ourselves?"

I sighed. "You can be yourselves, just . . . maybe a less intense version of yourselves. Remember that he's . . ." I took a deep breath. "He's very old fashioned. Like, nineteen-tens old fashioned."

Kamen's jaw dropped. "Does he ride a horse?"

I thought about the Friesian picture. "He would if he could."

"Can we tell him about the time you tried to pee in a bottle on our road trip to Boston and instead you peed on the car seat?" Gould asked.

"No!"

Kamen leaned off the couch. "Yeah, should we tell him about the Log Blog and how it was your idea?"

"Kamen!"

Miles grinned. "Or about the time you tried to make ribs in the slow cooker and left it on overnight and the barbeque sauce turned into a solidified crystalline substance at the bottom of the pan and we had to use a paint scraper to get it out?"

"Classic Dave!" Kamen agreed.

I glared at them. "You guys. No embarrassing stories about me. And do *not* mention the Subs Club."

Miles's grin slipped. "Have you not told him?"

"Of course not," I said defensively.

"Hmm."

"Don't 'hmm' me, Miles. He doesn't need to know everything I do. And even if he did know, it wouldn't be a big deal."

Silence.

Gould finally shrugged. "Well, I'm looking forward to meeting him."

"He'll love you guys. Just accept that he's weird, and try not to judge him."

Kamen saluted. "We shall make you proud, David."

Gould snickered. "Yeah, we already love your weird boyfriend."

"He is not my boyfriend!"

"Really?" Kamen stared skeptically at me. "You invited him to Black Friday: The Revenge."

"Yeah." Gould nodded. "It kinda sounds like you want to marry him."

Miles folded his arms. "Mmm. I have a great idea for a theme wedding."

"You guys are going to be murdered," I informed them. "Legit murdered. I hope you like being murdered, because that's what's going to happen to you."

Miles sat back down. "Dave. I think this is really good. I'm happy for you."

"Yeah, dude." Kamen slid his hand palm up across the couch for a low five.

I smiled and fived him. "Aw. You guys."

Miles glanced at the others, then fixed his gaze on me. "We've been worried about you since Hal."

"*You've* been worried about *me*?" I looked at Gould, who didn't say anything.

"I've been worried about all of you," I informed them.

"You've been, like, kind of . . . different," Kamen said. "Not as relaxed."

No one seemed to know what to say then, so Kamen unmuted the TV and we watched the teaser of the next *Law & Order* episode, but I couldn't focus on the murdered shopkeeper.

"Do you think we're like the sisterhood of the traveling pants?" I asked finally.

"Sort of." Gould turned from the TV. "Except we don't have a pair of pants that fits us all."

"I've never actually read that book. Is that what it's about?"

"Uh, yeah," Kamen said. "The pants are magic and the girls all look hot in them."

"Huh. I always assumed 'pants' was like a metaphor or something."

"For *what*?" Miles asked.

"I dunno, like a friendship that fit them all perfectly, or whatever."

"It's totally symbolic," Kamen agreed.

I glanced at him. "Have you read it, buddy?"

"I've seen the movie."

"Well, at any rate . . . I'm glad I have all of you." I paused. "But if you screw up this Black Friday dinner for me, you will wish you were in a PG movie about magic pants instead of trapped inside the nightmare I will unleash on you. Got it?"

"We love you too, David," Miles said.

Onscreen, the theme music started.

CHAPTER NINETEEN

I opened the door to D at precisely six o'clock on Black Friday. I was wearing ridiculous jeans but a totally serious button-down. *"How, precisely, do you intend to manage Black Friday: The Revenge in jeans that tight?"* Miles had asked me earlier. It was a fair question. But I really wanted D to spend all of dinner thinking about my ass.

I greeted D with an awkward kiss on the cheek. He'd brought whiskey. Expensive, by the look of it. I led him into the kitchen, where the others were waiting like good little minions.

I made introductions.

"This is Gould," I said. Gould nodded shyly. "Miles." Miles waved. He was wearing a blazer instead of a cardigan. "And Kamen."

"Hey, man!" Kamen got up to hug him. "We got so much food."

"Hello." D awkwardly returned Kamen's hug. "Thank you for having me."

"Sit." I pulled a chair out for him. We all immediately started filling our plates, passing serving bowls around in a mad frenzy.

"I am pleased," D said, "that you have both turkey and roast beef."

I took the potatoes from Gould and threw a spoonful down on top of my turkey. "D believes that meat makes a man."

Kamen chased a pearl onion that was rolling across the table. "That's pretty crazy you two have the same name."

I started cutting up my turkey. "It's a good name."

"Indeed," D agreed. "The only acceptable men's names come from the Bible or past presidents. A boy named Grayson, for instance, will grow up to be a miserable human being and will probably host a red-carpet special."

"Oookay." I took the green beans from him. "You do remember you're sitting across from a Kamen, right?"

D looked at Kamen. "I am deeply sorry for you."

"It's cool, man." Kamen popped the onion in his mouth. "I like my name because I can make 'came in' jokes. Like, I *Kamen* his ass last night."

If I had worried that my lecture to my friends about being on their best behavior would prevent them from being themselves—I needn't have. Miles went on an incomprehensible tangent about tryptophan. Gould was so adorable that I just wanted to punch him in his adorable Gould face. And Kamen and D absolutely hit it off. They talked about tools. They talked about football. They talked about . . .

"So an octodile would be, like, an octopus's body with a crocodile's head," Kamen was saying. "And an eelion would be an electric eel with lion claws in its fins. Or *instead of* fins." He made a *think about that* gesture.

I hid my grin behind my water glass.

"Son, you have a lot going for you," D told Kamen. "A fantastic physique, a marketable brand of creativity, and a wide range of practical interests. You ought to start thinking of yourself as a 'Matthew' or 'George.'"

"Or Millard?" I muttered. D pinched me without even breaking eye contact with Kamen.

None of my friends said a word about the Subs Club, and I started to relax on that front. I wasn't obligated to share everything I did with D—in fact, he preferred when I didn't. And he hated using the internet for anything but Fetmatch—and now not even for Fet, since he had me. So probably he'd never know about the review blog, and if he did see it, he'd understand why we were doing it. He was one of the good doms. He had no reason to feel threatened by the club he was never ever going to know about.

But how long was I going to have to keep it a secret? Ricky had helped increase our site's privacy, but then yesterday a feminist blog had written an article about the Subs Club, and the article was getting retweeted like crazy. People were starting to Google the Subs Club with alarming regularity. Almost one-third of our members were nonlocal. No way would we be able to remain small and secret forever.

And there was something else bugging me. Something I couldn't quite put my finger on. I was halfway through my sessions with D, and the idea of letting him go after session six physically hurt me. I wanted him to keep pushing me. I wanted to give him more control.

Make me fucking listen to you, I'd shouted at him the night of the crossword.

But that wasn't exactly what I'd meant.

Make me listen to me. *Make me do the things* I *know I need to do.*

The lists are fine. They're fun. But I need you to make me do more than stand on a mat. I need you to push me to do more than take a paddling.

I forced those thoughts out of my mind and tuned in to the ongoing conversation between D and Gould.

"—often used under harness for show and for labor—"

I elbowed D. "Oh my God. Are you talking about Friesians?"

He half turned toward me, blinking several times in annoyance. "Is that a problem?"

I grinned and leaned my head briefly on his shoulder. "It will be if Gould dies of boredom."

"No, hey, I like horses," Gould insisted.

D finished his presentation on Friesians while I stole the last of the cranberry sauce. And while I was making the cranberry sauce my bitch, D put his hand on my leg. All casual and under the table. I froze. Burped up a cranberry. Then tried very hard to continue eating as though his touch wasn't giving me all the damn tingles.

"Whose guitar is that?" D asked as the feeding frenzy wound down.

Kamen gestured with a spoonful of mashed potatoes. "Mine. I have one for my house and one for here. So I can play anywhere."

"He's really good." I was damn proud of my weirdo friends.

"Dude." Kamen glanced at me and lowered his voice, as though he imagined he was in any way discreet. "Do you want me to play 'Figging Me Softly'?"

No, I mouthed.

"You sure?"

I nodded and mouthed, *I'm sure.* Out loud, I said, "Who wants pie?"

Later, when we were all sick and moaning, Kamen played us a cover of "Down on Main Street," substituting "Wayne Street" for "Main Street." D shared some Davy Crockett fun facts. Eventually everyone was tired, and D said he needed to get going. He helped us clean up a little, though. And totally threw his napkins and uneaten salad into our recycle bin despite the three arrows on the bin's side. I wasn't sure if I should offer to go home with him or stay here, but he kissed me good-bye at the door and said, "I had a very good time. I like your friends."

I was so happy I almost hugged him. Then got weird and embarrassed at the last second. "Thanks for coming over. I'm really glad you were here."

"I'll see you next Thursday?"

"Of course."

I watched him leave, and once he was in his beat-up Chevy, I closed the door and did a total cliché turn-around-lean-against-the-door-and-sigh-dreamily. I went back into the kitchen, where Kamen was spraying Reddi-wip directly into his mouth and Miles was washing dishes. He shut the water off as soon as I entered.

"Well." Miles dried a bowl. "A strange but intriguing gentleman. I give him five floggers."

I rolled my eyes. "Oh God."

"He's way cool," Kamen said through a mouth full of Reddi-wip. "He told me I was going places."

"You really like him, don't you?" Gould asked on his way to the sink with a stack of plates. "Wanna marry him?"

"If I didn't weigh eight hundred pounds I'd run over there and tackle you."

"Uh-huh."

I ended up waddling over, grabbing him around the waist, and squeezing. Then I squeezed Miles so hard his glasses fell off onto the turkey platter he was washing. Then I went over to the table and squeezed Kamen, who sprayed whipped cream in my hair. "I love Thanksgiving!" I announced. "And I love all of you."

I went to my room and flopped on the bed, getting Reddi-wip all over my pillow. Smiled until my face hurt.

D answered the door in pajamas the next night around eleven thirty. "Sorry," I said. "I know it's late, but—"

He pulled me in and kissed me hard, and I felt it in my cock, a hot, almost stinging pleasure that made me twist and press against him.

I groaned as his hands went to my hips, holding me. I took one hand and guided it to the front of my pants. He stroked me there, and I gasped against his lips.

"I don't want to stop at six sessions," I whispered.

"Me either."

Okay. Okay, wow. Fine. Great, yes. Pornstache and Little d 4evs.

I was so startled by our shared desire to spend more time with each other that I immediately tried to distract myself.

I ran a hand down the front of his shirt to his groin. "May I?" I teased his fly, and he nodded. He unzipped me while I undid his drawstring. I paused as he slid his hand into my pants, groping my cock through my underwear.

When I could see straight again, I got his dick out of his pants. I went to my knees and licked his cock in long, eager swipes.

"So good," he whispered.

My spit ran down his shaft and pooled in the hair at the base.

I circled my tongue around the thick head, lost in the taste of him. I squeezed my lips around the shaft and dragged up to the head. He was having trouble staying quiet, offering little groans that fueled my performance. I flicked my tongue back and forth across his slit and pulled back just as he came, letting him hit my face.

I took my shirt off and wiped my cheek with it.

"Good," he murmured, swaying slightly. "That was good."

I grinned and got to my feet. "I'll bet you say that to all the boys."

He yanked his drawstring tight. "Just the good ones."

I draped my arms over his shoulders, and he wrapped his around my waist. We stayed like that for a minute. Then I leaned slowly back and met his gaze. "Can I tell you what I want?" I asked softly.

I hated to spoil the mood, but I was worried it would be a while before I got the courage up again to make this sort of confession.

"Please."

I couldn't be sure, but his cheeks seemed a little pinker than usual. Maybe it was just exertion. But no, there was something boyishly anxious in his expression.

I didn't know where to start. My heart pounded, and I wished I could put him inside my head so he could feel this confusion with me. So that he would understand—not just what I was trying to ask, but why it was so hard to ask.

"I'd like to try . . . if *you'd* like to try . . . a relationship where you discipline me. *Really* discipline me."

His brow furrowed. "What have we been doing?"

Nicki Minaj's "Only" blared from my pocket.

I took out my phone. "Hold on a second." I ignored the call and turned the ringer down to vibrate. Pocketed the phone again. Blew out a breath. "Domestic discipline."

He didn't say anything.

"I know we're not domestic. And I know you've had me bring you lists every week of the things I've done wrong, and then you come up with a punishment, and we . . . we have fun. I think. But I feel like we both know it doesn't matter what I put on the lists. You're going to punish me because that's the game we're playing."

He didn't say anything, so I went on. "But there are things I really want to change about how I live my life. And if someone doesn't hold me accountable, I don't . . . know how to change." I shrugged helplessly.

"What things?" he asked quietly.

"I want to go to hair school, but every time I tell myself I'm gonna research schools and apply, I end up putting it off."

He nodded, but didn't say anything.

"And then there's the way I talk to people. Sometimes I'm not sure how much of it's an act, and how much is that I actually can't control my mouth. And I usually know when I've taken something too far. The way I talked to you that night with the crossword . . . I don't feel good about that." I studied my feet. "I was wondering if you'd consider punishing me for real for those things. Not a game. No dom script. No brat act. Just you and me, and you making me do the shit I suck at doing on my own."

"Completing your applications."

"And talking more respectfully to people. That's all for now. If we try this and it works, I might think of more stuff."

"And what kind of punishment are you thinking?"

I wished I could close my eyes and just listen to his voice. Wished I didn't have to look at him while I asked for this. "I don't know. Honestly. You've done a lot of stuff to me, but it mostly turns me on. And I don't want you to have to beat me until I'm bruised to get me to feel punished. So . . . I haven't figured that part out yet."

"May I make a suggestion?"

I shifted. "Sure."

"Canes."

I stared at him, openmouthed.

"Just hear me out," he said. "I know how to use canes safely and effectively for punishment. You find them genuinely unpleasant. I could see a caning being a real deterrent."

"I said I wanted to be disciplined, not tortured," I snapped.

"David."

"Well, it bothers me that your first instinct is to go to something I told you was a hard limit."

"Just give it some thought. If you hate the idea, we won't do it. But if you want a punishment that doesn't feel fun . . . that might be it."

I chewed my lip. "How would you do it?"

He thought about it. "Six-stroke maximum. I'd put you over the back of a chair. You'd keep your underwear on. It would sting a lot and be over fast. No broken skin, no deep bruising. There could be some superficial welts, but they'd heal fast."

No. No, no. The worst idea. Don't do it.

But I want to try it.

I fucking trust him. Which is stupid. But I do.

I nodded warily. "You can lecture me. But no script. No weird dom clichés. It needs to come from you."

"I'll try my best."

I closed my eyes briefly. "And . . . no safeword."

So, so stupid.

I thought back to the paddling. He'd known when to stop. He'd pushed, but he hadn't forced. He would be fair. He would be careful.

His expression was soft. That admiration was there that I'd seen the night of our second session, when I'd first dropped the act. "All right."

"Just for the domestic-discipline stuff," I added quickly. "I still get a safeword for whatever potty-chair, clothespins, Vick's VapoRub nonsense you decide to do."

"Agreed."

"All right, then. Cool." I felt light-headed. "And I'll try not to fight you. I'll try to take it like a man. Like the kind of man I am. Which might not fit your exact definition."

"David." His voice was almost sharp. I looked at him. "You are a man, and a fine one."

That almost destroyed me. In the best possible way.

What do you mean when you say you don't want to stop at six sessions? Do you mean we could be, like . . . ?

I glanced at the floor. "Hey, D?"

Don't ask. Because what if he doesn't feel like you do? What if all he means is that he wants to do seven sessions?

"Hmm?"

"Do you—"

My phone buzzed. I pulled it out. "God damn it. Hold on."

Kamen.

"Sorry, one minute." I took the call. "Hey, buddy. What's up?"

"Dave?" he said. "Sorry, can you come home? We've got a situation."

CHAPTER
TWENTY

"I'm fine," Miles said. But I could see he was shaken up.

"What happened?" When he didn't answer, I filled the kettle with water and put it on the stove. Pulled out the chair next to his and sat. "Miles?"

Kamen had left work and picked Miles up to bring him here, but he'd had to go back to the restaurant. I hadn't gotten the whole story, just that Miles had met with some guy and something had gone wrong.

Miles didn't appear physically hurt, but he was definitely out of it. He wouldn't look at me while he talked. "The guy seemed normal when we were messaging on Fet. I met him for lunch a few days ago and he seemed fine too. I was gonna do a knife scene with him. I'd heard from other people that he was good with knives. I let him tie me up—nothing too crazy, just my wrists and ankles. Quick release. The scene was going fine, but then . . ." He sighed, burying his face in his hands. "Fuuuuck."

"It's okay."

Miles kept his face buried a moment more, then looked up, his hands still on his cheeks. He gave a nervous laugh. "He had the knife next to my cheek. And he said, 'You gonna put me on your blog?' He knew who I was. And he kept saying stuff like, 'You gonna give me a good review?' while he was dragging the blade along my cheek. I thought he wasn't gonna let me up. I thought . . ."

My stomach twisted.

"But then he untied me, and . . . He just let me go."

"Miles. I'm so, so sorry." I didn't know what to say or do to make this better.

He shrugged. "Not your fault."

It is, though. You told us the review blog was a bad idea. "Who is he? Tell me what he goes by, and we'll call the police, and . . ."

And what? The guy hadn't technically threatened Miles. Hadn't hurt him physically.

Miles shook his head. "I wasn't like you and Hal." He stared out the window. "The way you just sort of jumped into it. I had my first bondage fantasy at age six. I learned everything I could about the lifestyle, the theories behind it, the different subsets . . . By the time I actually started looking for partners, I had BDSM built up in my head as some kind of self-regulating, sex-positive paradise."

"Miles. I'm serious, we can't let him get away with—"

"I mean, it had *rules*. Rules that kept people safe. And I thought it was kinky people against the world, you know? Fighting stereotypes and proving we're mentally stable and—and *believing* we were somehow even better than our vanilla counterparts. That we were more in touch with our emotions, our bodies. Better at communicating."

He finally looked at me. Gave me a weak smile. "Then I learned BDSM is just people. And people suck."

"Not all of them," I said quietly.

"But a lot of them."

The kettle started boiling, and I got up and fixed two mugs of tea. Miles was staring at the table when I got back. I put a mug in front of him. "We've got to do something."

He shook his head again. "I don't want to do anything. I just want to forget about it."

Forget about it? When we'd created a whole fucking club to fight exactly this kind of thing?

But this was Miles. My friend. And he was telling me what he wanted. I had to listen.

"Are you disappointed in the experiences you've had?" I asked.

"No." He smiled sadly. "I've met a lot of good people. Nights like tonight just . . . make me miss being younger and less cautious."

"I can't picture you ever being less cautious."

"I was, though. I filled my head with all that *information*, and then I still went out and followed my dick. I miss that."

I laughed. "I still follow my dick."

He was starting to look and sound more like himself. "But doesn't your brain hold a little more sway now?"

"Possibly," I admitted. "A little. It's crazy; now I see kids like Ricky and I want to protect them. He told me the other day he's been playing with some guy, and I wanted to know who it was. In, like, a parental way. Not a juicy-gossip way. Even though doing stupid shit is, like, part of the learning process."

He nodded.

We drank our tea in silence. "I need to tell you something," he said finally.

"Uh-oh. What?"

He ran his finger along the handle of his mug. "I have to leave the Subs Club."

My stomach dropped. "Oh."

"And I'll probably give up the scene too. For a while, at least."

"*What*? You can't let this guy—"

"It's not because of tonight. Though tonight made the decision easier. I'm making some big changes in my life. Workwise, and . . . personally. I can't talk about everything that's going on just yet, but I really do think it's important that I take a step back from sexual deviance. Trust me."

"Okay, you can't just drop a bomb like that and be like, 'Trust me.' What changes are you making?"

He gripped his mug. "I'll tell you soon, I promise. I'll tell all of you. I just need a little more time to figure things out."

I tried not to think melodramatically. Just because my friends had secrets, and my club had nearly gotten Miles killed, and I was going to work in a mall forever . . . It was going to be fine. Everything would be fine. I just had to hold everything together. Including myself.

"Okay," I said numbly.

He seemed like he was drifting again. His eyes were far away, his cardigan hanging off his shoulders, his hands clasped neatly around the mug. "Do you remember back when Riddle was new? They'd just gotten that giant ladder in the middle of Chaos. There was that play party on New Year's, and everyone kept asking GK and Kel what the ladder was for."

I grinned. "And Kel said, 'For anything you want.'"

"Uh-huh. That couple—I can't remember the guy's name, but the woman was Ava—did that scene where he attached dildos to different points on the ladder, and she had to climb the ladder and fuck herself to orgasm on all of them."

"Yes! And then all the tops started having their bottoms do it, and they were timing them, like *American Gladiators* . . ."

"And GK was standing by with a tub of disinfectant, making everyone take the dildos off and sterilize them and put new condoms on them between contestants . . ."

I shook my head. "Kel told me later that's when she knew everything would be all right. She said she'd been so nervous about opening the club, but that night, she saw that she and GK weren't alone. That this really was a community, and lots of people were going to contribute their creativity and energy to it."

"Yeah."

"That's what I miss," I said after a moment. "The newness. That feeling that everything I did and every person I met was exciting and intimidating and awesome. I miss being Ricky."

I stared at my Fetmatch feed in horror.

New Group Invitation: Rate the Subs of the Subs Club.

I clicked the invite and visited the group. Someone had created a list of a fair number of Subs Club members. And people in the group were commenting on the names.

My name was at the top of the list.

Dave43221 cries like a girl when he's spanked. he's a awful fuck. Thinks he is hot but he's nothin special if you play with him, you should beat him hard then shove your cock deep down his throat so he can't talk. Choke the little bitch or he'll never shut up.

I read it over three more times, too shocked to feel much of anything. I clicked on the poster's name. The profile was brand-new, had no photos, and obviously had been created just for the purpose of posting in this group. This person was also the one who'd sent me the invitation. They'd wanted me to see this.

Stay calm. Don't panic.

I sent a message to the administrators flagging the entire group as abusive, and then refreshed every couple of minutes as I waited for a reply. While I waited, I checked to see who else was on the list. Kamen and Gould weren't, but Miles was. He had a couple of comments. One was *This guy's hot.* The other was *I like hot chocolate.*

I logged on to the Subs Club site. People had started posting comments on the review blog about the *Rate the Subs of the Subs Club* Fet group. A lot of Subs Club members had seen their names in the Fet group and were freaking out. I commented on as many of the freak-outs as I could find, assuring everyone that I'd written to Fet's admin and that the group would be taken down shortly.

But as I scrolled through the reviews, I noticed something. The Disciplinarian's name had been posted a few days ago, and he had four ratings totaling an average of three floggers.

Shit. Who had put his name up? My friends would have known better. Then I remembered Miles had given a couple of other members administrator access so they could help moderate comments.

I hovered over the link for a moment, then decided I didn't want to read the reviews. Underlying my guilt and fear about D's name being up here was a righteous anger. Three floggers? These people didn't know what they were talking about. D was five million floggers, all the way. I waved my admin wand and deleted his name, feeling even guiltier. I knew I shouldn't be using my power to give D special treatment. But . . . shit, it was my club. My rules. And nobody was gonna rate *my* dom.

I went back to Fet. Still no response from the higher-ups.

Gould came home, and I quickly put my laptop aside and pretended to be reading a hair magazine. I was hoping he'd go right to his room. I really didn't feel like talking.

But he came over to the couch, moved my laptop, and sat. "I met with Kel today."

Great. Just great. I wanted to shake my fist at the heavens and demand a fucking *break* from all this. Once upon a time, I had actually maintained a life outside of thinking about kink and talking about kink and doing kink. "What? Why?"

"To talk about the tensions between our club and the rest of the community. She might have an idea for a compromise. A way we can work together."

"I don't want to hear it." My panic rose. I wondered if Kel and GK had seen the new Fet group. God, they were probably members. "She's overbearing. And GK annoys the shit out of me. And neither of them cares what we're trying to do."

"Dave?" Gould was looking at me nervously.

"What?"

"I'm going to try a scene with them."

I stared at him, confused. "A scene with who?"

"Kel and GK."

What. The. Fuck? "You're gonna play with them?"

"Yeah."

I closed the magazine. "Gould, you can't do that. They're the enemy."

"They're not the enemy. They're offering us—well, you—an opportunity. If you'll meet with them this Saturday, and—"

"Why the hell would I meet with them this Saturday?" I threw the magazine on the table. "What do they have to do with my life?"

"They want—"

"I don't need *them* to offer *me* anything."

"Stop interrupting me," Gould snapped.

I fell silent.

"Seriously, Dave, I get that you're upset, but I'm trying to have a rational conversation about something that matters to both of us. You need to grow up."

The sting of the words cut deep, and I was left with this instant of blankness where I didn't know what to do or say. I stood.

"Dave . . ." he started.

I could tell he was going to apologize, and I didn't need that. "Whatever. You wanna play with two people who've as good as admitted they'd rather cover up abuse than deal with it? You're gonna end up just like Hal."

I turned and stalked to my room.

CHAPTER

TWENTY-ONE

T hings got steadily worse in the days that followed. First, Mandy got voted off *Space Camp*. The good news was that she'd fallen in love with Parker, the mathematician, who'd been voted off the week before. The tabloids were abuzz with news of their engagement. "Yeah," Mandy said in her closing sound bite on the show. "I told him to make like Saturn and put a ring on it." She flashed her rock, then glanced away from the camera. "I'm sicka throwin' up in the gravity chair anyway."

A day later, I got a message from D:

Dear David,
I regret that I will not be able to meet with you this week. I will get in touch if something changes.
Best,
D

What the hell kind of message was that? Seriously, what the fuck kind of paltry-ass message was that to give to someone you'd spanked, slept with, let read your screenplay . . . We were more than "Dear David" and "I regret" and "Best," weren't we? But I couldn't shake the awful feeling this had something to do with the Subs Club.

I messaged him back.

Dear D,
Why not?
David

David,
Best if we don't see each other for a while.
D

I spent the whole day worrying about it. Evening found me on my knees by my living room window, staring out at the darkening sky with my arms folded on the sill. Gould arrived home from work and didn't speak to me. I'd spent all day waiting for him, hoping I'd have the nerve to apologize when he showed up. But he walked past me, and I couldn't even make myself open my mouth.

I waited for him to go to his room. Then slipped out of the house and drove to D's, passing the brightly lit Finer Things, where I'd called him a drooling cartoon wolf. Where he'd pinched my ass. I pulled up to his house, hopped out of the car, and slammed the door. I strode up to the porch. Knocked furiously and then rang the bell for good measure. No answer, but the lights were on and I could hear a TV. I knocked again. I kept knocking, I don't know for how long, until D answered the door.

He was a mess. He had on a T-shirt and rumpled pants, and his hair stood up. His eyes were bloodshot and he looked, for a second, like he didn't even know me.

"Hey." I was too surprised by his appearance to say more than that.

"What are you doing here?" he asked.

"What do you think, *Sir*? You blew me off. I was worried about you."

He glanced past me into the dark yard.

"Hey," I said. "What's going on?"

He rubbed his forehead. "I was on Fetmatch the other day to make some adjustments to my profile. There was a lot of hullabaloo in my feed regarding what I'm told is a project of yours."

Shit. No.

Panic didn't quite eclipse anger. "So you thought you'd dump me over Fet message instead of talking to me about it man-to-man?"

"I don't know that you have any business yelling at me," he said quietly.

My stomach sank. He let me follow him into the kitchen.

He went right for the coffee. "An acquaintance of mine saw that I was online and messaged me about what was going on. He said my name was on some blog that you ran. A blog where you rated doms." He still spoke softly, but I could hear the edge in his voice.

"That blog is meant for submissives only. It's supposed to be a place where we can talk about what sorts of doms are safe and what sorts are assholes."

"I don't like being discussed behind my back. Not by someone I thought was . . ." He shook his head. "'Man-to-man?' What about you? If you have a problem with me, talk to me. Not the internet."

"I never rated you. I never even wanted your name to go up there. Someone else put it up. I deleted it as soon as—"

"What about the other doms on your blog? You think they don't want to keep their private lives private?"

"Put the damn coffee down." I walked up to him. "If you'd give me a chance to explain—"

"Please, do." His voice sounded rough with an emotion I couldn't quite identify. It wasn't just anger.

"I'm sorry if it hurt your feelings. But this project is important to me." *It's just gotten massively out of hand.* "I wanted to stop people from getting hurt. You know Fet wouldn't let abuse victims c—"

"How is it okay to rate dozens of people who are doing something incredibly intimate, that involves so much trust and care, like they're—like they're sellers on eBay?"

"That's not what we're doing! We're having *discussions.* I want to know what's so bad about—"

"Because what you and I do here is *private!*" He was as close to shouting as I'd ever heard him. "And what I've done with my other partners is private. I would think that's common sense."

"Nobody's talking about your cock size or debating whether you're a good lay. They're talking about your ability to be safe and respectful in a scene."

"I don't care what they're saying. I don't want to be fodder for your *discussions.*"

He wouldn't face me. I got angrier and more panicked.

I tried again. "Well, then—"

"All my life! All my goddamn *life*, I've tried to stay out of peoples' way. I've tried to live quietly. I haven't even made *friends* because I don't want to—to have to worry about what people think of me. Don't want to have to worry that I'm failing them. But I have this one thing—this one damn thing, David—that I *need* from other people. And I thought I was getting it from you."

"You . . ." I had no idea what to say. The magnitude of what I'd done was slowly sinking in.

He was breathing hard. "And I thought maybe I wasn't doing such a bad job of giving you something back."

God, had I ever fucked up.

I couldn't hold it together. Not myself, not my club, not my friends. Not D and me. And that realization scared me like nothing else.

I had *hurt* him. This giant, meat-loving, mustached manly man. I'd hurt his *feelings*.

And I'd turned myself into someone he couldn't trust.

I swallowed hard. "Please, I need to tell you—"

"Just stop talking," he said without looking at me.

I stared at him, anger slowly overtaking fear. I wasn't *wrong*. The Subs Club wasn't wrong. But if he wasn't going to talk about it with me, then we were going nowhere.

You don't get to snap your fingers and order me onto the mat for this. I am trying to tell you something important.

"I'd like you to leave." His voice was rough.

That did it.

"No problem!" I snapped. "Thanks for letting me explain. Thanks for trying to understand the one fucking thing I've done in my life that's made me feel *useful*."

I left.

I went to Riddle. The weather was lousy and it was too early for more than a handful of people to be inside.

Kel was refilling spray bottles of disinfectant by the front counter. "David." She sounded surprised.

I walked past her without speaking, worried that if I opened my mouth, I'd lose it.

This was a fucking nightmare. D hated me, Miles was out of the club, Gould was mad at me, and probably everyone in the community knew I was behind the review blog and wanted me to die.

I couldn't control how they felt.

I couldn't control who lived or died or fell in love or got hurt . . . anything.

Give it up.

I found myself in Tranquility, staring at the bench where Hal had died. "Fuck you," I said to the bench. "Seriously, fuck you."

I kicked it.

And then I kicked it again, because kicking it felt wonderful.

"David?" Cinnamon stepped out of the shadows at the far end of the room. She was wearing a harness and a hood with ears, tall black boots, and her butt plug tail made of real horsehair.

"Oh God." I rubbed my temples and sank down onto the bench. "I'm so not in the mood right now."

She came over to me. "Relax."

I looked around. "Where's your jockey or whatever?"

"He's getting some stuff out of the car." She sat beside me on the bench, sweeping her tail underneath her as she did.

"How can you sit with that thing in?" I asked.

"I'm used to it." She didn't sound as haughty as usual, and she glanced at me with what might have been concern. "You don't look so good."

"I'm not so good. I hate Bill Henson. I hate that he's allowed to play here. And I've fucked up pretty much everything I could possibly fuck up over the last few days. You've probably seen the Fet group dedicated to how much I suck."

She didn't answer. Yep, she'd definitely seen it. It had probably made her day.

"And none of the stupid shit I've done or tried to do has brought my friend back. So . . ." I raised my hand and let it fall.

She let out a long breath. "I want to tell you something. If you don't want to hear it, that's fine. But I thought you might like to know what I saw that night."

No. That is the last *thing I want.*

"I know what you claim you saw." My voice was bitter. "You took Bill's side."

She stared at her . . . hooves. "What I said at the trial was true. I didn't see Hal try to safe signal. I didn't see anything that indicated he'd been pressured into the scene, or that he was nervous about it. I'd been stabled right over there—" She pointed across the room.

"Don't say stabled."

"Hal and Bill were talking. Hal was laughing. I didn't even notice they were doing breath play at first. I just saw Bill standing behind Hal and kinda yanking him by the hair and stuff. The next time I looked over, Hal looked deep in subspace. I mean, Bill would say something to him, and Hal would just moan and sort of laugh."

The poppers. Hal had probably been giddy. Relaxed.

"Bill left the room. I saw Hal's legs move a couple of times after that—not—not frantic or anything. Just little movements. And then Hal was lying so still, and I started to feel uncomfortable about him being there with no one, like, checking on him. So I walked over. The rope was really tight around his neck. It had gotten caught on one of the screws in the bench. But he never . . ." Her eyes welled up. "I'm sorry. But that's what I wanted you to know. I never saw him struggle. He just looked really peaceful. Like he was sleeping."

My hands were shaking so bad I had to ball them into fists. "You don't leave someone tied up alone. Ever. There's no excuse for that."

"I know. I know, but Hal had one arm free. The knot was a quick release. And Bill only left to get Hal some water. It really was an accident."

"Oopsy-*fucking*-daisy."

Her voice was quiet. "I understand if you don't want to give Bill a second chance. But he's going to be fucked up for the rest of his life, and—"

"Shut up!" I rose. "Please, just shut up. I'm so tired of hearing how Bill's fucked up for life. Hal's life is *over*."

She stood too. "I know you think I messed things up at the trial. But I only told what I saw. There's always a slight danger in what we do, and . . . I . . . just . . . I'm not on anyone's side."

I didn't have the energy to shout anymore. I put my face in my hands and shook my head. Inhaled through my nose and looked up, my fingers steepled under my chin. I started laughing, and I was afraid I wouldn't be able to stop. When I finally calmed down, I gave the bench one last kick, but it was more affectionate than angry. "I'm also *so* fucking sick of hearing about how BDSM's a dangerous game, when the only reason I ever played it was to feel safe."

I left her there and returned to the front of the club. GK was with Kel now. My stomach churned, but I made myself walk up to both of them. They gazed at me warily, and when I opened my mouth, I wasn't sure what would come out.

"I'm ready to talk," I told them. "I *need* to talk."

CHAPTER
TWENTY-TWO

I was waiting to ambush Gould when he got home from work the next day.

"I'm sorry," I blurted before he was even all the way through the door. "I'm so sorry for what I said. I don't mean to try to control everything. I just love you guys so much. I really do. I don't want anyone else to get hurt. Not you or Miles or Kamen or Ricky or Kamen's mom or even fucking Cinnamon. I'm never going to be okay with the fact that I wasn't there when Hal needed me. Never." I stood there in the entryway, my head buzzing. Gould just looked at me, so I kept going.

"Every time Miles does anything with knives, even though he knows what he's doing, I'm always afraid someone's gonna stab him. Either on accident or for using words like 'ergo.' And Kamen's such a doofus, I'm worried he's gonna be involved in some random disaster. And I'm always, *always* afraid that the people you play with will never love you like I do."

For a second I thought he was going to tell me to go fuck myself.

Then he sighed. "No one loves me like you do," he agreed softly. He hung his jacket up and turned to me. "But that's okay. There are lots of ways I can be loved."

"I worry about you. I think you miss Hal more than any of us."

He went to the couch, and I went with him, and we both sat. "Hal and I had more baggage than he had with any of you."

"But you'd tell me, right? If you were having trouble dealing with it? If you still wanted to murder Bill?"

"I never wanted to murder Bill. Just punch him in the face. And I did."

I stared at the pine boughs on the mantel I hadn't even realized he'd started decorating for the holidays. The Pez-dispenser-and-birthday-candle menorah Kamen had made him last year was up too.

"D found out about the review blog," I said quietly.

Gould looked at me.

"His name was on there for a few days. I don't know who put it up. And someone told him about it. Told him I was one of the Subs Club founders." I tried to smile. "He's pretty pissed. And I definitely didn't help things with what I said to him."

Gould's expression was genuinely sympathetic. "I'm sorry."

"Yeah." I sighed. "Me too."

I didn't know if I should tell him about talking to Cinnamon. I wasn't sure I was ready to go there. So I stuck to talking about poor, poor me.

"Do you think I ruined everything with him?"

"Probably not."

"How? I mean, I took his name off the blog, but isn't that unfair to the other people who don't want their names there either?"

"Maybe what we need to do is take the review portion down. Go back to what the blog was originally supposed to be—what *you* wanted it to be, before I messed things up with my dumb idea. We make it a forum where people talk about kink."

"It wasn't a dumb idea. It's just… hard to please everyone." I tucked my legs up under me. "It's so hard to moderate all those comments and not know who's being too aggressive or spiteful or . . . you know?"

"Yeah."

"I talked to GK and Kel last night. They, um . . . asked me if I wanted to lead a roundtable discussion in a couple of weeks. To talk about the Subs Club and why we . . . what it was supposed to be."

He nodded. "What do you think?"

"I think it's a good idea. I said I'd do it." I groaned and leaned back. "*People* are gonna be there, though. Like, people who got reviewed on the blog and hate us. What if they heckle me?"

"I don't think GK and Kel will let you be heckled. And I'll be there. And Kamen and Miles."

"Promise?"

"Of course."

"So now all I have to figure out is how to win back my man." I stared at the ceiling. "I feel like such a romcom heroine. Like this is totally the part where a sad song plays over a montage of me doing stuff with D. Except my montage would be really weird. Like, he'd be putting Vicks up my ass and beating me with homemade paddles. And we'd be reading his monster-movie screenplay."

"So. What would a romcom heroine do next?"

"Eat a whole tub of ice cream."

"And then?"

"Watch a movie that makes her feel better."

"Okay, but what about after that? After she's spent two weeks crying and her eyes are all puffy and she decides she has to take action to make this situation right?"

"Adopt a shelter cat?"

Gould jostled me. "She'd go to the guy. And she'd tell him . . ." he prompted.

"Tell him," I agreed, nodding.

"Come on, Dave, you've so got this. Tell him . . ." He motioned for me to take over. "She's . . ."

"Pregnant?"

"Sorry."

"What?"

"Tell him she's sorry."

"Noooo." I picked up a throw cushion and hid my face in it. "D hates me. He'll never forgive me."

"You won't know until you try."

I refused to come out of the cushion.

Gould squeezed my thigh. "But we'll do this in order, okay? Pick a movie." He stood and headed for the kitchen.

I sat up. "Are we eating ice cream?"

"If we've got any."

"We don't. Kamen ate it all when the Seahawks lost."

I heard Gould opening the cupboards. "We could go to Mel's to get milkshakes."

"I'm in *sweatpants*."

"You're entitled to a couple of public appearances in sweatpants. Come on."

We walked to Mel's. I fished in my wallet as we entered. "Do you have a penny?" I asked Gould.

He handed me one, and I placed my order. "That'll be three twenty-nine," said the girl at the register. I immediately handed her exact change.

She smiled. "Wow, you were ready with that!"

"This is not our first rodeo," I informed her.

Once we had our milkshakes we headed back to the house, where I curled up on the couch and made my selection from the streaming menu.

"What're we watching?" Gould settled beside me.

"*21 Grams.*"

"Seriously? That's depressing as hell."

"I love Sean Penn."

So for the rest of the night I lay on the couch with my head in his lap, and we watched *21 Grams* and drank our milkshakes. And I tried to think about what I'd say to D.

CHAPTER
TWENTY-THREE

I spent several days preparing my apology. Part one was verbal. And if he was willing to listen to that, we might just get around to part two. I was sweating as I sat at his kitchen table a week later.

He listened. To the whole story, start to finish, of how the Subs Club had come to be and how it had spiraled out of control. He listened to my apology, and to my explanation of what was going to happen now.

"A member of the Subs Club is going to lead a roundtable discussion each month at Riddle. And we're going to keep the educational portion of our site—the articles and the resources for victims and stuff. But we're getting rid of the review blog. I know that doesn't undo the damage, but . . ."

I tried to look at him and couldn't. I continued.

"I'm also going to serve as an advocate, and so are some other members. We'll be available to anyone in the community who's been a victim of abuse but maybe doesn't feel comfortable going to the police, or isn't ready to yet. Kel and GK are helping with all of this."

"That's good. I'm glad to hear that." He still seemed a little stiff with me.

"I know it hurt your feelings," I tried. "Being rated. I wasn't trying to be sneaky, though. I swear."

Way too much silence. I almost got up and bolted.

"David. I like you a lot. And I admire . . . everything you do. And I know you weren't being malicious. I never thought that."

Really?

He shook his head. "It's hard to explain. How do you feel when you're bent over someone's lap for a spanking?"

"Um . . . What?"

"Just tell me how you feel."

"Pretty embarrassed. Nervous as fuck. But also kind of sexy."

"Then let me tell you this. I like being dominant. I like feeling confident and in control and giving a boy what he needs. It does make me feel 'kind of sexy.'" He paused. "But things rarely go as planned in a scene. And when I'm domming, there's a part of me that feels like you do when you're bent over—exposed and embarrassed. And that's why this public rating business is difficult for me. Because what I do in this house with you or with anyone else is very, very personal."

That kind of blew my mind.

But it made a lot of sense.

"I'm so sorry," I told him. "I wanted to tell you, a couple of times, about the club. But I didn't know if you'd . . ."

Hate me.

He nodded. "I know I'm not easy to talk to."

"What? No. You're incredibly easy to talk to. I just wasn't sure at first what we'd end up being to each other. And the club really was— *is*—personal to me. I wasn't sure how to share it."

He was silent a moment. "I'm sorry I didn't give you a chance to explain before."

"I'm sorry about the review blog." I paused, offering a hesitant smile. "Will you let me make it up to you?"

"David, there's really no need. I—"

"No, I actually have something really cool planned. If you think you can forgive me, I'd like to show you."

He looked wary. "All right."

My smile broadened. "Tomorrow is Thursday, after all. So why don't you come to my place? Seven thirty?"

"I am . . . somewhat frightened."

I laughed. I still felt kind of wrecked—but hopeful too. "Don't be. Or only a little."

D arrived at my place at exactly seven thirty the next night. I answered the door and ushered him in. He didn't kiss me, which stung, but I tried to let it go as I took his jacket and hung it up.

I led him into the kitchen.

"This is your surprise," I told him.

He glanced around the table. Miles, Kamen, Gould, and Ricky all gazed back at him, looking nervous. Except for Kamen, who looked pumped as all fuck. They had tablets and phones in front of them.

"We're doing a table read," I announced. "Of your script."

D whipped around to face me. It was possibly the fastest I'd ever seen him move. "What?"

Oh God. Please don't freak out. "I thought it would be fun for you to see your work brought to life."

"My . . .?" He sounded incredulous. I hoped in a good way.

"*Crocopython*," I confirmed. "I want you to know you're, um . . . You're way more to the Subs Club than a rating. You've made my life better. And I hope we can make yours better for, like, half an hour."

"The script's not even finished." He kept glancing at the group assembled at the table.

"I borrowed what you had. D, I want you to meet Jake Mandragon." Kamen saluted. "Tank Kevlar." Ricky waved enthusiastically. "Dr. Brittany Sands." Miles nodded. "Twix." Gould looked like he wished the crocopython would eat him quickly and put him out of his misery. "And, of course, the crocopython." I gestured to myself.

"Oh God."

"What, you didn't think I was gonna play the big-titted doctor, did you?"

D just stared. "I truly don't know what to say."

"Then just sit down and listen." I pulled a chair out for him. "And I might need you to jump in to play a doomed lab assistant or two."

The reading began. Kamen committed fully to his role as Jake Mandragon. Ricky was the most enthusiastic, adorable Tank Kevlar imaginable. Miles brought gravitas to the tragic part of Dr. Brittany Sands. And I was a pretty fantastic crocopython, leaping up to attack victims—even dragging Gould's Twix out of his seat and gnawing on him until we were all laughing too hard to continue. D kept his arm around me for most of the reading— except when I was eating people—and I leaned against him, glad beyond words that he was here.

It took a while for things to go completely back to normal between D and me. We didn't have a Thursday night session for a couple of weeks, but we spent a lot of time together. And we talked. About continuing to play, and about incorporating something into our relationship that wasn't quite play.

The weekend before Christmas, D and I agreed I'd do two applications. Just two. They had to be completed and submitted by Sunday at 11:59 p.m., and I was supposed to send him the online submission receipts.

I didn't do them. On purpose. Terrifying as the prospect of a caning was, I needed to know what it would feel like. So on Monday afternoon I stood, not in the Den of Horrors, but in D's living room. He'd placed a wooden chair from the kitchen in the center of the room and set a long, thin rattan cane on it. I couldn't stop looking at it. Every time I did, I wanted to bolt. But I stayed put and waited for him to tell me what to do.

D sentenced me to three strokes for not doing the applications and a fourth for purposely trying to get punished.

"That's not fair," I argued. "You can't do that."

"This isn't going to be a battle, David."

I took a deep breath. *Give it up. Trust him.*

He indicated the chair. "Bend over the back. Hands on the seat."

I obeyed, leaning slowly over the chair back and adjusting myself until I felt relatively comfortable. The height of the chair meant I was on the balls of my feet. Panic, resentment, excitement—it was all there, and I didn't know what to do with any of it.

"What's this punishment for?" His voice was quiet, familiar.

"Not doing my applications." I paused. "And trying to get you to punish me."

"You told me you were going to complete two applications yesterday. You told me you wanted to be held accountable for doing them, and yet you sabotaged yourself in order to get punished on your terms."

"I didn't . . ."

"Didn't what?"

I forced myself to exhale. "Yeah," I admitted. "That's what I did."

"So four strokes. You'll hold that position until we're done."

He straightened, and I tensed, glancing to the side in an effort to see him. My heart was pounding out of all proportion to the situation. "D?"

"Yes?"

"I . . . maybe can't do this."

He hooked an arm around me and tugged me up. I stumbled into his arms and felt them wrap tight around me again. I clung to him for a moment, breathing him in. "Tough time with the applications?" he asked softly.

"No, Sir." We weren't playing, but for some reason it felt right to call him "Sir." I raised my head and nuzzled the side of his neck. "I just . . . I wanted to find out how bad this is gonna be," I admitted. "Sorry."

"Hey. It's not the end of the world."

I sighed, resting my chin on his shoulder. "I like that. That's a good thing to say to me."

He held me like that a moment longer.

I hoped Bill had said all the right things to Hal. I hoped he'd whispered to Hal that he was just going to get him some water, and then he'd be right back. And I hoped Hal had relaxed and closed his eyes and sunk into some beautiful place, secure in the belief that Bill would come back and take care of him.

And I hoped Hal had understood that no matter how exasperated I got with him, I had always loved him.

One more deep breath, and then I stepped away. "I think I'm ready now."

I'd never be ready. But oh fucking well.

He nodded toward the chair, and I bent over the back of it, placing my hands on the seat. He put his hand on my lower back and pushed gently until I flattened it and stuck my ass out. Then he reached around me and undid my fly. Slid my jeans down to my knees.

I heard him pick up the cane and closed my eyes, wondering if it would be worse with them open or shut. He swished the cane through the air a couple of times, and I tensed. I nearly jumped when he touched it to the seat of my briefs.

I could do this. It wasn't really that different from being paddled, was it? Except canes were Satan's masterpiece and I wasn't even remotely hard and I was wishing to hell I'd just done the stupid applications.

"You will do those applications," spaketh Mind Reader Dom. "As soon as we're done here."

I gripped the edges of the chair. The cane swished again, then cracked across my ass.

I stood straight up and clapped both hands to my backside. "Oh, Hell and its fiery lake and all its outer circles, *no*." I turned to face him, rubbing furiously to diffuse the sting. "No. Absolutely no."

"Dave." He looked slightly amused, and I was pretty sure I was going to punch him, but I couldn't take my hands off my butt to do it. "Turn around and bend over."

"Are you *kidding*?" I kneaded my ass, which hurt like a thousand Mandys being sent home from *Space Camp*.

"Yes, April Fool's, David, let me snap this cane in half and we'll go out for ice cream." He pointed the cane at the chair. "Bend over."

"It's too much!" I was aware even as I protested that the sting was subsiding.

"Listen." He didn't raise his voice at all. "If you want this arrangement, then you have to trust me. Nothing terrible is going to happen to you beyond a sore ass. And if you think about *why* this is happening rather than the fact that you don't like it, the discipline might be more effective."

Nope. This was, without a doubt, the worst idea I'd ever had. It had been all well and good to fantasize about domestic discipline. To see a beautiful pornstache in Riddle that night and think, *yeah, Pornstache, spank me. And stay with me and change my life and be a thousand times better than anyone has ever been to me.* To play a game with D for a few weeks. To invite him to Black Friday: The Revenge.

But this was going too far. This was giving up a level of control I'd never given to anyone. And I was afraid I'd never get it back. Even if I broke up with D, I'd always be Dave, the grown-ass man who let someone cane him because he was too fucking stupid to get his shit together on his own.

Why the hell would I drop the act, when the act was what was keeping me safe?

I stared at him. Then I turned to face the chair. Bent over the back and placed my hands on the seat. I flinched as his hand circled my hip gently. I exhaled. Willed myself not to tense up when he took aim again.

A second later there was a whoosh, and the cane struck slightly lower than it had the first time. "Shit!" I shifted my weight from foot to foot, gripping the chair hard enough to turn my knuckles white. "I'm sorry. I'm sorry," I repeated, more softly.

"Two more."

Think about why this is happening.

Because I'm seriously messed up?

Because I'm a man-child?

That wasn't right.

Because I need it to happen.

Because I really don't like being alone or trying to do things without help.

Because he always throws his trash in the wrong bin, and for some reason it makes me want to trust him with my entire soul.

I'd been stupid enough to think this would be simple. What D was asking for—what *I* was asking for—was true submission, and maybe I wouldn't succeed in giving it today. But over time, hopefully I'd learn. I'd trust him more and more. Because maybe it wasn't Bill I was scared of. Maybe it wasn't the thought of ending up dead on a piece of dungeon furniture.

I was scared of this huge capacity that I had for love, and for hope, and for forgiveness.

And for hurting people.

As long as I focused on what Bill Henson was, on what he'd done, then I didn't have to think too hard about who I was, and who I wanted to become. As long as I focused on Hal's absence, on what I'd been *left* with, I didn't have to think about what I might still gain.

If I just fucking pushed myself.

D struck me on the lower curve of my ass, catching some bare skin. I cried out and kicked the carpet. Boxers. From now on, I was going to start wearing boxers.

"Take a minute." He still spoke quietly, patiently.

"It *hurts*," was my profoundly compelling statement of the obvious. It hurt way, way below the skin.

"I know."

It clicked for me then. He *did* know. He knew I was afraid; he knew I was sore. He knew I missed Hal. He knew BDSM was dangerous—that not just people's bodies got hurt, but their feelings too. He knew, and I wasn't in this alone. For the first time since Hal, I felt the fight leave me, in a real and lasting way. I wanted this. *I* had asked for this.

It stopped hurting so much.

The fourth stroke fell across the tops of my thighs.

Fuck. Fuck fuck fuck all the fucks.

I didn't cry, but I was breathing hard and shivering as I waited for him to tell me I could stand.

He helped me up and hugged me so hard I groaned. I hugged him back, and we were both silent for a moment as I tried to get my ragged breathing under control.

It's okay. It's going to be okay.

"Hey," I said finally into his shoulder.

"Hey." He stroked my hair.

My laugh was awkward and unsteady. "That was fucking awful."

"You were—" he kissed me "—very brave."

"Don't patronize me."

"Don't downplay it." He ran his hand down my back and over my ass. I winced.

Maybe, I thought, there was something at least a little brave, a little grown-up, about knowing what you needed and asking for it. About being vulnerable in front of people who could cover you with a new kind of strength. A strength that wasn't about hiding your moments of fear and uncertainty and stupidity, but was about being a whole person, boldly.

"It was awful," I repeated. "But . . . thank you."

He didn't actually make me do my applications right then. We had dinner and watched TV for a while. Then we headed up to bed. And the next day, I did two applications; did them sitting on a sore ass, rocking slightly every now and then to reawaken the pain, to remind myself how lucky I was.

CHAPTER
TWENTY-FOUR

T he overhead lights were on in Riddle when I arrived. Christmas decorations covered the walls, and there were about thirty chairs set up in the lounge. As the room filled, I became increasingly convinced I ought to leave now and hope no one would miss me. However, Miles, Gould, and some other Subs Club people arrived before I could flee. Kamen had to work, but I'd received his *Dude, you got this* text. Plus a video file of him singing "Don't Stop Believin'" into a meat mallet.

I hadn't told D this meeting was tonight. I figured he could find out about it on Fet and attend if he was really interested. But this was actually something I wanted to do without him.

I kept watching the door, half terrified that Bill would walk in. Half wishing he would. Probably if there was anyone who needed to come to this discussion, it was Bill.

I just never wanted to see his face again.

Mrs. Pell entered, and came over and hugged Miles, Gould, and me before taking a seat in the row behind us. Ricky arrived. And Dennis the spank weasel. Oh God. I so couldn't do this. BellaSade, one of Riddle's DMs. The woman whose boobs Jimmy X had wanted to touch. GK had to go for more chairs, and eventually dragged a spanking bench into the lounge so people could sit on it.

I sat with my friends until the meeting started. Kel went through the usual business, reminding people about membership dues and upcoming events.

Finally she launched into my introduction. "A lot of you are curious about a project that was started recently by a group of Riddle members called the Subs Club. Though the Subs Club is not in any way affiliated with Riddle, we have invited the club's leader, David, to talk about its purpose and maybe clear up some questions and concerns you have. I'm gonna turn this meeting over to David."

I received a smattering of applause as I stood.

"Um, hi," I said. "I'm David."

"Heya, David," called Josh, the sub who'd sent the request that we review D. I threw him a wave.

I took a deep breath. "I don't really know a lot about making speeches, but I'm good at running my mouth, so . . ." A couple of people laughed. "I was invited here to talk about some issues facing our community. Both Riddle and the kink world at large. Over the past couple of months, the Subs Club has worked to identify and call attention to abusive and irresponsible behavior. We came up with the review blog, where we critique sessions we've had with doms in this area and point out any abuse or unsafe practices." There was some murmuring and whispering, but mostly a lot of blank stares. "Unfortunately, we've strayed from that purpose, and that's what I'm here to apologize for. I do think submissives and bottoms should have a private place to talk about issues that are specific to what we do. But I know a lot of feelings have been hurt, and it's embarrassing that what started as a way to help became a thing where we, um, undermined our cause."

I looked at the faces and wondered how many people hated me, how many were bored. How many were on my side.

"I feel like the president of the Students Against Drunk Driving society," I went on. "Like the least cool kid ever, standing up here and lecturing about safety and proper behavior. But this is important to me because too many friends have been hurt in scenes where doms crossed lines. And, um, obviously . . . I lost a really good friend recently."

A man in the second row spoke up. "I don't think any top in this room would hurt a bottom intentionally. Most times it takes two to make a scene go bad."

"Very true. And if you've ever had me as a sub, I pity you." There was a lot of tittering. "Honestly, if you're in this room listening to this, you're probably not one of the people we're upset about. But what our club really wants is to have a dialogue about things that can go wrong in scenes. To encourage communication between doms and subs, so it's not just like, 'Oh great, I'm a dom, you're a sub, get on your knees and suck me.'"

There was some hearty affirmation.

"Nobody plays like that," a woman called from the back.

"You'd be surprised," I said.

Another woman turned to address the first woman. "*Tons* of people do."

The first woman shook her head. "I'm a sub. I've played with plenty of doms in Riddle and outside, and I have never felt disrespected or unsafe. The problem is in the way people perceive what's going on in the scene. What feels like a violation to one sub might be a fantasy come true for another."

"Which is why it's not enough for individuals to talk about limits," the second woman fired back. "We have to talk about attitudes. Because I have had problems with doms overstepping my boundaries, and I know other subs have too. Even when we're very clear about what we want or don't want."

Some people murmured agreement.

The first woman was getting more agitated. "I just don't see why we have to turn this into a drama."

Mrs. Pell turned. "Honey, this isn't a drama. This is progress."

"Yeah, what's the harm in talking about these things?" a man in the second row practically bellowed. "If you play safely, then you've got nothing to fear about *talking*."

I wasn't sure how to break back into the conversation.

"Because it's gonna be a witch hunt against dominant *men*," another man said. "I know all kinds of guys, they do everything to try to be good doms, and they're getting no complaints, and then the girls they play with turn around and are like, 'I didn't want that.' Sorry, babe, but that's what a safeword's for."

"I know you didn't just call women 'girls,'" said a woman to my left.

Then everyone started talking. And shouting. And no one even listened to Kel's scary dom voice.

I heard one man say, "That blog said I tied my ropes too tight. How the hell am I supposed to know that unless my bottom *tells* me?"

A woman yelled that the review blog said her wardrobe looked like it came from the Mormon Goodwill.

Another man said he didn't feel comfortable domming at all anymore, because he was afraid he was going to hurt someone without knowing it.

Witch-hunt Man boomed that all of life was tough titties, and that he wasn't going to stop playing the way he liked to play just because society was degenerating into a politically correct cesspool.

Then Ricky yelled at Witch-hunt: "Someone *died* because of the way people like you think!"

Everyone went silent. Ricky dropped his gaze.

I looked at Kel, who was very pale.

"Well, it's true," Ricky muttered.

Kel stepped in. "Nobody died because of . . . anything that's been said here tonight. But we do need to start thinking about attitudes, as Dave said."

"Listen." My voice was shaking. "What happened with Bill and Hal was an accident. But it's not an acceptable accident. And, um . . . um . . ." I'd lost my train of thought. I glanced at Miles and Gould, who both nodded at me. "It's an extreme case, but it's still not okay. In the same way that *all* violations of a partner's limits are not okay." I turned back to the group. "And that goes both ways. Bottoms have to respect tops' limits too. So as these discussions continue, let's focus on bottoms' concerns, but also what factors make it hard for tops to know what a sub's really asking for."

I thought about the mixed messages I'd been giving D. *Make me. But don't force me. Push me. But don't scare me.* I wouldn't want to be D for the world.

Witch-hunt spoke again. More calmly this time. "How about bottoms ask for what they *really* want? A lot of them do; I'm not criticizing. But if you can't say 'stop' and 'go' and *mean* it, then you've got no business playing."

"Hey." Kel stepped forward. "Let David finish. Then we can let these feelings out. Civilly." She shot me a smile.

I looked down at my notes. My hands shook on the paper, and I saw flashes of *cries like a girl. Awful fuck. Choke the little bitch.* This would never work.

"GK and Kel have agreed to set up a network through which subs can anonymously report abusive behavior." I glanced up. "Later this month there's gonna be a workshop on safety and communication—I told you, you're gonna wanna knock my glasses off and give me a wedgie, but this shit matters. It's about making sure we can all feel good doing what we do. I want to apologize on behalf of the Subs Club for the things we've done that are counterproductive to that goal. The review blog will be taken down, and in its place there'll be a discussion blog that's open to the public. So we can continue to have conversations like this one."

I paused. "If you're a dom who's ever done anything that wasn't consensual, you deserve a lot worse than a one-flogger review. But if you're someone who's trying their best and occasionally fucking up—in ways that don't leave someone, like, seriously hurt, I mean—then I guess you're just human. We're all works in progress here; we're all learning. So I hope we can learn together, and not—not be at odds. Thank you for listening."

People clapped. A *lot*. I looked around the room and started to wonder if maybe things would be all right. Not perfect. But better.

I let out a breath, too relieved to move. There was a brief Q&A, which Kel and GK fielded. One dom asked if we were gonna keep the good reviews up on the blog, and if not, could we email him a copy of his? When I got back to my seat, Miles and Gould congratulated me.

I sat there trying to focus on the rest of the meeting, willing my heart to stop racing. I should have told D this was happening tonight. He could have come, or he could have refused. But I might have just done a grown-up, unselfish thing, and I wished I'd given him the opportunity to see it.

It was easy to be a leader behind a keyboard. And much harder to stand in a room full of people who had actually been hurt by something I'd done.

"You were extraordinary," Miles said as we drove home. He and Gould had taken a cab to Riddle, so they were riding with me. "A little too willing to concede and apologize, but on the whole, very impressive."

"I got people to do a slow clap."

"That wasn't a slow clap. That was just a regular clap."

"It slowed down at the end."

"That's just natural clap fade. Slow claps start slow."

"Like so." Gould clapped once. Pulled his hands apart. Clapped again. Miles joined.

"Okay, I get it," I said.

Miles stopped clapping. "It'll be good, I think. This advocacy thing. Our new, review-free, nonexclusive site."

I stared out the windshield, half listening to Miles chatter on.

It'll be good, I said to myself.

And to Hal, in case he was listening.

CHAPTER
TWENTY-FIVE

The Sunday meeting of the Subs Club came to order.

"I hereby announce the end of the review blog, and the birth of the new Subs Club Sounding Board." I turned my laptop to show everyone the new site. "A little sounding joke for ya. Has anyone here done that?"

"Sounding?" Miles asked.

"Yeah."

"Yes, David. I have been sounded."

"Probably with, like, a fucking hot dog–sized sound," I muttered.

Kamen made a face. "That's stuff in your dick, right? Hell no."

"I've done it too," Gould said quietly.

We all turned to him.

I stared. "Gould. Why don't you tell us these things?"

I happened to know some other things he wasn't telling us—namely that he'd gone out last night to play with GK and Kel and hadn't gotten back until just before this meeting. That was a little hard for me to deal with. But apparently the world didn't center around me.

He blushed. "The new site looks nice."

"It does," Miles said. "And we still have a link to the Danger List, where we kept the reviews of the worst of the worst."

"And there's links all over the damn place to the abuse hotlines." I scrolled up and down the page. "We concede on this fourth day of January, that some doms suck. But that doesn't mean we're going to rate all of them like they're sellers on eBay."

"David." Miles solemnly placed a hand on my shoulder. "It's been an honor to have you fight by my side. *Vive la révolution.*"

"I'm not giving up the revolution," I assured him. "The Subs Club is still going strong. And, like, eight billion people want to write articles for the Sounding Board."

"We're pretty awesome." Gould slid beers down the table to each of us.

I popped mine open on the table's edge. "There's even more to celebrate. Maybe. I guess."

"Oh?" Miles gazed at me expectantly.

"The Disciplinarian and I have embarked on a domestic-discipline relationship."

Kamen tried to open his beer using the table and failed. "What's that?"

I looked at Gould, who smiled at me. Then at Miles, who gave me a brief, wise-looking nod, as though he wasn't surprised in the least. I turned to Kamen. Took his beer and popped the cap off, then handed it back to him. "It means that sometimes, when I do something wrong, D canes my ass. But it's, like, for real. Not a game."

Miles raised his eyebrows. "You? Canes?"

"Yeah, they're awful. They hurt so fucking much. But I haven't died yet. And they *work*."

"Dave, that's awesome." Kamen picked up his guitar. "I mean, not the getting caned part. Actually, it all sounds like a shit-ton of suck. But if it floats your boat . . ."

"It's just something we're trying."

He started playing a jaunty acoustic version of Pink's "Try," and sang:

"Where there is a David there is gonna be a cane

"Where there is a cane, someone's bound to get hurt

"But just because it hurts doesn't mean you're gonna die

"You gotta bend over and—"

"Okay, Kamen, thank you."

Miles slowly pushed Kamen's guitar away. "David, I'm thrilled for you. You've found a winner. I'm envious."

Gould looked up from checking out the Sounding Board. "You're gonna find someone too."

A moment of tension. I watched Miles, wondering if he'd told the others about his plan to leave the scene for a while. He still hadn't given me his reasons, and it was driving me crazy wondering. Miles smiled, a bit woodenly. "Maybe I'm better off solo?"

Gould didn't seem to notice Miles's discomfort. "Oh, you're telling me you don't want to find that one special person who'll drag a knife along your skin, stick a sound in your dick—"

"Paint trails of rubbing alcohol on your ass and light them on fire," I said.

"Hook a battery to your balls," Kamen added.

"Well." Miles looked, for just a second, incredibly sad. Then he smiled again. "I do want all that."

I exchanged a glance with him and held out my beer. "To Miles."

"Why are we toasting Miles?" Kamen asked.

"Because he's great." We all clicked beers.

Kamen played for us after that, and we had an impressive dance party. Miles and I ended up on the floor doing the worm while Gould stood over us, doing the "screw the lightbulb." We consumed all the beer in the fridge, and eventually the dance party turned into a bed party, which turned into me waking up the next morning to see Miles hurriedly pulling his cardigan on. Gould was awake beside me. Kamen was snoring on the floor.

"The last trolley left, Mr. Rogers," I mumbled groggily, rubbing my forehead and half sitting up. I collapsed again with my arm over Gould.

"Ha-ha." Miles tied his shoe. "I have to get to an appointment."

Appointment?

He left a moment later with a hastily muttered, "Good-bye."

"He's been acting really weird lately," Gould said.

I yawned. "Maybe he's a superhero."

"CIA," Gould whispered.

"A time traveler."

"Having an affair with a married man," Kamen murmured from the floor.

"Or Torchwood." Gould stretched. "He could work for Torchwood."

Kamen stayed for breakfast, then headed out around noon. That left Gould and me.

Gould gazed through the living room window. "Sunny out."

"Nice try. How was your scene with Kel and GK?"

Poor Gould couldn't stop grinning. "Good."

"Yeah?"

"Fuck, yeah, David, it was so good."

"You look like it was good."

"She's really . . . and he's . . ."

"Is this a madlib? Should I pick two adjectives? Luminous and puce."

"They get it. Why I'm so quiet. They don't mind."

"That's awesome." I wrapped an arm around him. He put his head on my shoulder. "You hurting today?"

He shook his head. "It wasn't rough. We're gonna try to play together every once and a while."

I nodded. "You deserve good people."

"I've always had good people." We sat in silence a moment. "I noticed you texting a lot last night. During the dance party."

I tried to play it cool. "D's just checking in to see how I'm doing."

"Uh-huh. Planning a big date?"

"Tuesday. We're going to the maritime museum. And I'm going to convince him to fuck me in the bathroom."

"Beautiful."

"You know, I've lived in this city almost my whole life and I've never been to the maritime museum?"

"Well, it is a maritime museum."

"I told D I want to go on dates to all the touristy stuff around here. See the city anew, sort of. I want to help him get out of the house and do stuff with other humans. And I want to, like, *know* him. See how he reacts to stuff like ships in bottles."

"I see."

I picked some dust bunnies off my shirt from last night. "Hal would be making fun of me so bad right now."

Gould smiled. "He'd never believe you'd found someone who can make you listen."

"Don't tell him. When you talk to him. Okay?"

"Oh, I've already told him all about it. He's happy for you, though."

We were both quiet for a moment. "Do you really talk to him?"

"Sure. Why not?"

"I feel weird when I do. I mean, he's gone."

"So? He still likes us to talk to him."

I laughed. Offered Gould one of my dust bunnies. "I want to keep playing," I said. "Even though it's a dangerous game. The most dangerous game."

"The most dangerous game is hunting man."

"I know." I paused. "I'll bet D would be good at that."

"He wouldn't. He's a big old softy."

I snuggled closer. "He is, isn't he?"

"At least where you're concerned."

"Whatever."

Gould jostled me. "Hey, Dave. What if the most dangerous game . . ." He waited until I looked at him, his expression dead serious. "Is love?"

We held the stare for a few seconds, and then we both burst out laughing. "You're an idiot."

"Okay, but seriously, it might be."

"Oh, yeah, totally. Good thing I'm not in love."

"Whatever you say."

"Seriously, how could I be in love after a couple of months of spanking?"

"Deny it all you want."

"Uggghhhhh. Gould, what if I love him?"

"What if you do?"

I punched the couch lightly. "That's terrifying."

"It's good, isn't it?" he asked.

No. Maybe.

What did being in love even mean? Did it mean I was going to get my house with wainscoting, and a forever companion who made me feel meaningful and amazing? Did it mean this domestic-discipline thing would continue for the rest of my days? Because I wasn't sure I was ready to make getting caned a permanent fixture in my life. I mean, I'd survived one caning. So, like, give me a participation award and never make me do it again.

If I was in love with D, then what did I need to learn to do for him? Besides listen? I was going to have to learn more about his existence before me. I was going to have to help him get his screenplay in front of agents. I'd have to remember that being in charge made him feel exposed and terrified, and exploit that at every opportunity. Slash support him through those moments of terror. I'd need to make sure he had the best life, full of meat and obedience and long stretches of companionable silence.

On his part.

I was going to talk nonstop until we were geriatric.

I stared at the Pez menorah.

Oh my fucking God. Love really is the most dangerous game.

And I want to play it.

"I think I'm hard for danger," I whispered.

"What?" Gould asked.

"Nothing." I looked at him. "What if I'm wrong? About how he feels?"

"Are you wrong about how you feel?"

I shook my head.

"It probably wouldn't hurt him to know. How you feel, I mean."

"Are you trying to make me do the final part of the romcom?"

"Hey, I sat through all of *21 Grams* while you drooled on my pants and snored. You'd better fucking bring this home."

I thought it over. D had said I could come over anytime, right? Why not today? It was Monday, and he didn't work until two. Why not go over and announce I either loved him or felt such a deep and abiding affection for him that it was likely to turn into love if we weren't careful. Or maybe I'd play it cool—go over there and kiss him passionately, take him into the bedroom, get him hard, and then Meatloaf him. Tell him stop—I needed to know right now, before we went any further, did he love me? Would he love me forever?

This is it, Pornstache. We need to make some decisions. About wainscoting and test-tube babies and canes and how to give each other the best lives.

I stood. "I have to go."

Gould snorted. "You sure you don't want to wait until it's raining, or he's about to catch a flight out of the country?"

"I'm sure," I called from the kitchen.

I stopped in my room to put on white briefs. It seemed highly unlikely I was going to stand quietly on the mat and wait to be addressed.

But when D took me over his knee or bent me over his desk or finally just fucking put his mustache between my legs, I wanted him to see I'd made at least some effort to be good.

Explore more of *The Subs Club* series:
riptidepublishing.com/universe/subs-club

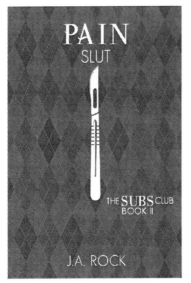

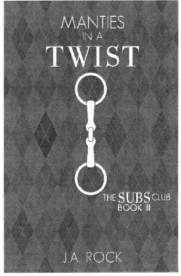

Dear Reader,

Thank you for reading J.A. Rock's *The Subs Club*!

We know your time is precious and you have many, many entertainment options, so it means a lot that you've chosen to spend your time reading. We really hope you enjoyed it.

We'd be honored if you'd consider posting a review—good or bad—on sites like **Amazon, Barnes & Noble, Kobo, Goodreads, Twitter, Facebook, Tumblr,** and your blog or website. We'd also be honored if you told your friends and family about this book. Word of mouth is a book's lifeblood!

For more information on upcoming releases, author interviews, blog tours, contests, giveaways, and more, please sign up for our weekly, spam-free newsletter and visit us around the web:

Newsletter: tinyurl.com/RiptideSignup
Twitter: twitter.com/RiptideBooks
Facebook: facebook.com/RiptidePublishing
Goodreads: tinyurl.com/RiptideOnGoodreads
Tumblr: riptidepublishing.tumblr.com

Thank you so much for Reading the Rainbow!

RiptidePublishing.com

ACKNOWLEDGMENTS

Thank you to Del, Sarah, Michelle, and John.

ALSO
BY
J.A. ROCK

The Subs Club Series
Pain Slut (Coming February 2016)
Manties in a Twist (Coming April 2016)
24/7 (Coming June 2016)

Minotaur
By His Rules
Wacky Wednesday (Wacky Wednesday #1)
The Brat-tastic Jayk Parker (Wacky Wednesday #2)
Calling the Show
Take the Long Way Home
The Grand Ballast

Playing the Fool series, with Lisa Henry
The Two Gentlemen of Altona
The Merchant of Death
Tempest

With Lisa Henry
When All the World Sleeps
The Good Boy (The Boy #1)
The Naughty Boy (The Boy #1.5)
The Boy Who Belonged (The Boy #2)
Mark Cooper Versus America (Prescott College #1)
Brandon Mills Versus the V-Card (Prescott College #2)
Another Man's Treasure

ABOUT THE AUTHOR

J.A. Rock is the author of queer romance and suspense novels, including *By His Rules*, *Take the Long Way Home*, and, with Lisa Henry, *The Good Boy* and *When All the World Sleeps*. She holds an MFA in creative writing from the University of Alabama and a BA in theater from Case Western Reserve University. J.A. also writes queer fiction and essays under the name Jill Smith. Raised in Ohio and West Virginia, she now lives in Chicago with her dog, Professor Anne Studebaker.

Website: www.jarockauthor.com
Blog: jarockauthor.blogspot.com
Twitter: twitter.com/jarockauthor
Facebook: facebook.com/ja.rock.39

Enjoy more stories like *The Subs Club* at RiptidePublishing.com!

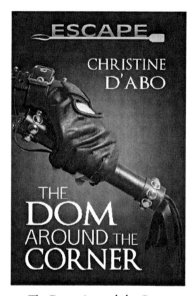

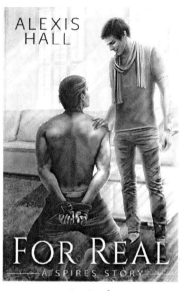

The Dom Around the Corner
ISBN: 978-1-62649-325-4

For Real
ISBN: 978-1-62649-280-6

Earn Bonus Bucks!

Earn 1 Bonus Buck for each dollar you spend. Find out how at RiptidePublishing.com/news/bonus-bucks.

Win Free Ebooks for a Year!

Pre-order coming soon titles directly through our site and you'll receive one entry into a drawing for a chance to win free books for a year! Get the details at RiptidePublishing.com/contests.

CPSIA information can be obtained at www.ICGtesting.com
Printed in the USA
LVOW06s1512191115

463342LV00006B/846/P

9 781626 493445